Praise for *Gossip of the Starlings*

"De Gramont's debut novel is the kind of smart and riveting read that fans of a certain kind of campus drama—think Donna Tartt's *The Secret History*—will devour . . . There's romance, betrayal, a gorgeous scholarship boy and a spot-on rendering of the queasy regret you sometimes feel when friends from separate orbits meet. Grab this one and share it with your teenage daughter."

— *People*

"It's a rare book that draws you into the tiny, idiosyncratic world of its characters so completely, and de Gramont's descriptions are often so vivid you'll want to give them a closer read . . . Grade: A-."

— *The Washington Post*

"The prose sparkles with an intense exuberance . . . It trumps *Catcher in the Rye* and *A Separate Peace* . . . *Gossip of the Starlings* will join that shelf reserved for literary classics."

— *The Providence Journal*, Best Books of 2008

"[*Gossip of the Starlings*] must be the savviest and scariest book of the season. And the reason it's such a stunner is that North Carolinian Nina de Gramont's smooth, sinuous syntax sharpens the reader's sense of terror, a horror that emanates from the ease with which the author's teenage protagonists sabotage and shatter their parents, teachers, and friends."

— *The Louisville Courier-Journal*

"When almost-good-girl Catherine Morrow, just sixteen, crosses paths at boarding school with the blithe, brilliant daughter of a senator, their friendship seems destined to soar, and it does—but too close to the sun. Nina de Gramont has written a stunning story of youth at its zenith and the tragic allure of a reckless zest for life that masks something far darker. I inhaled this novel in one breath."

—Jacquelyn Mitchard, author of *The Deep End of the Ocean*

"[A] charged and unforgettable debut novel . . . In prose brief and powerful as poetry, *Gossip of the Starlings* is reminiscent of classics such as *A Separate Peace* and *The Bell Jar.*" —*Body and Soul*

"De Gramont writes with uncommon grace about the hypnotizing effect of fame." — *Time Out Chicago*

"The book [is] a page-turner. Reading it is like indulging in the guilty pleasure of gossip." —*Winston-Salem Journal*

"Welcome to Nina de Gramont's first novel, a synonym for *tour de force*. My heart started racing on page one and never stopped. Rarely has a book married such finely wrought lyricism with such a page-turning plot. You want a story about prep school? *This* is a story about prep school."

—Alicia Erian, author of *Towelhead*

"De Gramont's prose, graceful and visual, stays with the reader. She's a writer to watch." — *The Charlotte Observer*

"The secret lives of prep-school girls Catherine and Skye come to life in this fabulous debut novel." — *OK! Weekly*

"Inspired by the true account of an '80s drug bust, de Gramont recalls [a] destructive relationship in graceful, poetic language . . . Make sure you stick around for the surprising finale."

—*Daily Candy Boston*

"[A] poignant novel . . . De Gramont's coming-of-age story distinguishes itself with sincere prose and complex characters."

—*Publishers Weekly*

"Think Donna Tartt and Bret Easton Ellis with the wisdom of hindsight . . . [A] compelling coming-of-age novel . . . [*Gossip of the Starlings*] excels in its honest depiction of the interrelationships among teens and with their families and circumstances. Recommended."

—*Library Journal*

"Though the world within Nina de Gramont's debut novel is well-known terrain to readers of *Prep* or *Catcher in the Rye,* the tale itself . . . transcends ready comparisons . . . The grace of de Gramont's prose acts as seductively upon the reader as Skye does on her peers . . . Rich characters . . . and a taut narrative keep the story pulsing to the (inevitable) tragic end."

—*Bust* magazine

"Memorable . . . When de Gramont focuses her gaze on her naïve, doomed muses, the book soars . . . A transfixing confessional about the secret lives of dangerous girls."

—*Kirkus Reviews*

"*Gossip of the Starlings* grabs hold of you and does not let go for a minute . . . I am not exaggerating when I say that I stayed up all night reading this book. Nina de Gramont shows us the conflicts that come with loyalty, the ease with which we choose right from wrong, and the moral consequences of both. Unflinching, wise, terrifying, and beautiful, this is a book that will resonate long after it ends." —Ann Hood, author of *The Knitting Circle*

"An elegant page-turner, *Gossip of the Starlings* is a compelling and beautifully nuanced story centered on the heightened emotions of adolescents. Against the backdrop of the privileged class, de Gramont skillfully captures that willful unknowingness regarding consequence and action that teenagers often have, deftly reminding us this quality does not belong only to the wealthy and the young." —Elizabeth Strout, author of *Olive Kitteridge*

"Exquisite. Nina de Gramont's prose seems wrought from gold filaments. The story lifts off the page and hovers around you as you read. Real people and real feelings in a performance that is full-bodied and—more impressively—full of real soul. I won't forget this book." —Luis Urrea, author of *The Hummingbird's Daughter*

"Nina de Gramont's novel glitters with beautiful and deceptive surfaces; her teenaged characters live comfortably in their aesthetically cosseted world yet simultaneously feel compelled to smash through those surfaces to see what's on the other side. The narrator is achingly sensitive and unique, but the story strikes universal themes: our false sense of immortality at the very moment we act most recklessly, our nostalgia for our own youthful intensity of perception and emotion. The book is also about the attractive and deceptive nature of danger itself, and how sometimes the people we encounter in our lives who are at greatest risk are also those who make us feel most alive."
—Wendy Brenner, author of *Phone Calls from the Dead*

Gossip of the Starlings

Gossip

of the

Starlings

a novel by

Nina de Gramont

ALGONQUIN BOOKS OF CHAPEL HILL 2009

Published by
ALGONQUIN BOOKS OF CHAPEL HILL
Post Office Box 2225
Chapel Hill, North Carolina 27515-2225

a division of
WORKMAN PUBLISHING
225 Varick Street
New York, New York 10014

First paperback edition, Algonquin Books of Chapel Hill, June 2009.
Originally published by Algonquin Books of Chapel Hill in 2008.
Printed in the United States of America.
Published simultaneously in Canada by Thomas Allen & Son Limited.
Design by Anne Winslow.

This is a work of fiction. While, as in all fiction, the literary perceptions and insights are based on experience, all names, characters, places, and incidents either are products of the author's imagination or are used fictitiously.

Library of Congress Cataloging-in-Publication Data
De Gramont, Nina.
    Gossip of the starlings: a novel / by Nina de Gramont. — 1st ed.
        p. cm.
    ISBN 978-1-56512-565-0 (HC)
    1. Teenage girls — Fiction.   2. Best friends — Fiction.   3. Boarding schools — Fiction.   4. Identity (Psychology) — Fiction.   5. Psychological fiction.   I. Title.
    PS3557.R24G67 2008
    813'.54 — dc22   2008005883

    ISBN 978-1-56512-676-3 (PB)

10 9 8 7 6 5 4 3 2 1
First Paperback Edition

For Danae and Leslie

Gossip of the Starlings

Everyone has a moment in history which belongs particularly to him. It is the moment when his emotions achieve their most powerful sway over him, and afterward when you say to this person "the world today" or "life" or "reality" he will assume that you mean this moment, even if it is fifty years past. The world, through his unleashed emotions, imprinted itself upon him, and he carries the stamp of that passing moment forever.

JOHN KNOWLES
A Separate Peace

FALL

1

Now, WHEN I SEE teenage girls laughing. When I see them loosed on a summer evening—their limbs tanned and gossamer, their imagined freedom radiating like nuclear light—I can't help but fast-forward two decades or more. I know the curve of their bones has already made an imperceptible bow to gravity. I see the decay in slow motion, even or especially through those stunning and immortal years.

But Skye could see it then. At seventeen, she spoke about her childhood with the most yearning nostalgia, like an old woman looking back at youth.

"I used to swim past Tautog Rock in October," she told me, sitting in the open window of my dorm room. "I used to ride my bike down Scargo Hill without ever touching the brakes."

She threw out her arms—so freckled and slender, they might still have belonged to that ten-year-old, tearing around Cape Cod.

I sat on the floor, cutting lines of Colombian cocaine on top of my toaster oven. With the flourish of a Japanese chef, I used a razor blade to fan, dice, and separate. The coke was fine and completely pure. It coursed through our bodies with none of the usual side effects: no gas or worried jaws. Only wide open lucidity, exhilaration, confidence.

"Fearless," Skye said, pronouncing the word with greed, as if the quality had long since left her, and she would spend the rest of her life chasing it down.

The autumn air hung behind her in complete darkness. If headmasters were smart, they would employ floodlights—no shadows anywhere, to slip between. But at the Esther Percy School for Girls, we saw not a glint of orange or red from outside, just heard the wind soughing through brilliant leaves.

"But it's okay," Skye said. "Nobody stays young forever, right?"

I laughed and said, "I don't think you're ready for dentures just yet."

She stretched in the dimly watted light. The strap of my white eyelet nightgown—bought by my mother in Paris—slid off her shoulder.

"At our Cape house," she said, "we've got powder post beetles in the beams. You can hear them at night, gnawing away like little buzz saws. Sometimes I think I hear them in my bones. *Chzz chzz chzz.*"

I lifted the toaster oven toward Skye, and she collected her long, red curls. With a plastic straw, stolen from the dining hall and snipped in half, she inhaled a line. Before tonight, Skye had never done coke—or any drug, other than sips from her father's wineglass. But she wielded the accoutrements with surprising grace. When the line vanished, she sat up and ran one finger across the bridge of her nose—her face smooth and white as a teacup.

She sniffed and shivered, then asked me if I believed in an afterlife.

"Sure," I said.

What I really believed in was this life, continuing on indefinitely. Sweet, acrid powder melted and dripped down the back of my throat. I blinked like an animal—completely and deliciously awake. What we lacked was a fire to dance around. Deer to chase down and slay. Instead of this small wooden room and the most simplistic metaphysics.

"Me too," Skye said. "I believe in heaven."

"But you don't have to be good to get in," I said.

Skye laughed—a piping sound, loud but not easy. She climbed down from the window and held out her hand for a turn with the razor. I watched her press the sharp edge into the powder, her brow furrowed with a perfectionist's concentration. Determined to master this new skill.

From the other side of the room, I heard a knock and a sleepy voice. One of the conditions of my admittance to Esther Percy was sharing a wall with the dorm counselor.

"Catherine?" Ms. Latham called. Skye swept the toaster oven—as forbidden as the contraband on top of it—under my bed. It was a perfunctory gesture. Ms. Latham was far too lazy and kindhearted to put on a bathrobe, walk around to our entrance, climb the stairs, and catch us. Instead, she always accepted whatever explanation I called back.

"Sorry," I said. "I must have been dreaming."

We turned out the light and crawled into my single bed. With the covers pulled to our chins, we blinked at the ceiling, completely awake. Our limbs twitched against each other with restless clarity.

Skye had crept here after evening bells, navigating the wide lawn and gnarled oaks, her sneakers caked with mud and pine needles. I lived in White Cottage, on the old part of campus, with clapboard siding and black shutters. Skye's room lay on the other end, where dark wooden buildings had slanted skylights and low flush toilets.

At my last school, we'd snuck out to boys' dorms or they had come to us. At Esther Percy, there were some girls who traded labored breath and bare skin. But most of us, like Skye and me, traded secrets. I missed my boyfriend John Paul—pining patiently for me at Waverly—but a part of me preferred this more intense intimacy: fueled by disclosure and a feeling of permanence. I knew that any boy, no matter how loyal, would ultimately be fleeting. While we, the girls, would stay friends forever.

"I'll tell you what," Skye said. "If anything happens to me, I'll come back and fill you in. Tell you what it's like."

"Me too, you," I said.

She laughed, another loud burst. Growing up, she had often traveled under the imposing watch of bodyguards—and so had faced her mortality early. She probably didn't consider me important enough for serious peril.

"Hush," I reminded her.

"Unless you get thrown from a horse," she whispered, "I don't think you're going anywhere. And even if you did, you probably wouldn't tell me anything."

"I will," I insisted. "I promise."

My eyes adjusted to the dark, and I could see Skye raise her brows doubtfully. I was better at keeping secrets than sharing them. In the past few weeks, she had handed me every exciting detail of her infamous and unjust expulsion, while I'd revealed only the dullest outline of my exile. I never corrected her assumption that I'd been expelled from Waverly. I told her almost nothing about my fam-

ily and less about my friends. I refused to tell her where I got my
coke.

So in this instance, she would not take me at my word. "Blood
oath?" she said.

She opened her hand to reveal the razor blade, still resting against
her fingers. I held out my hand obediently, waiting for a gentle slice
of my thumb; but Skye did herself first, carving from the base of her
middle finger to her wrist.

"Jesus Christ," I said.

She sat up and cupped her fingers to catch the blood, which gathered in her palm — voluminous enough to sip from. I felt a sharp
rush of nausea — the kind that usually accompanies one's own grave
injury. The green of Skye's irises was almost entirely swallowed by
black pupils. I listened to her shallow quiver of breath and regretted
this corruption — which I'd never meant to be so complete.

"Now you," she said. "Hurry up."

I took the razor and held it over my palm. My hands didn't shake,
which surprised me. But I did hesitate.

"Come on," Skye hissed, faintly maniacal.

"Shut up," I said. And scratched a faint, horizontal line, one third
the length of hers. I had to squeeze it to bring out blood, but Skye
thrust her hand into mine like our wounds were equal.

"There," she said, our hands creating one man-sized fist, Skye's
blood trickling between our fingers. "It's a pact."

I got a T-shirt from my top drawer, which she wrapped around her
hand. She settled back in bed, holding the ballooned cloth against
her chest like a battle veteran. If I'd been able to see clearly in the
darkened room, I'm sure her fair cheeks would have been flushed
with color and an eerie sort of pride.

Skye's hair fanned out across my pillows, and her breath quickened. Something inside me went gray, as if I'd lost more blood than I'd realized.

My premonition lit the room as if we'd struck a match. Its glow settled around her in a flickering updraft. And I thought that whatever story we had together — Skye and I — she would be dead by the end of it.

2

In the fall of 1984 there were three teenage girls whose names we all recognized. Phoebe Cates, who skipped—with a smiling mouthful of braces—through our outgrown subscriptions to *Seventeen*. Brooke Shields, who had disrobed on film at the exact moment our own bodies became a desperate source of uneasiness. And—in Massachusetts, at least—there was Skye Butterfield: who had appeared on campaign podiums since her head barely grazed her father's elbow. Who became particularly visible in that election year—when the world's fate teetered in the Sturm und Drang of the cold war, and her altruistic transgressions worked to the best advantage of her father's campaign.

"Why can't you be more like Skye Butterfield?"

For years, mothers across the state had issued this demand during the evening news, pointing to our senator's beautiful and accomplished daughter. Her curly ponytail and tailored wool coat. Her direct gaze and her straight, obedient shoulders. Her merit scholarships and her wholesome, supportive smile.

None of these mothers had recanted when she was suspended from Devon, after writing a series of English papers for a student on a football scholarship. They only sighed in heightened esteem, wishing their own children's misbehavior could be so high-minded. A few months later, Skye made headlines again—expelled this time, for sneaking away from school to protest Chanticleer, a plant that produced plutonium triggers. Even the more conservative parents appreciated her bravery and selflessness. At a press conference, the sag of her shoulders looked more instructed than sincere; she stared at the ground with fixed determination as her father rushed to eloquent and modest defense. Douglas Butterfield had never seemed like a practiced politician, but completely sincere—never more so than when speaking on his daughter's behalf. Not so much defending her actions as casting the reasons behind them in a compassionate and admirable light.

The local media had run away with both stories, with the tacit blessing of Senator Butterfield's campaign. Skye's rogue charity for the scholarship student only legitimized her father's status as handsomer-than-a-Kennedy-and-just-as-liberal. And his opponent in the Senate race supported Chanticleer—a position that Skye's protest made increasingly unpopular.

The cameras loved Douglas Butterfield more than ever: shining and honest, generous to share the mantle of crusader. And we, Skye's peers, loved him, too—believing entirely in the promises he made from the glossy palette of the television screen.

Not that we often watched the news. Prep school was its own insular world. TV sets lived far away—at home. None of us listened to the radio. What little political awareness I had amounted to a certainty that Ronald Reagan's reelection would presage a nuclear holocaust. Our president's hoary, schoolboy demeanor inspired nightmarish visions of underground silos across the Midwest, shuddering open to launch their warheads.

THE MORNING AFTER OUR blood pact, Skye didn't show up for English, an absence made especially noticeable by our teacher's preoccupation with her empty seat. Mr. November was Esther Percy's youngest faculty member, just two years out of Haverford, and one of only a few males. With a slight, youthful build and an unremarkable bearing, his most impressive quality was his wife—who played guitar, sang in a lilting contralto, and rarely deigned to address the students directly. Any crushes we had on Mr. November bore deep connections to Mrs. November's elusive cool.

That morning he scanned the room for Skye at regular intervals, finally interrupting his own lecture on *The Great Gatsby* to question me directly. "Catherine," he said, "it's not like Skye to be missing. Do you know if she's all right?"

I shrugged and shook my rattled head, certain that my sudden and violent blush communicated everything: the coke, the wounded palm, and the sleepless night, along with the fear that Skye had been seriously damaged in a way that would not only be irreversible but traced back to me.

Mr. November returned to topic with a wistful and deflated air, as if Daisy Buchanan had somehow managed to remove herself from the text. I tried to remember if he'd been as concerned the week before, when Laura Pogue-Smith had come down with the flu.

By late afternoon classes had ended and I still hadn't seen Skye. I thought about going by her dorm room, but instead punished myself by riding in a sitting trot around and around the outdoor ring. It was an exercise in battling wills—not only against my own discomfort, but against my horse's longing to break into a gallop. Pippin was an eager, high-strung animal, never easily contained. I squeezed the reins insistently and ground my heels down deep: perversely enjoying the clattering of my bones, which had been awake for thirty-six hours straight—enduring classes and communal meals. My teeth felt like icicles, ready to shatter on impact. My brain moved through a foggy sludge, and a deep and anxious guilt scuttled beneath my rib cage. I imagined an important nerve in Skye's palm severed, or an essential facet of her self-image lost—and feared that she had awoken so appalled by her swollen hand and altered state that she'd rushed to the headmistress and turned us both in.

I returned Pippin to his stall and walked back to the main campus, dragging my crop along the dusty road. In good weather my hometown in western Mass was just a two-hour drive from Esther Percy's southern Vermont campus. Everything felt familiar. Wood smoke dissipated in the New England air. The mulchy, grass scent of manure. A light, horsey steam rose from the sweat on Pippin's bay coat, and a kaleidoscope of damp leaves wilted beneath my boots. The deep, dull sun of midautumn pulsed on my bare neck, hair pushed under my helmet, and the unlikely heat snaked down my spine even as afternoon darkness loomed.

My head pounded, my vision separated into pixels, and I imagined crawling into the bed my mother had covered in goose down and French linen on the day she'd left me here.

Skye stood on the steps of White Cottage, waiting for me. My footsteps quickened with the need to inspect her, but relief had already descended. From a distance, she could easily be mistaken for an adult, her height and carriage belonging to a different league than the rest of us. But with every step closer, she lost a year — her face so smooth and round that her features looked delicate to the point of unformed, like a very small child's. The air around her crackled with wellness — physical health and beauty — so that despite the thick, professional gauze encasing her hand, it seemed ridiculous that she had ever been the subject of my concern.

"What did you tell her?" I asked. We knew from Lisa Zuckerman's miscarriage that the school nurse could not be trusted.

"I said I was helping you in the barn and cut my hand on a rusty nail. She gave me a tetanus shot."

"Probably not a bad idea," I said, trying to remember the razor blade's origin.

I pulled off my helmet and shook my stringy hair loose. At Esther Percy, with no boys around, we prided ourselves on going days without showering. But now I longed for a hot bath, followed directly by twelve hours of sleep.

"Okay," Skye said, when I told her this, and followed me upstairs like she'd be joining me in both. I didn't object. On our first day at Esther Percy, Skye had chosen me — inexplicably striding across the dining hall to slide her tray next to mine and sit down beside me. The rest of the girls had looked on in envy. I had yet to shake the sense of privilege her friendship afforded me.

At the top of the stairs, we politely averted our eyes from Amanda and Amanda — my across-the-hall neighbors — kissing in their doorway. Skye stepped over my threshold and picked her way through the general debris, the week-old laundry and stolen dining-hall plates.

"I like this place better in the dark," she said, and sat on the edge of my unmade bed, looking prim in khakis and a Peter Pan collar.

"I don't know how you can be so chipper," I said.

Skye's eyes were green and bright, her complexion fine. No evidence of our debauchery. Whereas my own lank, blonde looks stared back from the mirror, decimated—eyes rimmed with pink, their pale blue faded to gray. My clavicle protruded violently beneath a blotchy neck, making my slender face appear gaunt and waifish.

"That was fun last night," Skye said. "I felt so wide awake. I still haven't slept. Have you?"

"No," I said. "But I'm not quite as happy about it as you are."

"I like it," she said. "This restlessness. Even this hangover. It's exciting."

Skye had already told me everything about herself. I knew that her daredevil streak long preceded the new urge to rebel. She had skied Tuckerman's Ravine in blinding snow. She had sailed to Nantucket in heavy wind. On a hiking trip in Colorado, she had not backed away when she came upon a bear, but walked up close for a better look. Skye had a careful eye for detail, and I could picture the animal exactly: a young black bear, rangy and lean, his winter coat shedding and rumpled. Returning Skye's curious regard as he gnawed on a stick of hackberries.

No wonder she loved this new feeling, its faux exhilaration made real by the consequences of discovery.

"That's coke," I said. "Especially this coke."

Skye got up and began straightening my bed. "I was thinking," she said, tucking the sheets into neat hospital corners. "Maybe next weekend we could go to the Cape."

"With your parents?"

"No," she said. "Just us. Maybe you could invite your friends from Waverly. That's not far from Cape Cod, right? I'd really like to meet them. And we can get more. Of the cocaine, I mean."

"I'll ask them," I said, knowing that of course they would come.

I gathered my bath oil and shampoo and turned to examine Skye, who had sat back down on my now-perfect comforter. Long legs tucked underneath her, long red hair spilling over her shoulders. We had come together at cross purposes — me to shed wild ways, her to cultivate them. So far, her resolve had proved stronger than mine.

I tried to imagine Skye on Cape Cod with my old friends — who of course would be dying to meet her — and felt a strange combination of jealousy and protectiveness. I preferred the picture of the two of us, Skye and me, walking along a rocky beach.

Which surprised me. Usually it was difficult to imagine anything without Susannah, who had been my best friend since first grade. At our private elementary school in Old Lenox, I had sat behind Susannah in chorus. We all huddled unnaturally close together on the narrow risers, and I would sit there and stare at her shiny black hair — worthy of an Indian princess. My hands would tremble with the effort of staying in my lap, longing to plunge into that thick, black curtain, so much more luxurious than my own stringy corn silk. I was young for my grade, only five years old. Perfectly common, in those days — at private schools — to start children too early. Both of my older sisters had entered kindergarten months before their fifth birthdays.

The school was in an old Episcopal church — gray stone and stained glass. Restored murals covered by Plexiglas to protect them from children's grubby fingers. Everywhere, things we weren't allowed to touch, hands by our sides as our Mary Janes padded down beige looped carpets. I knew how to keep my hands to myself. But the back of Susannah's head looked so electrically beautiful. Not touching it would have been like not singing. And who could resist joining in the airlifted rising of little voices?

It must have felt like an errant firefly: my light fingers, scuttling down from the crown of her head. Susannah whipped around, startled and indignant. Her face settling upon mine in a puckish, gap-toothed smile of discovery. From that day forward, I knew everything about Susannah's life. She narrated it to me in endless letters, and even more endless conversations. She told me her important events, and she told me her philosophies. She told me her fears and her disappointments — describing every interior and exterior view. What I told her amounted to scarcely nothing, and at the same time more than I told another living soul.

My second day at Esther Percy, a few hours after I met Skye, I had called Susannah at home. Fall semester at Waverly hadn't yet started.

"There's always something wrong with him," Susannah said, when I told her I'd met Senator Butterfield's daughter.

"What do you mean?" I asked, surprised. "I thought you liked him."

"Oh, I do," Susannah said. "I like his politics very much. It's just when you see him on television, there's always something wrong, like a stain on his collar or a cowlick or something. It distracts me."

I tried to picture Senator Butterfield on-screen and couldn't imagine any kind of imperfection.

"Anyway," Susannah said. "You sound happier."

I realized immediately she was right. With Skye's appearance the world had widened — sun breaking through my resigned fog.

"Get the details." Susannah's disembodied voice — deep and smoky — was a distinct contrast to her tiny, ethereal form. "Find out everything about that scholarship kid, and what really happened."

"Okay," I said.

"Really do it, Catherine."

I nodded into the phone to her exasperated sigh. She knew me well enough to know: I would find out everything, and tell her nothing.

Now Skye kicked her legs out across my bed and leaned back against the pillow.

"This is the best time of year on Cape Cod," she said, closing her eyes—the first hint that last night had affected her. "The beach is empty, the weather's just right."

Her breathing had slowed slightly, and I had the feeling she would still be there, fast asleep, when I returned from my bath. Remarkably, no blood stained my bed from the night before. But watching Skye, her pink-cheeked stupor and her bandaged hand, I felt a sinking sensation—the sort of panic teenage mothers must feel. As if Skye were my own creation, and here I stood: distinctly unprepared to care for her.

"Skye?" I said. "Maybe you should go back to your room and get some rest."

She smiled, eyes still closed. "Eleanor's clattering around in there," she said. "It's more peaceful here. I wish I'd asked for a single."

In the two months since we'd been at Esther Percy, Skye had spoken to one other person besides me: her roommate, Eleanor Blakeley. Eleanor's father was a congressman, and the two girls had known each other since infancy. According to Skye they'd always been close, but I hadn't seen much evidence of that this fall. Eleanor was short, shy, and bookish. She worked hard at concealing her beauty with thick glasses, shaggy hair, and oversized clothing. Slouched and morose, next to Skye she looked like a charcoal smudge. Apart from academic excellence and glamorous families, I couldn't guess what they might have in common.

"How do we do the permission slips?" Skye asked. "Do we forge them? Or is there some other trick?"

"I'll sign yours," I said, with the careful tone I sometimes used with her, this visitor from a foreign planet. "You sign mine."

She nodded, memorizing the new ways even as she drifted off to sleep.

3

I DIDN'T HAVE TO forge a permission slip. The next weekend my mother showed up at Harrisburg, my last important event before the National Horse Show. The year before I had been disqualified at Regional Finals for going off course — ruining my chances after a year of championships. My mother and I had agreed she wouldn't come to any of the top shows this time, not wanting to add extra pressure. She had already skipped Regionals and the indoor show in Washington, DC.

I spotted her in the stands after my first blue ribbon, in the Under Saddle phase. With no jumping course to worry about, only a circular exhibition of Pippin's paces and my seat, we won easily. The announcer called my name and Pippin's show name: *Catherine Morrow on Corner of the Sky.* I pressed Pippin forward and let my eyes roam up toward the stands. My mother was instantly recognizable — disguised like a movie star, the only person in the sunless arena wearing a big hat and sunglasses. Born and raised on the outskirts of Paris, my mother had a Frenchwoman's way of looking bored even in the most high-pressure situations.

My trainer, Captain Zarghami, saw me locate her. He plucked the ribbon off Pippin's bridle and snapped his fingers in the air, willing my attention back to him.

"Catherine," he said, in his crisp Middle Eastern accent. *Cat-er-ene* "You have important things to accomplish this weekend."

I never once saw my trainer wear anything but riding clothes — jodhpurs, high leather boots, white button-down shirt. His silver hair combed back behind his ears. Ready to lead a cavalry squadron rather than coach equestrians at a girls' boarding school. He tapped his crop against my custom-made Vogel boots, then adjusted the scarlet bow on one of Pippin's braids. The horse shook his head in protest and pawed the dusty floor.

"Do not think of her," Zarghami said, jerking his silver head toward my mother. I wondered if he'd known she planned to come. I wondered if he knew John Paul was also in attendance — feigning injury, he had stolen away from a soccer game at the Phelps School. I concentrated on not glancing toward where he sat in the stands.

Zarghami answered my question by picking up his crop and pointing behind me, to where John Paul sat on one of the front bleachers. I hoped my mother didn't notice.

"You're far too good," Zarghami said, "to have spent all these years without ever getting to the National Horse Show."

Despite the implied admonishment, this was as close to a compliment as I'd received from him. What's more, it was the truth. I regularly appeared in the *Chronicle of the Horse* as a first- or second-place winner in the Medal Maclay division. Even as champion. Every year I entered the fall indoor shows as a front runner, then managed to blow it — disqualification last year, seventh place in Under Saddle the year before after I'd lost my stirrup during the canter. Nine times out of ten, my performance in the ring was flawless. But the tenth time—the time I failed—always seemed to occur when it mattered most.

"You just need to focus," Zarghami said, tapping his temple with his forefinger. "Head on the horse, not in the clouds."

Pippin backed up a few steps and did a quarter turn, as if he wanted to avoid this scolding—as if it were directed at him rather than me. I could see John Paul now, leaning on the empty seat in front of him, dark hair grazing the collar of his soccer jersey. My mother had only met him once, when I was suspended from Waverly. I hoped her usual vagueness would keep her from recognizing him in the crowd, but I doubted that it would. John Paul was hard to forget, even in the most ordinary circumstances. His good looks would have made him memorable enough to most women, and my mother especially would recall his humble but confident calm. John Paul possessed a certain air of exiled royalty—the kind of boy you'd expect to step forward and pull the sword from the stone.

I threw my leg forward while Zarghami tightened Pippin's girth. John Paul saw me watching him and lifted his hand. I waved back with a barely perceptible shake of my head, telling him not to come over.

Zarghami absorbed the entire exchange in one glance.

"Catherine Morrow," he said, lowering his voice to fatherly modules. "You can pursue greatness or you can pursue girlhood. Eventually, you will have to choose."

He kept on talking, the sound of his voice in fierce competition with the day's sensory overload. I loved the indoor shows: the rising whorls of dust in the foggy spotlights, the grassy scent of manure and the musky, steaming sweat of horses. Black velvet helmets rose and fell, posting or sailing over jumps. A swirl of colorful ribbons on the sidelines — triumphant blues and disappointed pinks.

And in the midst of it all, John Paul, whom I hadn't seen in months, respecting me too much to come forward even while my reasons remained a mystery. Gazing at me, the preposterous blue of his eyes visible from our hundred-foot distance.

A loudspeaker droned announcements of winners through the clip-clop of horse hooves, the same names I'd heard for years. Pippin jittered beneath me, and I gave his withers an absentminded pat. My first Thoroughbred, we had bought him last year. My mother — convinced that I needed *un vrai cheval* to reach the next level of competition — had talked me out of my devotion to Bloom, the chestnut mare I'd been showing since I was a child in the Short Stirrup division.

With Bloom, I'd shared a deep and intimate love. Growing up in a house full of animals, she had been my most cherished pet. After battles with my father, I'd cried gallons of tears with my face pressed against Bloom's golden withers and even slept nights on the bales of straw in her stall.

My feelings toward Pippin were strictly business, with a little admiration thrown in. I patted his neck as he twitched restlessly beneath me. Zarghami held a finger to his lip as they announced the final Under Saddle class. When they called my name he smiled and clapped his hands, then went into the stands to talk to my mother. I was still in the saddle when John Paul appeared, standing on the other side of Pippin so that the horse blocked Zarghami and my mother's view.

"Congratulations," John Paul said, stroking Pippin's neck and looking up at me — a vantage point I seldom had, his face tipped upward. Never mind the importance of this event. In John Paul's presence I always wished the world away: no outside noise to impede or threaten our relationship.

"My mother's here," I told him. As soon as the words escaped, Pippin back-stepped, exposing John Paul. Even if my mother didn't remember him, she couldn't miss WAVERLY emblazoned across his chest in bright blue letters.

He ducked back behind the horse. "I have to go soon, anyway," he said. "The team bus leaves at four."

I told him about the possibility of meeting on Cape Cod. He squeezed my leg in the improbably personal spot between the knee and the rim of my boot.

"I'll see you next weekend," he said. "Good luck."

I watched him walk toward the nearest exit. I could see my mother's eyes following him, a heavy enough gaze that he must have felt it, her curiosity boring into his handsome back. He turned and waved at me, then looked up into the stands. His already straight shoulders lifted—not defiant, or prideful, so much as determined.

John Paul wasn't especially tall, but he had long strides. It only took him a few minutes to reach my mother. I saw her stare at him dubiously from beneath the rim of her hat. I imagined the habitual twitch of her lower lip. He held out his hand. I could see his lips move and guessed that he was speaking French. My mother smiled and gave him her hand in a distinctly European manner—limp, as if she meant for him to kiss it. He hesitated a moment, then turned her hand over and shook it. My mother patted the seat next to her, and he sat down. As John Paul threw his head back—a quick gesture, too nervous to be triumphant—my mother looked over at me and wagged her finger. But I could tell she was smiling, properly charmed.

HALF AN HOUR LATER I rode Pippin through his flatwork with nine other riders. We rode through our paces—walk, trot, canter—wearing identical custom boots and wool blazers. All of us bone thin, with our hair tucked into our helmets. Perfect seats and easy hands. I felt John Paul's eyes on me, and my mother's. Zarghami's and the judges'. I willed my body to relax in precise synch with Pippin and not glance at the other riders, which would have deducted points. My competitors formed a blazered, peripheral blur as I felt my body—erect but relaxed over the daisy cutting of Pippin's hooves, skimming the ground just so.

All my anxiety had melted away. John Paul's courage seeped into my marrow, and I knew clearly as hindsight: I would win.

4

AT THE RESTAURANT in Harrisburg, the waiter didn't question my
mother when she ordered a bottle of wine and two glasses.

"Your young man is lovely," she said, running a hand over her
sleek dark hair. Its perfection confirmed, she tilted her head and
waited for my reply. I stared hard at my plate, knowing that if I
didn't respond this would be the last I heard of it.

"So," she said, after a minute. "You've made friends at the girls'
school?"

"Just one, really. Her name's Skye Butterfield. Her father's the
senator?"

I watched my mother's face respond, impressed and then gratified.
Even though she never followed politics, she recognized the name
instantly.

"There, you see?" she said. "You don't meet people like that in the
public schools."

My mother—whose own tuitions had been paid by benevolent
relatives—considered private education as imperative as oxygen.
Whereas my father had reluctantly agreed to send me to another

boarding school on two conditions: that it be all girls and I spend the summer working as a maid in a local hotel.

"No horses," he'd said, when my mother tried to commute this sentence to a stable. The sounds of Lowell were clear in his voice as he made his favorite pronouncement. "Catherine's problem is that she's never had to work a day in her life."

My father had a particular grudge against each of his children. My brother, Etienne, disappointed him by going to law school instead of showing proper interest in the family business. Beatrice spent too much money on too-skimpy clothes. Claire spoke very quietly; my father always took his inability to hear her as a personal affront. But it was for me, the youngest, that he reserved this accusation: I exhibited a woeful lack of industry.

That summer, the scent of Clorox and Murphy's Oil Soap didn't seem to reverse his assessment—as if these chemicals only represented the lowly station I had brought upon myself. My father would never be impressed by the glamour and old money of Skye's family. But I knew they would hold great sway with my mother, and I poured her a little more wine.

"Actually," I said, "the Butterfields have invited me to Cape Cod next weekend. They have a house on the beach. May I go?"

"Of course," she said.

I swirled the good wine in my glass, not tasting it. I thought how if my father only understood my current physical state—the flushed warmth, the sore legs and clear head—he couldn't help but approve. The sense of accomplishment from a strong performance. If my father could just occupy my body for this single moment, he might understand that I had indeed arrived at this state through hard work, instead of insisting that horseback riding—no matter how much I achieved—constituted nothing but leisure.

I imagined my mother showing him the ribbons as proof of my virtue. Telling him that I'd finished in the top ten. Outwardly he would dismiss the news with a craggy scowl. "She won plenty of ribbons last year," he would say, logically denouncing their worth as testaments to my good behavior. But one spark in his skeptical blue eyes would betray an oblique sort of pride. That I'd be going to the National Horse Show. To Madison Square Garden. Whatever my father might think of my character, he appreciated excellence. He couldn't help but respond when glimpsing it in his own daughter. All I had to do was qualify tomorrow, and even he would not be able to withhold his approval.

On the drive back to the hotel, I stared out the passenger window and waited for my reflection to reappear with passing headlights. In the periodic glare, my eyes looked huge and watchful, my face luminous and childlike. I thought that maybe I wouldn't go to the Cape after all, but spend next weekend studying for my history test and making up new jumping courses for Pippin. Getting ready for November.

"Has she talked to you," my mother asked, "about that whole business?"

We hadn't mentioned the Butterfields in over an hour, but I knew exactly what she meant: Skye's ardent activism—rallying against the production of plutonium, saving Massachusetts at the expense of herself. Her misguided championship of the scholarship student, who'd turned out to be barely literate.

"He wasn't stupid," Skye had told me. "He was good at math.

He'd just gone to such bad schools, came from such an unfortunate background."

Away from Skye, it could be hard to believe the things she'd told me. How her father had reproved her actions behind closed doors but defended them under the glare of the spotlight—even publicized them when the media took its complimentary spin. On television, her father never seemed like he was reading a speechwriter's script. He sounded like he was *speaking*, from the top of his head and from his heart.

"Catherine," my mother prodded.

"Only a little," I said, to the looking glass of the car window.

My mother had booked her own room at the Hilton, not wanting to interfere with my sleep. Riding up the elevator after saying good night to her, I ran into Billy Frye, another rider from the Medal Maclay circuit. He'd placed third in our class today.

"Hey, Catherine," he said, still wearing his riding clothes. "Congratulations."

"Thanks."

"This your last year to qualify?"

"No," I said. "I'm not seventeen till December."

He whistled. Not much taller than me, he had fair hair and very red lips.

"A whole 'nother year," he said. "Lucky. The rest of us are up against the wall."

We got off at the same floor and walked down the hall together. "Want to come in?" he said, when we reached his door. "I've got some coke."

I hesitated. Not because I worried about him making a pass—like most boys who showed seriously, Billy was gay—but because I wanted to be clear and sharp the next day. I wanted to win. To come home with a championship ribbon from Harrisburg: that would be infinitely better than the very best cocaine.

"Come on," Billy said. He opened the door, and I saw there were already several riders in his room, drinking and snorting lines from a glass table. "You did so well today, you barely even need to place tomorrow."

I wondered if he remembered what had happened to me last year.

"Catherine," someone called from inside. "Come join us."

The night stretched out in front of me—restless and full of worry, alone in my hotel room. I wished John Paul had concocted a way to stay with me.

"Okay," I said, to the as yet unrecognized friend. And followed Billy into his room.

IT WAS WELL PAST midnight when I got back to my room, wishing I were drunk—so that I could fumble for the lights, then collapse and pass out in my bed. Instead my instincts operated on overdrive, my eyesight nervously keen. I found the light switch immediately, knowing I would never be able to sleep, and praying the hotel had HBO.

The fluorescent bulbs flickered in a nervous haze, and John Paul sat up in my bed.

"Hey," he said, squinting at the clock. "Where've you been?"

I dove across the room and landed on top of him, too overjoyed to curse the wasted hours in Billy's room. John Paul flopped back and stretched his arms behind him.

"You're here," I said, sitting on his stomach, my legs straddling his rib cage. "How did you get into my room?"

"Let's just say I'd like to see you in a hotel with better security."

He sat up, pushing me slightly backward, and took my face in his hands. I submitted to his careful examination as the fantastic and intimate scent of his sleep settled around me, along with the probing gaze I would have found intrusive from anyone else in the world.

"You're very high," he said, and I laughed at this diagnosis. John Paul never did coke. Though he appeared placid to the outside world, beneath his veneer of calm anxieties roiled. He disliked any added intensity.

"Here," he said, and reached into the drawer of the hotel night-stand. I slipped off of him and lay on the polyester comforter, staring up at the ceiling. My toes beat an uncontrollable beat. The drugs, more speed than cocaine, had plastered my eyes wide open. I could barely blink, let alone close them to rest. But John Paul—in addition to the glorious fact of himself—would provide relief. He would roll a joint, which we would smoke together. He would make love to me for the first time in a long and aching eon. Beyond that, the promise of sleep—at least a few hours—resting in his arms. I let my fingers walk across his broad, bare back as he fiddled with rolling papers.

At his home in Saw River, John Paul kept a cockatiel named Pretty Girl. He and his mother had found her one summer, abandoned in an Essex house they'd been hired to clean. The bird and her mate had been left in their cage for at least a week, and the male had resorted to feeding on Pretty Girl. She was close to death, starving, bald, and despondent from the repeated attacks. John Paul's mother sent him to the vet with both birds. Though the male was thriving, and Pretty Girl close to death, John Paul had the male put to sleep. He worked out an installment plan to pay for Pretty Girl's revival.

I had only known him a few weeks when we took the bus down to his house in Connecticut, where he introduced me to the bird. Then and there I decided: let the other girls love John Paul for his bluer-than-cornflower eyes. I would love him for that scrawny and hideous cockatiel, pressing her face against his cheek with all the urgency of her posttraumatic stress disorder. She was overjoyed at his return, and furiously jealous of my presence. I would love John Paul for the way he kissed Pretty Girl's beak and scratched her terrible neck, which never had regrown its feathers.

Now, in the hotel room, I let him bring the lit joint to my lips like desperately needed balm. And I thought about telling him how much I loved him, and all the reasons why. I may have even opened my mouth to do so.

But before I could speak, he laughed.

"What?" I said, staring into his face, which stared back at me with the fondest and most intent regard. "What?"

"You look like you should have hearts and flowers floating all around your head."

"Well good," I said. "Because that's how I feel."

I wrapped my arms around his neck and let his nearness float me through what ought to have been a long night, tortured with jittery regret.

The best thing about John Paul: wish for him and he'd appear. Think how much I loved him, and he'd say, "I love you, too."

HE LEFT BEFORE first light, not wanting to risk being caught by my mother. I washed the smoke from Billy's room out of my hair, even though it would still cling to my blazer. Then I went downstairs to my mother's room, where she ordered breakfast. Under her direction, I ate in a miserable haze—gulping coffee and forcing down a croissant with jam.

"I really, really can't," I told her, when she pressed me to eat the plateful of scrambled eggs.

At the stadium, Pippin acted like he was hopped up on coke. From the moment I saddled him he pranced and back-stepped, pulling on the bit as if it sat under his tongue. I dismounted three times on my way to the ring, to make sure the bridle was on properly, then finally decided to lead him instead. He shied away from a girl in the audience, her Walkman barely audible through her headphones. My only hope for calm had vanished along with John Paul. Nerves shot, I barely contained myself from giving the reins three sharp and punishing yanks.

"Hush," I said instead, stroking the gorgeous line of his neck. Already sweating, and we hadn't even reached the ring. "It's okay," I told him. "It's okay."

I longed for Bloom, who had always been able to sense and accommodate my moods—one of those rare, empathic animals. Whereas with Pippin, I had to be aware of his state, no reciprocal allowances made. I had to cater to his unpredictable spirits, finding a way to calm him even when my hands shook and my eyes stung.

"You smell like cigarettes," said Captain Zarghami, meeting me by the gate, and I pictured the thin whorls of smoke curling up from Billy's hand.

"Some men were smoking in the hotel restaurant," I said, the lie evident in my husky voice.

He frowned at me, then went to Pippin's head and whispered in his ear. The horse jerked his head away—he didn't like men, no matter how familiar. Zarghami continued to pat his neck, looking worriedly back at me, as if he couldn't figure out what happened between last night and this morning.

We both turned to the ring as the announcer called Billy Frye's name. Watching him ride his exquisite gray—half Arab, half Thoroughbred—felt like agony. Billy had beautiful carriage, slim as a girl, and he flew through the course with perfect form. I hated him—not only because he had so easily talked me into partying while John Paul lay waiting in my room but because he could perform so well, so serenely and seamlessly. Not the barest evidence of the coke and the cigarettes, or even the Jack Daniel's he'd been throwing back between every line. Billy couldn't have slept any more than I had. Why did I feel so wrecked and ruined? Why could my friends perform perfectly well, the saturnalias undetectable, while I suffered such sabotaging hangovers?

Pippin startled at the applause for Billy. Zarghami held his reins while I mounted. As the next rider trotted into the ring, I ran through the course in my head for the last time—determined to remember the order of the jumps, despite my foggy brain and quivering hands.

Number fourteen, Catherine Morrow on Corner of the Sky.

If it had been Bloom, I might have been able to survive on automatic. With Pippin, I had to consider and monitor the slightest movement. I squeezed the reins on every post. Watched his head, his ears, his shoulders. Took an extra circle before approaching the first fence. The moment I let him have his head, we sailed over the uneven white poles. I heard the echoed pounding of hooves, muffled by the dirt floor. I had a strange, nervous sense of performing underwater, an unnatural throb all around me. Stands stood in unearthly

silence—noise drowned out by my concentration—as I steered
Pippin toward the vertical wall. Nearly four feet high and we cleared
it with inches to spare. A faint spattering of applause, and for a moment I felt a streak of panic—that I didn't know which fence to
head toward next.

The image of Billy's equitation came into my head, and I remembered him turning to the right. A too obvious command, I
realized—recalling the way his hand had moved to the inside, his
knuckles rotated in an error the judges would not miss. His performance had not been flawless after all. I shifted the slightest weight to
my right boot, my hand work invisible. Pippin and I galloped toward
the brush box, my body out of the saddle. We were just about to leave
the ground when a flashbulb popped from the front bleachers.

Pippin stopped short, sending me forward, over the jump without
him, my hip smacking the edge of the flower filler with a thwack.
Landing on the opposite side, dust rising up around me as my back
hit the dirt floor.

I knew the wind had been knocked out of me, and tried to sup-
press the terrible noise issuing forth from my lungs—reverberating
in the quiet arena, everyone standing to see if I was hurt rather than
simply humiliated.

IN MY LIFE I had been injured by horses again and again. I'd
been thrown and kicked, bitten and stepped on. Pippin himself had
dragged me, the day we first went to look at him. When his breeder
handed me his reins outside the stable, before I could mount, Pippin
broke into an uninstigated gallop. I fell forward, onto my stomach,
the reins still clutched in my hands. And instead of letting go, I clung
with the fiercest clench of adrenaline. I let him drag me the quarter
mile to the riding ring, while my parents chased after us, screaming

at me to let go. I bumped over the dust, perilously close to his flying hooves but hanging on as tightly as if the reins had been tethered to my wrists. Eventually my slight weight bore down on him. As we approached the riding ring his gallop eased into a trot. I pulled myself up on the reins and dug my heels into the ground, forcing him to a stop. My mother marched over for a brief inspection. She bent both my arms at the elbows, checking for breaks, then dusted off my jodhpurs and pointed to the saddle. The cardinal rule of horsemanship: get right back on immediately or risk never riding again.

My hands and legs had tingled with long, painful scrapes. A million times, I had been hurt by horses but never in such concert with my own stubborn will. I climbed onto Pippin's back, every muscle trembling. The breeder had watched, horrified and frowning, certain that he'd lost the sale. Not knowing that my father had been dubious until he saw the tenacity of my ill-conceived grip.

Now, with a thousand eyes watching, I got to my feet and held up my hand to indicate I hadn't been hurt. Zarghami changed his direction—stopped heading toward me in favor of chasing down Pippin. I didn't bother to help him but picked up my crop and marched out of the ring. Ripping the number off my back and heading to the stables.

"You still have next year," my mother said, back at school, walking me up the path to White Cottage. On the seven-hour drive from Pennsylvania, she had repeated this phrase again and again. Along with other insincere words of comfort, disappointment apparent in her strained tone and deflated carriage.

Ms. Latham saw us approaching and came outside to introduce herself.

"Mrs. Morrow," she said, holding out her hand and hunching over in a way that would surely irritate my mother. A tall, broad woman, Ms. Latham wore her thick blonde hair under a kerchief, and a Mondale/ Ferraro button pinned prominently to her chest.

"Catherine's doing wonderfully well here," she said, although she would have had scant knowledge of how I fared in school. Ms. Latham lived at Esther Percy in exchange for her monitoring duties and worked in town as an apprentice to a potter. But my mother did not know this, and so the assurance from an apparently reasonable adult seemed to relieve her. She accompanied me upstairs with an expression that nearly resembled a smile, finally shifting the conversation to everyday topics. Had I heard from Susannah. Did I like the French teacher. Was my bed comfortable enough.

Then she kissed me good-bye—a lipsticked peck on each cheek.

"I *am* proud of you, my darling," she promised, her emphasis only suggesting the many ways I'd failed her. She signed my permission slip, wound her cashmere scarf around my neck, and tucked a generous wad of bills into my coat pocket. "For your weekend," she said.

From my window, I watched her leave the building in what remained of dusk. Her trim, elegant form looked delicate and unadorned. I noticed that as she walked she looked around, turning her head toward the other students, as if she hoped to see Skye Butterfield—or even the senator himself—strolling across the commons. Funny, to think of my mother being starstruck by one of my friends.

I brought her scarf up to my nose and inhaled her perfume. Chanel or Joy. I was never good at identifying scents, but closed my eyes against the softness of wool and fragrance.

And I remember clearly: wishing to be more deserving of her pride, and vowing to become so.

5

THAT MOMENT IN THE WINDOW, watching my mother leave, the vow to behave: it only lasted until John Paul called, early in the week. At Waverly, students were allowed phones in their rooms. At Esther Percy, with so many of us sentenced to girls' school because of wild pasts, there were fewer personal privileges. I found his message on the community bulletin board and called him back on the rotary-dial pay phone in the student lounge.

"I don't get it," John Paul had said at the hotel, when I told him Skye's plans. "I thought she was famously well behaved."

"Not so much, it turns out."

On the phone, we ironed out the details, one hand curled over the receiver to muffle my words. John Paul would borrow his cousin's car and he, Drew, and Susannah would pick us up at the bus station in Hyannis. Susannah, putting her deep voice to use, pretended to be Skye's mother and called Mrs. Chilton, Esther Percy's student dean. She told her that a car would come for Skye and me on Friday afternoon.

If I hadn't been thrown at Harrisburg, if I'd been headed to the National Horse Show, maybe it would have given me a reason to abstain from this sort of behavior. But what else was there to do with the rest of 1984? When the shows started again in January, when performance became important again, maybe then I would tell Skye that I could no longer be her tour guide to delinquency. In the meantime, at least I had something to give the days a color beyond the fading foliage.

"It'll be fun to meet your friends," Skye said, as we walked down the long dirt road from school, our backpacks over our shoulders. There was little danger of being caught, even if somebody saw us: students were allowed to hitchhike into town after classes. Nobody but Mrs. Chilton expected a car to collect us, and she left school for Boston every Friday at noon.

We felt giddy with lawlessness and possibility. New England fall had taken one of its unpredictable vacations; we moved through the warm light of Indian summer. Skye's decadent hair rose and fell, and the damp earth felt like a springboard beneath my steps.

"I think this is the second time in my life nobody knows where I am," Skye said. She threw her arms over her head, twitching fingers through the crisp air, and skipped a step or two, perhaps affirming her continued existence.

"*Why didst thou promise such a beauteous day,*" she quoted. "*And make me travel forth without my cloak, / To let base clouds o'ertake me in my way, / Hiding thy bravery in their rotten smoke?*"

We stopped and stared up at the sky. Perhaps we expected rain clouds to gather at her bidding. Gentle wisps of white floated through the pale autumn blue.

"That's number thirty-four," Skye said. "I memorized all the sonnets the summer my Mom and I went to Stratford-on-Avon."

"I've been there, too," I said.

"It's pretty," Skye said, and I nodded.

We walked on, and after a long stretch of meadow and brush, began passing houses — lovely New England clapboard, modest and dilapidated country mansions, occasional ponies grazing in front yards. Skye wanted to stop at the apple orchard for a snack. We cut through the cider-scented trees, reaching the little harvest store just as Mrs. Gray turned the lock. Skye banged on the glass and clasped her hands against her face, pleading. A few minutes later we were back on the road, eating chunks of smoked cheddar cheese and Mrs. Gray's homemade cookies. It should have felt incongruous — the exhilaration and the unweighted happiness, instead of guilt and worry over being caught. But it felt so natural, almost innocent to impose our own messy rules.

With our thumbs pointed outward, Skye and I walked under an elm. Its low-hanging branches muted the strong light. An old, wood-paneled station wagon stopped on Percy Hill Road, and a young woman pushed open the back door for us. A guitar case, covered with sunflower stickers and political slogans, took up most of the backseat. US OUT OF NICARAGUA. NO NUKES. MONDALE/FERRARO. SAVE THE WHALES.

"You can throw the guitar in the way back," the woman told us.

Skye crawled in first and moved the instrument gingerly, balancing it on top of bags and boxes of clutter. Once we were settled, I recognized the driver as our English teacher's wife.

"You girls going to town?" Mrs. November asked, when we finally closed the door.

"The bus station," Skye said. I kicked her lightly in the shin, but she didn't seem to register that she'd said anything alarming.

We saw Mrs. November in the rearview mirror, frowning slightly.

The bus station was several miles past the general store and obviously out of her way. She tapped her fingers on the steering wheel in one progressive, rhythmic thump. Mrs. November didn't teach at Esther Percy, but sometimes she led singalongs after Wednesday night chapel. Probably close to Ms. Latham in age but somehow seeming much less adult—perhaps because of her once-removed status as authority. Certainly in a position to turn us in, but not obliged to.

She put the car into gear and drove down the road. I watched her long fingers on the wheel, noting the diamond-encrusted wedding band.

"What a pretty ring," Skye said, following my gaze.

Mrs. November didn't glance at her hand but lifted it off the steering wheel and waved in a slight, dismissive motion, as if she'd forgotten the ring were there and meant to shake it loose.

"It was his grandmother's," she said.

"I love that art deco jewelry," Skye said. "All those tiny diamonds and platinum from the twenties."

"You don't say." A lighthearted sneer. Mrs. November's voice sounded girlish as our own, but she infused it with just enough condescension to make us instantly adore her. She had long brown hair and a mannish face—beaky nose and narrow eyes. But her demeanor, confident and slightly amused, insisted on attractiveness despite these physical shortcomings. From steering to glancing in the rearview mirror, every movement carried the grace of expertise.

At the bus station, Mrs. November let the car idle a minute. With one arm sprawled across the back of the front seats, she turned to look at us—long enough to let us know she was taking in our features and, in Skye's case at least, our identities.

"Do you want to tell me where you're headed?" she said, in a tone too authentically casual to be teenage. "Just in case you turn up missing?"

"Oh, we have permission," I told her.

"Uh-huh."

"We're going to my parents' house on Cape Cod," Skye said, an almost exact imitation of Mrs. November's measured cool. "You're welcome to come along, if you like."

Mrs. November laughed. "Don't think it's not appealing," she said. "But alas I have this life to attend to."

We stood in the parking lot, waving as she drove away.

"She's so cool," Skye said. "I wonder how he ever snagged her."

"Don't you think he's good enough for her?" I asked. Skye rolled her eyes, refusing to entertain that possibility.

Early in the school year, I had come into the dining hall late after training with Captain Zarghami. Dinner was over, so I walked into the kitchen and begged a glass of milk and a peanut butter sandwich from the cook. As I settled alone at a corner table, Mr. and Mrs. November sat facing each other in the middle of the abandoned room. Their untouched plates were pushed aside, and they whispered fiercely, each one's clipped and breathy words running into the other's. Something about their pose—gesticulating fingers so close, foreheads nearly touching—struck me as very passionate. It looked so much more intimate and imperative than my parents' clipped and frosty arguments. From my considerable distance, I could see Mr. November's pale face taut with anger, a prominent vein red and swollen at his temple. He looked about to kill her, or else burst into tears. I picked up my sandwich and crept outside, not wanting to embarrass them, and worried that if they saw me they'd feel the need to explain themselves.

"I like Mr. November," I said now, to Skye—inanely, not even sure that I meant it.

We went inside to the ticket window. "I've never been on a bus before," Skye said. And then, like it had only just occurred to her that we'd have to pay, "Can you loan me the cash for my ticket?"

Skye's great-great-grandfather had founded the First Bank of Boston. Somewhere along the already wealthy line, the Butterfields had bought a television station as a tax shelter and then watched it balloon into a communications empire. Her father had divested from that empire when he entered politics, but the fortune itself remained. The Butterfields owned a house in Georgetown and three homes in Massachusetts. Yet Skye never had money for anything. Perhaps her family considered cash an unseemly form of currency. One fact the Butterfields had managed to keep out of the newspapers, possibly because it would seem so unlikely: Skye's scholarship student had paid her for every one of the papers she'd written.

I bought the tickets. Skye and I had been friends less than eight weeks, and already I couldn't remember a time when everything I owned wasn't gladly available to her.

But as the bus rolled over the highway, and the scenery around us darkened, I found myself drifting away from her, toward better-known friends. Toward John Paul, his memory looming larger as the distance between us lessened.

"Will I like him?" Skye asked.

"Sure," I said, though I wasn't sure. Apart from me, I hadn't met anyone Skye liked. And John Paul could be reticent, not at all a flirt. He would be polite to Skye, but he would refuse to be starstruck. Still, looking at her—the regal recline transforming her nylon seat into an overupholstered throne—I had a sinking feeling that John

Paul would see the two of us, stepping off the bus, and wish that Skye were his. He wouldn't reveal it — not a glimmer. But the wish itself would be unavoidable.

"Is John Paul cute?" Skye asked.

"No," I said. "He's beautiful."

She leaned back against the headrest, disengaging. I thought this piece of information — one of the few snippets I'd ever granted — would please her. But like so many beautiful people I'd known, she disliked hearing the word attached to anyone else.

"Your friends are always so *attractive*," my mother used to say, clearly bewildered. She became even more perplexed when I hit the teenage years and beautiful boys courted me surely as beautiful girls. I never knew how to explain: it wasn't that I loved gorgeous people, but that gorgeous people loved me. Maybe it was my looks — pretty enough to confer status but plain enough not to threaten. Or maybe something more, some cryptic message written on my body or in my carriage, decipherable only to a very particular kind of person.

Our bus pulled into the darkened station. I could see John Paul, waiting on the stoop outside, a worn cotton sweater loose over his broad shoulders. An unexpected swell rose beneath my ribs: just when I thought I'd gotten used to him.

"That's him," I said to Skye, and she leaned over my lap to look out the window. I tried to wave to him over her impossibly bright head.

We lifted our backpacks and filed off the bus, and the next thing I knew my nose was pressed against the dusky scent of John Paul's sweater. His chin on top of my head, and the good, honest grip of his embrace.

It wouldn't have surprised me when I turned around, if Skye had vanished into the night air, like an imaginary friend. *Where's Skye Butterfield?* the others would ask, when I reached the car without her. They would sympathize completely when I confessed to fabricating my association with her — which suddenly seemed too unlikely, too fantastic, to be real. Yet there she stood, a face from the newspapers and television, her hands in her pockets. Perfectly pale and poised. And I found I didn't want to continue with the weekend, which could only mean sharing her, or exposing her, or both. I couldn't help but feel: two worlds that should only be parallel stood on the brink of collision.

"Hi," John Paul said to Skye, holding out his hand. "Nice to meet you."

Inwardly, I winced. Just the other day, Skye had been going on about that very phrase, insisting that no well-bred person ever said "Nice to meet you."

"What are you supposed to say?" I'd asked her.

"How do you do," Skye said. "Or if you want to be less formal, How are you."

I couldn't tell if Skye had registered John Paul's polite faux pas. But I could see the barest trace of surprise in her face — at his working-class Yankee accent, which had been evident even in those few words. And it struck me that although Skye had spent hours telling me about her expulsion, she'd never once mentioned the scholarship student's name.

I held John Paul's hand a little bit tighter.

We walked over to the battered old Buick. Susannah and Drew sat in the back, saving shotgun for me. I saw their expectant heads — craning forward as we approached, waiting to catch a glimpse of Skye. I felt her slow down beside me, aware of their curiosity, and confused by the car itself, with its rusted and dented exterior. Her footsteps became too deliberate.

"Why Miss Butterfield," Drew called, in a British accent borrowed from *Monty Python*. "You're even more beautiful in person."

I slammed the front door, and Skye slid in back cautiously.

"Ignore him," Susannah said, leaning across Drew's lap. I could see her face, a floating vision in dark air lit by streetlamps. She looked like she always did: sad, beautiful, watchful, so that her dismissal of Drew sounded strangely compassionate. As if his inappropriateness were a reflection of the world's unavoidable ills and there was nothing to do but bear it.

Over Susannah's dark head, Drew smiled a little too broadly. Susannah didn't see his expression but must have sensed it, sitting back and placing a hand on his skinny knee. It disappointed me that Skye turned away from her so quickly. I wanted to see a moment of appreciation—to take in these two girls, recognizing each other. Instead of the brief, polite turning away, as if forced to sit beside a stranger at the movies.

Susannah wedged her hand around the headrest and squeezed my shoulder. "Hola, Catherina," she said, and I smiled back at her.

John Paul started the car. "Where to?" he said.

Skye rolled down her window, letting in the cool, briny air. She gave him directions and pressed her elbow against the door, leaving room for two more teenagers between her and Drew. Still, it felt companionable enough: our carload of outlaws, rumbling down the sandy and vacated streets.

SKYE'S BEACH HOUSE was in the town of Sesuit, on the bay side of Cape Cod. We made our last turn down a private road and rumbled over sand and shells—scrub oak and pitch pine on either side. Finally the vegetation gave way to the top of a clear hill and a wide, wild lawn. Even at night, the view of the Butterfield house was picturesque, the calm bay reflecting moonlight. The car stopped in a square parking lot in front of a multicar garage, and we climbed out into the evening to stare at the towering, rambling edifice before us. John Paul held my hand as we followed Skye along the dark path.

Skye spoke in practiced and modulated tones, like Jackie Kennedy describing the White House renovations. The original house had been built in 1857. She pointed to a modest, two-story wing, settled back on the edge of a wildflower meadow. The property had changed hands in the early 1900s and the first addition had been built—a single story closer to the ocean, now acting as a breezeway to the grandest part of the house, erected after the Second World War as a resort hotel. There were nineteen bedrooms, Skye told us, each with a private bath and an ocean view. Ceramic numbers still hung on every door. She pointed out yet another addition, built in the seventies, even closer to the water's edge.

"The ballroom," Skye said, "so they can host fund-raisers."

The house had gables and widow's walks. It had balconies and turrets, decks and piazzas. Skye's grandfather had bought the place in the late fifties, but renovations had been undertaken faithfully. As Skye led us through the cavernous front hall—once a reception area for hotel guests—we expected musty Oriental rugs and dripping faucets. Instead we were greeted by polished wood and cheerful white walls; picture windows exhibiting the bay like a gigantic, rolling mural. The only one who appeared nonchalant was John Paul—accustomed to feigning indifference in the face of his schoolmates' wealth. The rest of us were openly astounded. No one asked for a tour. It would have taken too long.

My parents' roomy and well-appointed three stories were no match for this. I thought how odd it must have been, growing up an only child in all this *space*. No siblings' voices, reverberating through the hallways.

"My parents used to close it up in winter," Skye said. "Boards on the windows, the water turned off. But then we always ended up coming for holidays and vacations, and my dad decided it would be easier to just keep it open year round."

We came to rest in a low, luxurious living room. Through the wide glass wall we could see the lawn lit by flickers of buoys and passing ships.

"Is that the bar?" Drew asked. He strode toward it on long legs, sandy hair grazing his shoulders. The sort of boy who was not handsome but — through some lucky combination of height, charm, and confidence — would always date beautiful girls.

For an instant, Skye furrowed an uncertain brow. Then she waved her hand, turning the place over to him.

"Go ahead," she said. "They'll never notice."

Drew opened louvered cabinets to reveal everything from Pims to Absolut. "Do we have this place to ourselves?" he said, inspecting wine labels.

"There's a caretaker next door," Skye said. "If you see him, just wave."

"Won't he call your parents?"

"The election's in two weeks," Skye said. "Good luck finding them."

She opened a drawer in a small table, then closed it. As Drew and John Paul mixed drinks, she circled the room. The furniture was antique and spare—only a few drawers to be found. Skye opened every one, closing each quickly, not enough contents to sift through.

"Looking for something?" Susannah said. Her voice sounded gentle, not unfriendly. But I knew her well enough to have registered her decision not to like Skye, which made me nervous. Susannah, too used to being courted, could be coyly outspoken.

"Money," Skye said. "I want to pay Catherine back for the bus ticket."

"You don't know where your parents keep cash?"

Skye shook her head.

"They wouldn't leave it in a living-room drawer," Susannah said. She ran her fingers over the gilt frame of an impressive-looking oil painting. "You want to look in their bedroom. Or if your father has an office."

"I'll help," Drew said. A cork popped cheerfully out of its bottle, and Susannah frowned at him.

"Catherine and I will go," she said, holding out her hand for a wineglass.

Skye declined a drink; Susannah and I followed her upstairs to the Butterfields' rooms on the third floor, carrying our wineglasses. The house—this section, at least—still retained the layout of a hotel, so despite the vast scope it was easy to navigate. The master suite—two rooms and two bathrooms on either side of an airy sitting room—had been constructed in the most recent renovation, everything designed around huge windows and the endless, sparkling view.

"It's amazing, when you think about it," Susannah said, searching the bureau drawers in Mrs. Butterfield's bedroom. She let her eyes roam around the room, the weight of her glance too significant to merely be registering decor. "Doesn't it seem weird that some people have huge houses like this? Summer homes that just stand empty most of the time? While some people live on the streets."

The personal challenge must have been so foreign; Skye didn't seem to recognize it. She replied with the affectless tone of a weary politician. "My father's done more for the homeless than anyone in the Senate," she said. She sounded more tired than defensive.

"I'm not criticizing," Susannah said quickly. "I love your father."

"Everybody does," Skye said. She stood on tiptoes and ran her hands across the top shelf of the walk-in closet.

"He's going to save the old-growth forest right by Catherine's house," Susannah said. "In Old Lenox."

"No he's not," Skye said. "They're already planning to clear-cut there."

"What are you talking about?" I said. "It's one of his campaign promises."

"That's why they're not announcing it until after the election." Skye gave up on the closet and strode into the sitting room. Susannah and I followed. We stood in the middle of the room and watched as Skye set immediately to searching.

"Are you supposed to tell us that?" Susannah said.

"Obviously not. But Catherine trusts you. And you know. She's my best friend."

Susannah narrowed her eyes at me. Then she smiled, confidently amused. Letting me know she understood: no one could ever displace her.

"Anyway," Skye said. "Who are you going to tell?"

"I could call the newspapers," Susannah said. "I could call the Republicans."

Skye laughed. "Be my guest," she said.

I couldn't be sure what she meant, that she didn't care whether Susannah blew the whistle or that she didn't think anyone would believe her.

"But I thought your father was this big environmentalist," I said.

"He is."

Susannah and I looked at each other, confused and disbelieving. It was one thing to know Senator Butterfield had used and exposed his daughter. We expected little more from a parent. But as a politician, as a public figure, I trusted Skye's father absolutely. Everything he said echoed our own vision of the world as it ought to have been. He promised to clean up Boston Harbor and heat inner-city homes. To shut down Chanticleer. He promised to fight for disarmament and ban nuclear testing. He wanted the United States out of El Salvador, out of Nicaragua.

It never occurred to me that he might not believe in his promises as deeply as we did.

"It's difficult to understand," Skye said. "That's what he would say if he were here. He'd give a song and dance about compromise and lesser evils. Who knows how much of it would be true? But I promise, you'd believe every word."

"Maybe you don't know him as well as you think you do," Susannah said.

Skye shrugged, dismissing this possibility. Either she didn't register Susannah's antagonism or she didn't care.

Which surprised me. For all her imperiousness, wounded people were drawn to Susannah. At Waverly, a mentally retarded man named Cory worked in the dining hall—mopping floors and wiping down tables. After meals, we all had to carry our trays to a window adjoining the kitchen and empty our dirty plates and utensils onto a conveyor belt. Every day Cory would go about his work intently, barely looking up at any of us. But whenever Susannah finished her meal, he would stop whatever he was doing and run to meet her at the conveyor belt, so that he could empty the plates from her tray. Susannah always said a simple thank you, never protesting but accepting his help with a child's flattered smile. I don't know exactly what Cory saw in Susannah, but it wasn't just her beauty. The Waverly dining hall was filled with pretty girls. But something about Susannah's dark, freckled face conveyed equal parts sun and rain, carrying the world's ills with a wistful air. I had expected Skye to keen toward this quality. But she didn't seem to notice it.

"There's nothing here," she said, standing up and putting her hands on her hips.

"We'll look in his office," Susannah said. "My father always has cash in his desk drawer. Or he did, anyway, when he lived at home."

We headed downstairs, to Senator Butterfield's vast and private enclave—all oak and Oriental carpet, the first non-sea-facing room in the house.

BACK INTO THE LIVING ROOM, Skye held a hundred-dollar bill in each hand. She held up her find to show the boys, who had just removed a long, oak mirror from the wall. They lowered it on top of the coffee table, then congratulated Skye on her discovery.

Susannah and I replenished our wine. "Sure you don't want a

drink?" I asked Skye. Not to pressure her. I just didn't want to be rude.

"Why not," she said, the barest sigh of acquiescence. For a moment she stared at the mirror like its removal constituted supreme disarray, then seemed to decide she might as well give into the bacchanal entirely. I gave her a glass and sat down on the silk couch next to John Paul, who put his arm around me. He held a tumbler of whiskey, which made him look strangely adult and upper crust. Across the room, Skye looked toward us for a moment, then flicked her eyes away. She had yet to address a direct word to him.

"I wonder if it will be warm enough to swim tomorrow," Susannah said. She kicked off her shoes and settled in a plush leather armchair, wriggling her toes through her stockings. She had a fondness for schoolgirl clothing, and on this day wore a field hockey kilt and white oxford shirt.

"I swim off this bluff during every month of the year," Skye said. "My father and I always swim on New Year's Day, no matter what the temperature is."

"I think I read that once in the *Globe*," Susannah said. "I seem to recall a picture of him all wet and shivering. I don't remember seeing you, though."

Drew pulled a small bag of coke from his pocket. I pictured him deciding on this non-hiding place; riding in the backseat as John Paul drove too fast and police cars cruised by. And then waiting for our bus, never once worrying about the drugs being discovered. In all our minds, getting kicked out of school was the worst thing that could happen to us. Local authorities — the police — never worried us in the slightest. We assumed their course of action would be to hand us back to the school, no matter the infraction. John Paul always joked that a Waverly student ID was a get-out-of-jail-free card.

"May I?" Drew said to Skye, jutting his chin toward the bill in her right hand. She handed it to him without question, and he rolled it into a tight, narrow tube.

Drew of course gave it back to her before using it himself—understanding that first honors always belong to the hostess.

WHILE THE REST of us sat around the mirror, John Paul walked outside to smoke a joint on the piazza. After a while he came back into the room, eyes red rimmed and fixed, bemusedly, on me. I smiled back. Stoned or not, he and I had a similar way of functioning in groups. We both tended to stand back, quietly observing, letting the dynamic unfold around us rather than contributing to it. So that although our blood pulsed just as quickly, and our vision widened just as far, it was the three of them—Drew, Susannah, Skye—who took over the bright, wide room.

Skye had proclaimed herself overheated and removed her sweater and shoes. She couldn't stop moving, circling the perimeters of the room like a nineteenth-century woman taking a turn or Pippin going through his paces in a riding ring.

"I love this drug," Skye said. She swung her arms as she moved. "It makes me feel like running. Or talking. Or just *doing* something. It makes me feel invincible."

"If only I had a camcorder," Susannah said, sprawling on the floor by the coffee table. "Think how much the networks would pay for footage of this famous good girl."

To my surprise, Skye laughed. "Let's see him put that in a positive light," she said. "Maybe I'd get him votes from the Betty Ford contingency."

Susannah stared at me from across the room, widening her eyes. I recognized the invitation to conspire but couldn't bear to reject Susannah or betray Skye. I just smiled shortly, then looked away.

"So, what really happened last year?" Susannah said.

"Hey," Drew protested. "Maybe she doesn't want to talk about that."

"Don't be so protective," Susannah said. "Of course she wants to talk about it. She just did."

"What could I possibly tell you that you don't already know?" Skye said. She halted, aware of the words' narcissistic tinge as soon as they'd escaped. "Not that I'm a big celebrity or anything."

"But you are," Susannah said. "Of course you are." She stood up and walked across the room to the bar. A good six inches shorter than Skye, at least twenty-five pounds lighter, she somehow managed to take up equal space.

"So tell us," Susannah said. "What happened?"

"Just what you know," Skye insisted. "They would have let me get away with Chanticleer if it hadn't have been for that scholarship kid. But that's their thing, once you've been suspended you get expelled on the next infraction. Stupid. Maybe they want plutonium leaking into our rivers? Or they're in love with nuclear bombs?"

"But what about the cheating?" Susannah said.

"It didn't seem like cheating. The truth is, I'd been doing it forever. Writing papers for other kids. In English, in creative writing. Everybody hated doing it and I loved it. I still do. I love typewriters. I love thinking."

"That's cool," Drew said.

Susannah laughed. "You're an idiot," she said fondly, and then turned back to Skye. "Not you," she promised. "Tell us more."

I waited for Skye to say something about the money. She cast the barest glance at me, perhaps waiting to see if I'd interject. Then she shrugged.

"There's not more to tell. I'd always done it, for all sorts of people, and then I did it for this one guy and I got caught. You know, I've won two national scholarships, but my parents never let me use them. They paid my tuition and gave the scholarship money away."

She made an oblique, half-conscious gesture toward the hundred-dollar bill on the mirror. "Doesn't that seem like stealing?" Skye said. "I earned that money for school. I should have been allowed to use it, if I wanted to. My dad always made sure the press found out about giving the money away. He made sure everybody knew that I was smart and he was altruistic. When I got expelled, he leaked that story to the press, too. So that he could prove we were all great crusaders for the good of the world."

"Perverse," Susannah said.

Skye looked at her, startled by the sympathetic insult, and recognizing that she had invited it.

"None of it sounds like a huge deal," Susannah said. "Catherine and I have done each other's homework our whole lives. I do her science. She does my French. I only wish there was a way she could take the AP test for me, since thanks to her everyone thinks I can ace it."

"The difference," Skye said, "is in getting caught. Right?"

She climbed up onto the windowsill and pressed her body against the glass. Black night and silver ocean surrounded her.

"I feel like I want to break out of my body," she said. "You know that James Wright poem? About breaking into blossom? That's what I feel like."

"Neat," Susannah said. Her voice didn't exactly drip with sarcasm, but it was there. I had hoped the poetry would be a point of connection between the two of them. Susannah loved anything to do with words. Last year, Allen Ginsberg had come to read at a Waverly assembly. We'd all sat reverently in our seats, not prepared for him to walk on stage carrying an accordion. He leapt about on stage, what few straggly curls he had left flying in the air around him—playing his squeeze box and chanting in a quavery voice. We tried our best not to laugh, but before long the entire auditorium erupted in laughter, even the most devout beatniks covering their mouths and shaking with embarrassed hilarity. All except for Susannah, who had leaned forward in her seat, brow furrowed in concentration, her eyes narrowed in disappointment over her schoolmates' lack of control.

"Don't they understand the man's a genius?" she asked me afterward, as we filed down the aisle, kindly forgetting—or ignoring—that I'd laughed right along with the rest of them. If Skye had been there, she and Susannah would have been in complete and somber solidarity.

Unlike now—Susannah's disapproving eyes following Skye's ethereal and possessed skulk along the windowsill. The room's bright track lights burned insistently, forbidding shadows of any kind. For a moment I thought Skye might levitate through the window, out toward sea—leaving the four of us staring, wondering if she'd ever really been here, with us, at all.

6

"Skye's not like I thought she would be," Susannah said to me, an hour later.

We stood alone at the bar, opening a new bottle of wine. The others had gone down to the boathouse to see the Sunfish and sea kayaks.

"How so?" I said.

"I don't know." She gathered her dark hair into a ponytail, unwinding an elastic from her wrist. "On TV she always looked so calm and controlled. But in person she has all this frenetic energy."

"We've been feeding her cocaine," I said. "Lots and lots of cocaine."

Susannah laughed. She lifted her hand and watched her fingers twitch, involuntarily. "Still," she said. "Before you met her, I would have expected her to be all elegance and serenity. Maybe a little prim. Then when you told me she wanted to bring us here, I thought she must be very sly. Slick. But she's not slick at all. She seems kind of desperate."

Her hand floated down to the counter but she kept her eyes on the same spot—as if her unkind words hovered in the air in front of her. "It's like she's Sybil," Susannah said. "At war with her various personalities. I keep feeling like one of them is going to pick up the phone and turn us all in."

My heart sank. I had probably known that it would be impossible, friendship between these two most important friends. But I had at least wanted Susannah to be impressed. To see the turbulent beauty, the layers of possibility. I had expected Susannah's estimation of me to rise through my association with Skye. Like carrying a report card full of A's back to my parents, or an armload of blue ribbons. *Look what I brought you.*

We crossed the room and knelt in front of the mirror, balancing our drinks near its edge. One day a cleaning woman would be perplexed by the perfectly round water marks.

"Skye's not desperate," I said. "She's incredibly smart."

"Yes, I know. She told me. Who quotes poetry like that?"

"She likes poems."

"There's something wrong with her."

"But there's not," I said. "It's hard coming into a group of old friends. And she's not used to all this. Breaking rules."

"She didn't have much trouble stealing that two hundred dollars."

"She's not used to coke."

"Nobody's used to this coke," Susannah said. Irritated with my refusal to excoriate Skye, she seized on another subject. She inhaled a line, then told me about a party she and Drew had gone to at Yale.

"The coke was like something the vet would give your horse," Susannah said. "It made us completely paranoid."

I nodded, appreciating the calm and cool exhilaration—like something tickling at the base of my throat, and spreading through all of my veins.

"I was thinking of going back to Venezuela," Susannah said.

"To visit your father?"

She made a motion with her hand, like shooing away a fly. Since her father had left their family to take up permanent residence in the tropics, Susannah refused any feelings for him.

"No," she said. "To get more coke. Even with buying the plane tickets, we could make a ton of money. If that guy wanted a hundred a gram for that swill we had last week? We could raise the money for the trip before we even leave."

She fiddled with her collar. Small appliquéd strawberries, where the buttons would have been on a boy's collar, matched the pendant on her gold necklace.

"So you and Drew would go?"

"Drew." She made the same fly-shooing gesture. "He's not going to last much longer, I can tell you that right now."

I didn't pursue this pronouncement, which she made often. I liked Drew but wouldn't necessarily have mourned if Susannah got rid of him. He kept a python in a glass cage beneath his bed. I'd watched him feed the snake live mice and considered him capable of anything.

"You and me," Susannah said. "We could go to Venezuela. You'd love these guys who sold me the coke. Rico and Alan. And oh my God, Catherine. The birds. I would love to show you the birds. It's like being in another epoch."

We each leaned over the mirror and snorted another line. The coke did a strange little tap dance up the back of my neck, clearing my brain of any misgivings. The dark shoreline outside gave way to lush jungle. Neon birds.

"Okay," I said, and worried for a brief moment that I would have to draw blood to seal the agreement.

But this was Susannah, who knew and trusted me. So she only grabbed my hand and led me out the door into the unseasonably balmy evening.

JOHN PAUL STOOD on the tiled piazza, smoking a cigarette. "Where's Skye?" I asked.

"She and Drew took out the kayaks," he said. I looked out over the water: calm, cold, and very dark.

"Drew went with her?" Susannah said. She sounded angry but resigned, like this were exactly the sort of thing she might expect from Drew—or any male. She took the cigarette from John Paul's fingers. "What were they thinking?"

He shrugged. "They're very high."

Susannah blew out an abrupt stream of smoke. She had lost the ability to stand still—her feet doing an odd, unrhythmic shuffle. The three of us walked closer to the water, and I thought I could make out two banana-shaped forms, gliding alongside the jetty. Heading toward open sea.

"You'd never catch me doing that," Susannah said. "I've seen *Jaws* too many times."

We stood quietly for a moment, listening to the tide. Ordinarily Susannah was good at finding the fun in these evenings, and her bristle disconcerted me. I suppressed the urge to apologize, reaching out to touch her elbow instead.

"At least they're not in the same boat," John Paul said, and Susannah kicked sand at him.

"Shut up," she said. "Like I care what that dirtbag does."

It was exactly the sort of thing she said about her father. John Paul and I each threw an arm over her shoulder as we stood there, listening to the lap, lap, lap of the tide.

"You seem different when you're with Skye," John Paul said, a while later. Susannah had insisted we go off by ourselves. We left her with both reluctance and gratitude, her mounting disgruntlement fueled by a sudden bent on snorting lines.

"We won't be long," I promised, as we headed up the stairs.

"Be all night," Susannah said, waving her hand and bending over the mirror. "I'll be fine."

I'd imagined the end of the world so many times—its vacated streets and deserted homes—that wandering through this empty grand hotel felt strangely familiar. Without Skye to direct us we settled on room 6, in honor of John Paul's soccer jersey. It was a nicely decorated room, completely lacking personal effects. The bed seemed about three miles wide. John Paul opened a window so we could hear the ocean. I climbed onto the bed and sat cross-legged. He waited for me to answer and, when I didn't say anything else, sat down in front of me. In the room's muted bed-and-breakfast light, I could see tiny pimples smattered across his forehead. I felt an irrational fondness for that barely perceptible acne. It seemed his one mortal—and therefore best—feature.

My heart beat too fast from the drugs. The past two months, I had lived and breathed Skye. Now, as she paddled farther out to sea, my closeness to her felt increasingly foreign. I worried it had left some kind of mark on me, then cringed at my own disloyalty.

That night in Pennsylvania with John Paul had been a strange and insulated reprieve. On the way to the Cape I had anticipated his presence with great relief, partly because I knew he wouldn't burden me with confidences. We would just coexist, quietly and companionably as ever. I didn't like this new line of conversation, this instant plunge into matters of the heart, as if he'd lost the ability to read my mind.

"Different how?" I asked.

"I don't know," John Paul said. He pulled off his sweater and threw it across the room. It floated heavily, then landed on an embroidered armchair. "Like you love me less?"

I couldn't help it. I laughed. His insecurity seemed so unlikely. He smiled, but not happily, and his sadness slowed my coke-induced giddiness. The year before, any separation from John Paul had felt like death. I remembered waiting for my parents' car before Christmas vacation, clinging to his shirt, feeling like a piece of my skin was about to be pulled away. But since the day we'd been caught in bed together and my father had taken me out of Waverly, I'd learned how to live without him. This never mitigated the happiness I felt when in his presence. Instead, it seemed a sort of elevation. I didn't need him anymore, but still I wanted him.

"I don't love you less," I said, wishing I knew how to explain in a more complete way. "How could I?"

He shrugged and put his hand on my knee, more aware than I of the various ways love could be withheld. John Paul's parents and mine shared the same age difference: eighteen years. But his father was married to another woman. He'd met John Paul's mother when she was just a teenager, with a summer job in the same Essex restaurant where she still waited tables. Like my mother, John Paul's father was French, and when summer ended so did the affair. He had gone back to his family in Lyons when John Paul's mother sent a letter to his office, announcing the arrival of her baby. Since then he'd sent checks, but not regularly or often. John Paul sometimes spent summers in Lyons, posing as the son of a business associate, living in a downstairs guest room and calling his father Monsieur Filage.

I picked up his hand and brought it to my lips. He smiled, because we usually left that sort of gesture to him.

We were worldly enough, John Paul and I, to know that despite everything we felt for each other our relationship would not continue. College applications had begun arriving for me in the mail, from good schools that would accept me because they had equestrian teams: Dartmouth, Amherst, Cornell. John Paul was a fifth-former, but like Skye a brilliant student, and certain he'd be headed to Harvard, Stanford, or Yale. We'd never broached the idea of coordinating. We knew that at college there would be other people, other interests, and our connection to each other would become thinner and thinner.

"But right now we're here together," John Paul said, uncannily.

His skin smelled like the kind of soap men used—sharp and drying. His hands—under my shirt now, just above my hips—felt cool and chapped. The shared mourning of our inevitable separation felt profound and unbearably sexy. John Paul was handsome enough to get away with being a brigand, a ravisher. But he always moved with amazing caution, every touch a tentative request for permission.

Our kiss was interrupted by Susannah's knock on the door. For a split second I felt furious, not caring what happened to Drew or Skye as long as nobody bothered me with it till morning.

THE BUTTERFIELD KITCHEN, once professional, was easily the size of White Cottage. The three of us stood around a long marble island. The industrial clock above the eight-burner stove read four thirty, but the windows didn't betray any signs of dawn. Just black night filled with the seaside movement of wind, shore, eel grass—and still no sign of Drew or Skye.

"Do you think a flashlight would help?" Susannah said, digging through utility drawers. She found two in the pantry—huge, square, and professional looking. She handed one to John Paul and one to me. I noticed, walking through the living room, that the mirror was clean. Susannah must have finished the three lines that had been left there when John Paul and I headed upstairs.

And it showed when we reached the water. Two days away from Halloween, she stood at the edge of the tide wearing wispy baby-doll pajamas, the cold water lapping over her bare feet. Her slim arms beat in a jerking motion as she paced up and down along the shore.

"I don't know what to do," she said.

John Paul shined his light across the water. I lifted mine, its cylindrical beacon meager and ineffective against the vastness of the jetty, the huge rocks emerging at low tide, the vague white caps on what had been—earlier in the evening—a completely calm sea.

"Should we call the coast guard?" I asked.

"That seems a little premature," John Paul said. "It's not like there's a storm or anything."

"And that's exactly what she wants us to do," Susannah said. "She wants us to freak out and call the coast guard, and get her back on the evening news."

"No she doesn't," I said.

Susannah wheeled around and pointed a delicate, tapered finger at me. She weighed exactly ninety-eight pounds, and I marveled again at how much space she could take up through sheer force of will.

"You can't see it," she said. "You're too dazzled. But that's exactly what she wants. She's using you, Catherine."

"She's not," I said. "She's my friend."

"Right. Your best friend."

"I never said that."

I would have added something more, some sort of assurance. *Of course she's not,* I might have said. *You are my best friend. You always will be.* But I'd never known how to make those sorts of statements, definite and emotional. Susannah always made them for me. Luckily, this ability did not leave her now.

"I am your best friend, Catherine."

I looked into her dark, freckled face, certain but unable to articulate: that one friendship did not contradict the other.

"Why is this Skye's fault?" I said instead. "Drew's out there, too."

"Look," John Paul said.

Susannah snatched his flashlight and held it up next to her face, as if it would enlarge her vision as well as illuminate it. In a minute we could hear the lapping of an oar as a single kayak rowed into the thin shaft of light. Until that moment, despite our upset, I don't think we actually believed anything bad might happen. We had simply been going through the motions of distress and worry, confident that any moment they would both appear, apologetic and shivering.

A tiny reddening of the horizon, and a sudden widening of light. We saw Drew get out of his kayak. Susannah ran through the water as he pulled the boat toward shore. His shoulders sagged with exhaustion as he returned her violent embrace.

"Where's Skye?" I said, as Drew scraped the kayak onto the sand.

"She wouldn't come back," he said. He unbent himself away from the boat and brushed sand off his soaking wet jeans. "She's kind of crazy," he said.

Susannah raised her eyebrows at me, victorious.

"What were you guys doing out there?" John Paul said.

"Paddling. We went out to this sandbar and walked around. I wasn't sure it was smart to paddle out so deep, but she kept saying the water was calm and the sky was good, and it would be a shame to row back so early."

I felt slightly relieved: no accidents, no tidal waves, no sharks. Only a triumph of romance over sagacity, which I understood far better than disaster.

Drew shivered. The morning had grown distinctly lighter, and I could see huge goose bumps on his bare arms.

"You better get a hot shower, " John Paul said. "How'd you get so wet?"

"We went swimming."

"*Swimming.*" Susannah shook her head in disgust.

"Now what do we do?" I said. "Call the police?"

John Paul looked out at the water. "Well," he said. "We've got a fair amount of coke here. And we're not supposed to be in this house in the first place. And her father is a senator. Campaigning for reelection."

"I'll tell you what I'm going to do," Susannah said. "I'm going back to school."

"What do you mean?" I said.

"We should all go. We should all get into John Paul's car and drive away. So when Skye paddles up, instead of a television news crew and coast guard helicopters, there's just this big empty house."

We didn't say anything. I stared back at the water, willing Skye's kayak to appear.

"Let's just wait a little longer," John Paul said, coming to my defense. "Let's say give it till it's totally light out, and then we'll call someone."

"You can do what you want," Susannah said. "I'm going home."

SHE BUNDLED BACK into her clothes and called a cab while Drew took a shower.

"There's still time to cancel the taxi," Susannah said, when she hung up. "John Paul can drive us all back to Waverly. Catherine can go back to Esther Percy on Sunday."

"I can't leave Skye," I said.

John Paul put his arm around me. "I can't leave Catherine," he said.

Susannah frowned. Drew appeared, damp and chagrined. "Put on your coat," she said, plucking Skye's hundred-dollar bill from the mirror and sliding it into her pocket. "We'll wait at the end of the driveway. Do you want to walk down with us?"

"We better not," I said. "We better wait for Skye."

"God," Susannah said. "I really hate that girl."

"I don't know why you're so angry," I said. "She could be in trouble. It's not like you to be so heartless."

"Heartless," Susannah said. "That's the last thing I am. I just know that Skye's not in trouble at all. She wants to get in trouble, and she wants to drag us down with her. If I really wanted to be heartless, I'd play along with her pathetic scheme. But I've got better things to do. You should, too."

For some reason I thought of Susannah's father—how he'd feel if he knew Susannah planned to visit Venezuela without contacting him. And I felt a sudden sinking fear, that I'd drawn the same kind of ire on myself.

"Please don't be mad," I said.

"I'm not mad at you, Catherine, I'm worried about you." Which sounded so much like something a parent would say we both started to laugh. She stepped forward and hugged me.

"Come with?" she said.

"I can't."

She touched my cheek with her fingertips, then she and Drew trudged out the door and down the long driveway to wait for the taxi.

John Paul and I went upstairs to our room. He rolled a joint while I pulled the down comforter off the bed; then he stuffed the rest of the pot—easier to come by at Waverly—into my backpack.

We walked back down to the shore and sat down on the sand, smoking the joint and staring dutifully out at the horizon. His arm linked through mine in silent and comradely sentry. Till finally the cocaine ebbed and morning arrived—the light and marijuana acting on us like phenobarb, and we both fell asleep in the sand.

I WOKE UP SHIVERING from a stark apocalyptic nightmare. An urgent but shaky relief—opening my eyes to so much color after the burnt gray of my dream, its obliterating mushroom cloud. Low tide had painted an entirely new landscape of sand, rocks, and tide pools, and the sun shone alarmingly central in the sky. Everything muted, green and orange, the clean brushed lines of an Andrew Wyeth painting.

John Paul was gone, nothing but a neat indentation in the sand.

Drew's boat lay where he had abandoned it, resting on its side like a beached seal. Out on the horizon, no boats—just a calm sea and a sudden drop, the route to falling off the edge of the earth.

I hoisted a comforter around my shoulders. In daylight, from the beach, Skye's house looked grotesque. Most of the shoreline was sparsely dotted with cedar-shingled cottages, dark and lonesome, their windows boarded. But the Butterfield house—with its convoy of additions—rode the bluff like a cruise ship. I walked toward it with a sour taste in my mouth.

John Paul had cleaned up the glasses and bottles and was spraying the mirror with Windex. "You'll have to help me put this back," he said.

"Did Skye come home?" I asked, and he shook his head.

"I don't think so," he said.

An abyss opened up around me, terrible and unreal. Skye, so alive and shimmering. I remembered her palm underneath the razor blade, and along with dread for her safety I felt a rising and newly familiar panic: like she were a patient in my care, and I had just realized my lack of credentials.

We balanced the mirror and heaved it onto the wall. John Paul stood back, directing my realignment.

"I think we have to call the police," John Paul said, when it was straight.

"At least the drugs are gone," I said.

John Paul nodded. Of all of us, he was the only one with anything real to lose. Susannah, Drew, me—everyone's parents could provide high-priced lawyers, and new schools, and endless bank accounts to pad every fall till the end of our days. But if John Paul lost his scholarships, that would be the end of his private education—perhaps any education at all. I never asked him why he was willing to risk everything he'd worked for. As opposed to my father, who liked to broadcast the differences between himself and the naturally wealthy, John Paul preferred pretending they didn't exist. Not that he ever misrepresented himself; he just refused to acknowledge that his background mattered.

Still, in this instance, I had to say something. "You can go, if you want," I said. "And I'll do this myself."

"No," he said. "I want to stay with you."

I knew I should have protested more and briefly hated myself for making the offer while knowing absolutely he'd refuse it. Even in that moment, I felt that instead of just admiring John Paul's courage I should have tried to emulate it. We stood there together, in the midst of the Butterfield riches. Every floorboard and tile and piece of art radiated staggering wealth, and it shouldn't have been difficult for me to insist on bearing this burden myself. But of course it wasn't only difficult, it was impossible. The thought of facing the authorities alone terrified me, and I could no more send John Paul away than I could swim through the icy Atlantic and find Skye. I reached out and grabbed his hand, thinking how funny it was that my father objected to John Paul, who embodied so many of the qualities he approved of most. Never mind the drugs and the unauthorized forays from school. I believed in John Paul completely. Not only in his intrinsic goodness and his sense of ethics: but his gallantry.

I picked up the phone and just as I knew he would, John Paul eased it out of my hand. Put it to his ear and started to dial.

"Who are you calling?" a voice said from the doorway.

And there, of course, was Skye. Wearing a thick terry-cloth robe, her freshly shampooed hair spilling over its lapels. Looking like she'd materialized from air, completely new. Comprising everything in the world that was wholesome, uncomplicated, and lovely. I didn't know if the intake of breath belonged to me, or John Paul, or both of us. I didn't know if it originated from anger, or relief, or admiration. I only understood that soon John Paul would leave this house, too, and that none of my friends would ever come back — to anywhere near Skye.

And I had the oddest vision, a three-second dream in the middle of the day. Skye and me, walking across the night on a rope made from stars. Our arms held out like circus performers, fair heads bent and focused on our precarious paths. The moon full and silver, shimmering down on us.

The vision burst, leaving only three teenagers and the ocean view. The rafters and fine leather. The silk upholstery and the good antiques and hundred-dollar bills hiding in drawers. All amounting to the exorbitant hush of safety.

7

THAT AFTERNOON, SKYE and I picked our way across the rocky bluff to collect her kayak. I stopped breathing when we came across the carcass of a seal—half rotted, the fetid scent of blubber and brine.

"This bluff is its own little graveyard," Skye said. "We find dead gulls, gannets, porpoise fish. Seals. Last summer we even found a dead coyote."

She brought me up to the bank where she and her father had dragged the coyote corpse—safe from the high tide, so they could track its decomposition. Young and slight, its glassy eyes open and staring. Astonishing white teeth.

"Probably it drowned," Skye said. "That's what the Audubon people said, when we called them."

We walked on with bent heads, to keep track of our footing. "In the winter, we find half-dead sea turtles," Skye said. "They wait too long to migrate because the bay's so warm, and then when they hit the ocean they get cold-stunned and wash up on shore. The year before last my dad carried one all the way back to the house. It weighed almost fifty pounds." Her voice was a strange combination of boastful and mourning.

We scaled a vast array of rocks and boulders, slippery with salt water. I looked around, wondering how anyone could spot a turtle shell amid this primitive expanse of gray and green.

"You won't see any now," Skye said, following my gaze. "It's too early."

Asserting herself on a subject where she was knowledgeable seemed to comfort her, but her skin still looked flushed from crying and her breath had a childlike catch.

"What happened?" I said, and then added, in case she thought I wanted to talk more about last night, "To the turtle, I mean."

"They brought it to the aquarium in Boston. We went to visit it there. Had pictures taken with it, all that. Then when it was better, they flew it down to Florida."

"That must have been good press for your dad," I said.

"That's not why he did it," she said, in a tone that hovered somewhere between neutral and plaintive. "It's why he does a lot of things. But not everything."

We stepped off the edge of the bluff onto a wide stretch of sandy beach. Weathered wooden staircases lined the battered, root-swelled beach wall.

"There it is," said Skye. The kayak huddled under a stairway, tied to a step to protect it from high tide.

"Once," she said, "my dad and I were kayaking and we saw a humpback whale. It breached right next to us. I thought the wake was going to lift my boat. You've never seen anything so big in your life as that whale. I thought I was going to die of fright. But then, after a few seconds, I realized it was just swimming by, minding its own business. I've never seen anything so beautiful."

Automatically, I looked out toward the water. Maybe I thought the whale would present itself above the waves. Skye watched me with a pitying and grateful expression.

"He didn't have to leave," she said.

"I know," I answered.

By the time John Paul had packed and driven away, the day was more than half gone. Now the sun had begun a startlingly rapid descent; from the slight gust of onshore wind, I could tell its dip signified not only the end of the day, but the stretch of warm weather. I tried to remember if I'd packed a sweater.

"You're cold." Skye reached out to touch her fingertips to my elbow.

I pictured her, soaking wet in the middle of the sea and night, impervious to any chill.

"No," I said. "I'm fine."

But the idea of herself as caretaker seemed to please Skye, so I let myself shiver a little. She untied the kayak, and we each picked up an end. Within twenty minutes we were making our way in the dusk, panting under our cumbersome load—tripping, laughing, and righting ourselves whenever we took a false, shaky step.

THE NIGHT BEFORE, out on the water, a few minutes after Drew had headed toward shore, Skye remembered the whale. Not the transcendence of the experience so much as the terror.

"It was so strange," she said, back in the enormous kitchen. She leaned on the counter while I uncorked another bottle of French wine. "I didn't want a chance to think. I just wanted to keep moving, keep going, keep having fun. And then when Drew paddled off, and I was all alone, I got the clearest picture of everything bad or evil that could happen."

I carried the bottle and two glasses, following Skye across the kitchen and into the ballroom: a huge, fairy-tale place, unfurnished except for the chandelier and the enormous arched windows that looked out to the sea. We sat down in the middle of the vast parquet floor and I poured our wine. Skye picked up her glass, running her fingers around the rim until it hummed, but did not take a sip.

Instead she told me about the night before: how she and Drew had paddled out to Sandy Neck, a spit of land that curved into the water—mirroring the tip of Cape Cod itself. They had done handstands and cartwheels on the beach, the waves that lapped their fingers so surprisingly warm that they took off their clothes to go swimming; Skye left her silver bracelet on a rock so its glint would not attract sharks. Then they raced through the frigid deep toward the first flashing buoy. But the deeper water was so cold, they barely made it a quarter of the way—Drew turning back first, then Skye following. When she met him onshore, he had already caught his breath and pulled on his pants. He put his hands on her shoulders, rubbing them to warm her up. Then pulled her close and kissed her.

"It felt nice," she told me. "He's not that cute, but I was freezing from the water, and his skin was warm."

She kissed him back for a minute, maybe two. She could feel the fine hair along her spine stand on end from the air, the droplets of water running down toward her legs. His lips. Then she pulled away.

"You have a girlfriend," she reminded him.

"It's okay," he said. "Susannah and I have an agreement."

Skye laughed. "Does Susannah know that?"

He tried to kiss her again but she pulled away, reaching into the surf and splashing him with an armful of water. She ran back to the rock, and as she collected her bracelet he appeared behind her, wrapping his arms around her waist. She bent to duck out of his grasp, but he held her tight. Drew was about five inches taller than Skye, but it startled her that he should be so much stronger. Her body felt suddenly meager and tiny in its attempt to move away from him. That she was nude, pressed against his damp but fully clothed torso, emphasized her vulnerability, and so Skye drew back her fist and landed it squarely against Drew's solar plexus.

He doubled over with a snort and infuriating laugh, releasing his grasp but snatching Skye's pants from the rock. She pulled on her shirt and called to him as he ran down the beach.

"Bring that back," she yelled, suddenly laughing again. She buttoned her shirt as she ran after him. The night air held only the vaguest chill; what cold there was pumped itself into the prickling skin along her spine, and down her legs. She shivered as she moved forward, a strange and delicious spasm—caught up short as Drew turned and stopped, so that she slammed directly into his chest.

His fingers dug gently into her shoulders, and he kissed her again, melting the chill into irresistible warmth. Skye kept her eyes open, watching the black sea lap the shores of Sandy Neck. She envisioned the kayaks, waiting for them a few yards back on the beach. The cloth of her pants brushed her shoulders, hanging limply from Drew's hands. From there, the usual results of manufactured closeness—the conspiracy of drugs and night and just the two of them. Skye stayed naked from the waist down, Drew kept his jeans firmly buttoned. Tongues and hardening, sinking into the sand below. Everything about this place a no-man's-land, with its ecotone of sea and shore, cold and warm. The tide worked its deep, slow way back to England, making Drew's traveling hands the most natural and inconsequential event in the world. Skye's breath quickened along with his, the coke pumping through her capillaries with rhythmic exaltation.

Afterward, she lay on the sand, staring up into the dark sand. She could hear Drew by the water, cursing and splashing.

"What are you doing," Skye called. Realizing with a pinch of inevitable sadness that Drew had left their limbo and returned to the world of consequences.

"Cleaning up," he said. Skye felt her face flush as Susannah mattered again. The trouble with any kind of climax, Skye thought, was the flatness that always followed. She sat up and pulled on her pants and wished for a way to bring the excitement back.

"Hey," she called to Drew. "I'll race you back home."

Running along the shore to her kayak and sneakers, she listened for equally playful footsteps behind her but heard only a resolute and guilty plodding.

She pushed off in her boat, floating out a yard or two. Drew plunged into the water, making the dampness uniform. Then he climbed into his kayak and rowed toward her. By the time he came close enough for her to see his face, he was shivering. Skye could also see that his mood had changed to grim, distant, and she instantly longed for moments ago, back on the sand, pressed together under a dark and moonless sky.

She laughed, hoping the sound would make her feel less lonely. It echoed hollowly along the waves, and she wondered if Susannah, John Paul, and I would be able to hear it from her father's house.

"Let's not go back yet," she said to Drew. "It's such a perfect night."

But she had already lost him. He didn't even mention the cold, or his wet clothes. He just said, "Susannah will be worried," and paddled past her, toward the vast row of lights that marked her own stretch of shoreline. The water, Skye said, was much calmer than it looked from where John Paul and I had stood—staring out with our anxious imaginations. Offshore, the sky hung so dark and low, she thought she might reach up and lay her hands flat against it. The boat rose and fell, and she had a sudden awareness of all the creatures swimming just below, unseen to her, their movements contributing to the swaying current.

"I called out to Drew," she said. "But he didn't hear me. Or maybe he was mad. Like it was my fault he cheated on Susannah."

The memory of this injustice—along with that of Drew distant and angry enough to abandon her to the sea—seemed to give Skye a moment of profound grief. She halted now, the wineglass suspended below her chin, and for the first time I understood why she might feel old. The sadness across her face reminded me of an expression my mother sometimes got—contemplating her sorrows and accepting there was nothing she could do to change them.

Instead of following Drew—his diagonal route back to her house—Skye paddled straight to shore. Abandoned her boat and walked briskly over the rocks. When she got inside, none of us were there, so she went up to her room and took a hot shower, then got into bed and fell asleep.

"Why didn't you come out and tell us you'd gotten back safely?" John Paul had asked the next morning, when Skye appeared in the living room.

"I guess I assumed you'd gone to sleep?" Skye said. "I couldn't exactly search every bedroom."

"We were worried," I told her.

"I'm so sorry," she'd begged. She dissolved, tears running down her face—inexplicably making her prettier, more luminous. Skye was one of those rare people who look best after personal tragedy and sleepless nights. "I didn't mean to upset you. Please stay, John Paul. There's a screening room downstairs, I'll set up a movie. There's plenty of wine. We can make popcorn."

He'd shuffled uncomfortably. If it had been Susannah instead of Skye, the three of us could have passed a weekend easily and naturally. But as I watched John Paul watch Skye, I knew he understood. That she only wanted him to forgive her on my account. She didn't really care about his opinion, and she did not want him to stay.

"It's okay," he said. He reached out to touch her hand, then changed his mind and grasped mine instead. "No blood shed," he said. "I'll see you another time."

From the elegant piazza, I watched him drive off—feeling furious with Skye, that her irresponsibility had first robbed us of a precious chance to make love, and then chased him away. I felt trapped at the luxurious house, longing instead to chase down the battered Buick and ride away on ratty Naugahyde, my head on John Paul's shoulder as he steered one-handed. So it was strange that later, listening to these confessions in the ballroom, John Paul's departure and Skye's presence felt inevitable and correct. I would never have said it aloud, or even acknowledged the formation of the idea in my mind: how much easier being there became, once the person who didn't belong had left.

Skye shook her head, then finally took a drink from her glass.

"You can't tell Susannah about Drew," she said. "Swear to me you won't tell her."

I had already decided not to tell her. Drew couldn't last forever, and news of his faithlessness would only confirm Susannah's bleak worldview. Still: my allegiance stretched tenuously enough that I couldn't bring myself to swear. Skye waited a minute, then decided to take my silence as oath.

"I hate this feeling," she said. "I feel so disappointed. Like such a failure. Do you know that feeling?"

I nodded.

"It makes me crazy," she said. "It makes me want to crawl out of my skin."

It might have comforted her — made her feel less crazy and alone — if I'd talked about my own guilty conscience. I knew, after all, how it felt to disappoint people. I could have told Skye about the terrible days during my suspension from Waverly and the way I would sit in my room, cringing, while my parents argued downstairs about what to do with me. It had made me feel so hollow and ruined, the way my father would glance away when I appeared — like he couldn't stand the sight of me. Even now a part of me shrinks, remembering his suit-coated back heading out the front door, leaving the house without so much as a wave in my direction.

Maybe if Susannah had left some coke, I would have been more generous than usual. A surge of adrenaline might have relaxed my guard and jostled confiding words loose. Instead, I reached over and patted her arm.

"It doesn't matter," I said.

Skye stared at a point over my shoulder, frowned, and took another sip of wine. "Do you want to see the old part of the house?" she said. "I never got to show you my bedroom."

We carried our wineglasses through one living room and another, through serpentine halls and the old causeway with its wide redwood beams till we came to a low, wood-paneled portion of the house—with knots in the grain and black footsteps on the ceiling.

"They modeled it after a sea captain's house." Skye said. "But a sailor would never build so close to shore. They always lived away from the sea, on higher ground. Out of the wind, out of the flood zones."

She headed up a narrow, enclosed staircase. At the top was an attic room with slanted ceilings and exposed beams. A large white bed, neatly made, tucked in the corner against an ocean-facing window. Low bookcases everywhere, crammed with picture books and thick novels. Her weekend clothes unpacked in her dresser drawers, nothing on the floor but the polished expanse of hardwood.

"It's fantastic, isn't it," Skye said.

I nodded.

"One time when they redid the main house, they fixed up a new room for me. We worked with an architect and an interior decorator, getting it just the way I wanted. But then when it was finished, I couldn't bear to move. I felt like this room would miss me, like I would break its heart. 'Rooms don't have hearts,' my dad said. But I just couldn't do it."

Skye sat down on her bed and looked out at the ocean. I sat in the white wicker rocking chair.

"I guess I was eight?" she said. "Maybe nine. Young enough so I thought rooms really did have hearts. It took me the longest time to grasp the concept of inanimate objects. I used to think the house would have a brain somewhere in the attic. That creaky noises at night were its internal organs gurgling."

I had grown up so attached to animate objects—so wrapped up

in my horses—that I'd never worried much about rooms or things. When I'd abandoned Bloom for Pippin, unlike Skye's room, she *had* minded. The horse had missed me, and I knew it. But I had abandoned her anyway, leaving her at home and taking Pippin with me to Esther Percy. In contrast, Skye's irrational loyalty to these unthinking walls represented a superior moral fiber. I felt lacking in the same way I had the day before, allowing John Paul to stand by my side and make that phone call. It frightened me slightly—as if I recognized myself as capable of doing harm to the people I loved.

"Wouldn't it be great if we had a choice," Skye said, "to go backward in time instead of forward?"

She leaned against the pillows. On her bedside table, there were two framed photographs—one of a joyfully freckled and skinny Skye, receiving a hug from her father. There was a sailboat in the background, impossibly blue seas and white sand. The two of them in matching windbreakers, looking so golden and happy that I understood Skye's longing to return to that time. I wanted to crawl into the picture myself. She followed my gaze to the photograph and picked up the one next to it, assuming it was the one that had caught my eye. I balanced the frame in my hands and looked at Douglas Butterfield, years younger, arm in arm with JFK. On a dock somewhere—faint clouds gathering in the sky behind them. I wanted to ask Skye if she'd ever been to the Kennedy compound. I imagined her laughing and insouciant in a blue bikini, putting her hand on John John's shoulder for balance as she stepped into a speedboat.

I waited for the details to come spilling out of her, but Skye—uncharacteristically—didn't offer any history.

"You should see him," she said. "You will see him. He's the shini-

est person in the world. He's got this light around him. All you'll
want to do is let it envelop you."

For a moment I thought she meant John F. Kennedy, who'd died
well before we were born. Then I realized with something like shock:
she was talking about Douglas Butterfield. Her father.

In a thousand years, I couldn't imagine saying anything remotely
like that about my own father. I looked back at the picture, with
the kind of longing I'd only felt watching Michael Landon on *Little
House on the Prairie*. There was a slight rash along Senator Butterfield's jaw, like an irritation from shaving. I ran my finger over it,
back and forth, as if to erase the imperfection.

"I found him with a woman last year," Skye said. She didn't look
at me, but out the window. "After the protest at Chanticleer, before
they found me, I came here. My dad was on the phone with the
Devon headmaster, pretending to be surprised I was missing. But really, he was the one who told me to go to that protest. He promised
that he would fix it somehow, that I wouldn't be expelled."

She watched me carefully as she spoke, gauging my reaction. I
wasn't sure what she wanted — vindicating shock, or a comforting
lack of horror. I sat perfectly still, conscious of my wide, unblinking
stare.

"Anyway," she said. "I walked into the living room, that one with
the bar, and there he was in his bathrobe. With this blonde woman
sitting on the couch, wearing this ancient pink robe of my mother's,
with a frayed hem and coffee stains. It seemed like the most horrible
violation of privacy, letting some stranger wear that ratty old robe."

I thought how much more Susannah would like Skye, if she could
hear this story. How much better she might understand her.

"Did you tell your mom?" I asked.

Skye shook her head, then nodded. "I promised him I wouldn't, but then I couldn't help myself. The way he backed off keeping me in Devon, when he could tell how much more press he would get if I were expelled. He broke his promise, so I broke mine. But I think my mother already knew. She seemed less angry about the woman than about my knowing. Still there were big, ugly scenes. Talk of divorce."

"But she stayed with him."

"She says she respects what he's trying to accomplish. As a man. For the world. He promised to get rid of the woman, but I don't think he did. I know she still works on his campaign."

"I'm sorry," I said.

I wondered if all husbands cheated on their wives. I thought of Drew out on Sandy Neck with Skye and couldn't imagine John Paul ever doing such a thing. I remembered Mrs. November, that scornful flick of her wedding ring, and wondered if her slender and unworthy husband sometimes strayed. I imagined my mother catching my father with another woman, and wondered how she would react. I pictured her narrowing her eyes and closing the door with a reprimanding click, then getting on with the rest of her day. She would saddle a horse and take a long ride through the old-growth forest, then come home to make a complicated dinner. Rolling out pastry dough, a taut tendon in her forearm and a slight hardness in her jaw would be the only indication that something had gone amiss.

Skye reached over and eased the photograph out of my hands. Put it back on the table in its precise original spot.

"Remember that poem," she said. "That Shel Silverstein poem, about the language of the caterpillars and the gossip of the starlings?"

"I think it's the language of the flowers," I said, grateful that for once I recognized one of her references.

"That's how I feel sometimes. Like there's this language I knew when I was a kid, and every year of my life it unravels just a little bit. Becomes more and more indecipherable. So that I'm left all alone, trying to figure it out. Trying to remember it."

She sipped from her wine again and grimaced, as if it were distasteful but necessary medicine. And I wanted to ease it out of her hands — returning her to the times before last winter, when nothing threatened her high ideals and grand illusions.

She broke my sympathy with a non sequitur. "John Paul's not what I expected," she said.

My spine straightened, an involuntary bristle, and for some reason I pictured my father: his weathered and grouchy intelligence. Never knowing or caring about the right fork, or what anybody — particularly the proper and wealthy — thought of him.

"Why not?" I said.

"I don't know, " Skye said. "I can't put it into words. Is he the one who gets the cocaine?"

"No," I said. "He's not."

Skye waited, a polite and abiding pause. Still on the defensive, I didn't feel the barest temptation to tell her. Any other time, Skye might have pressed me. But so soon after her disappearance and her dalliance with Drew, she felt penitent. Cautious.

"Okay," she said instead. "Tell me something else about John Paul. Tell me something I wouldn't guess."

"He speaks perfect French," I said, and she laughed.

"That's a very personal detail, Catherine," she said. "But does he speak the language of the flowers?"

I frowned, scratching my fingernails across the chair's embroidered armrests. Skye retreated back into her poem.

"Once I heard and answered all the questions of the crickets," she said. *"And joined the crying of each falling dying flake of snow, / Once I spoke the language of the flowers . . ."*

So many opportunities, and I missed them all. There was so much I could have changed, and rescued: if only I had given Skye and Susannah the information that might have brought them close together. Instead of always protecting and guarding.

"How did it go?" I asked, rather than tell Skye the truth. *"How did it go?"*

8

PIPPIN HAD COLIC. Two days after our return from Cape Cod, I found him in his stall — biting at his abdomen, then stretching out like he needed to urinate. The vet was summoned; he pronounced the condition mild and administered sedatives, instructing me to let him walk. I led him round and round the outdoor ring, a wool blanket draped over his back, the cold burning through my leather riding gloves.

Nobody knew what he'd gotten into — no evidence of crab apples or tipped-over barrels of grain. I felt sure that my own indulgences had somehow transferred to him. Sweat glistened on his neck, his nostrils flared. Every few rounds, I would stop to bury my face in his slick mane and inhale that musky animal smell, manure and sweet grass, like restorative oxygen. The illness — the fear that he might die — transformed my feelings for him. My resentment and antipathy evaporated into the frigid autumn air, and I found myself awash in anticipated grief. *Please,* I whispered, to whatever nebulous deity might have been listening. *Please let him be okay. I'll never do it again.*

What "it" might have been, I couldn't say specifically. Certainly I

didn't mean I'd never sneak away to see John Paul: I could still feel
his fingertips, sliding out of my hand as we said good-bye. But I was
relieved that Susannah, in her anger, had neglected to replenish my
supply of coke. I only had a scant half gram left and wished I had
the courage to flush it. Just thinking of the drug made my bones feel
rattled and poisoned, but I knew this aversion wouldn't be enough
to dissuade temptation. At least not as it would present itself: in the
form of Skye's insistence. Faced with Pippin's adversity, my friendship with Skye seemed painfully lonely and limited. If Susannah had
been there, or John Paul, they would be walking by my side, stroking
Pippin's neck and promising me that he would be all right.

That weekend on the Cape, with no ride to the bus station,
Skye and I had decided to hitchhike all the way back to Esther
Percy — Skye tucking her hair under a wool cap to keep from being
recognized. On the way, we received the usual lectures from concerned adults who picked us up.

"Some fella could take you for a one-way ride," one woman said,
after we'd clambered into the backseat of her battered AMC Spirit.
A menthol cigarette dangled from her bright red lips.

I leaned forward and showed her the pearl-handled stiletto I kept
in my coat pocket.

"You think that's going to help a little wisp of a girl like you?" the
woman said. "Pull that on some two-hundred-pound guy, it's going
to end up under your ribs."

"If you're so worried," Skye said, "why not drive us all the way
back to school?"

Skye may have been obedient, I thought. But clearly she'd never
been meek.

The woman considered this for a moment — assessing us through her rearview mirror. I could see the spiderwebbed wrinkles around her eyes, magnified in the reflection.

She shrugged. "I guess I'd rather take a little time out of my day than see the pair of you on the ten o'clock news." And she drove all the way to I-91, all the way to Esther Percy. Hours out of her way, as she pointed out several times.

At the end of the school's long dirt road, she let the motor run for a minute.

"What if I walk up with the two of you?" she said. "Tell your teacher how I found you on Route 2 with your thumbs sticking out?"

My heart skittered to a halt at the thought of my father's consciousness absorbing this image. But Skye just smiled.

"You wouldn't do that to us, " she said, leaning forward and patting the woman's shoulder. I thought of Obi-Wan Kenobi, controlling the storm trooper's thoughts.

The woman smiled back, a little chagrined but mostly charmed. Perhaps she recognized a small piece of her own reckless youth. Or else felt too pleased with her good deed to ruin it with betrayal. So she told us to take care of ourselves. She told us to behave. We didn't watch her drive away—the last piece of evidence that our trip had not had parental sanctions—but walked up the hill together. The air had become infused with seasonal chill; I worried for Mrs. Chilton's pumpkins, nestled among vines and leaves in the school garden.

"That was nice of her," I said to Skye. "Driving us all the way here."

Skye nodded. I worried for a moment that she would say something derisive about the woman. I didn't want to hear anything scornful about her rusty car or cigarette-stained fingers. And to her credit, Skye just smiled—more fond than superior. Still, she said nothing further, and I longed for Susannah, who would have taken a minute to reflect on the poetry of the woman's generosity, not only the ride itself but the refusal to betray us.

Now, Pippin snorted and pawed the frozen dirt. "That horse is too good for you," my father had said the year before, in the wake of his disappointment with my behavior at Waverly. I'd sneered openly. What did my father know about horses, beyond their price tags?

But now, watching Pippin suffer—and feeling responsible in a bleak, karmic way—I worried that it might be true. That the horse, too good for me—too pure of blood and spirit—somehow suffered whatever chemicals I ingested. My coke jangled his nerves, my alcohol infected his veins. The idea made me feel a connection to him approaching the one I had with Bloom.

"How is he?" a reedy voice asked.

Laura Pogue-Smith leaned over the rail, dressed in riding clothes and a bright orange vest. Another regular on the Medal Maclay circuit, I'd known her before I came to Esther Percy. My first week there, before the full-bore advent of Skye, we'd gone for a trail ride or two. Laura had a crisp, brunette prettiness—regular features and neat lines maintained by careful starvation. She hadn't qualified for the indoor shows this year because of time lost in treatment for anorexia, a common syndrome on the A circuit.

One time I'd introduced Laura to my mother at a dressage exhibition in Roxbury. "Pretty American girl," my mother had said, in a dismissive and slightly superior tone. I thought how immediately she would prefer Skye.

"He's okay," I said now, to Laura. "The vet says it's intestinal dysfunction. He should be fine."

"Good," she said. "My first pony died of colic. Very traumatic." She twirled her crop like a baton, a motion that would have spooked Pippin if he hadn't been so miserable.

"Are you going for a ride?" I said. "It's so cold."

She shrugged. "Doc needs the exercise," she said. "And I'm feeling a little stir-crazy, with midterms and applications and everything."

I nodded. There was a stack of college applications on my bureau, but I hadn't filled out so much as a line. The thought of contacting old teachers at Waverly for recommendations made my head hurt.

"Want to come?" she asked. "You can take one of Zarghami's horses. We can go up the ski trails. Just be mellow."

I started to reply, and to my dismay a sob came out instead. It sounded horrible, diseased: a struggling and pregnant honk.

I threw my arms around Pippin's neck and wept into his shoulder. I could hear Laura climb over the fence and walk across the ring to me. She patted my back lightly, with a soft and circular motion. "I know," she said. "I know exactly how you feel. But he'll be all right, if the vet said so."

I nodded in agreement but didn't unbury my face.

"Come for a ride," Laura said. Her voice sounded gentle and reasoned. "Let Pippin rest. He'll be better by tomorrow, I bet."

When I didn't answer, she said, "I shouldn't have said anything about my pony. Plenty of horses recover from colic, too."

I led Pippin back to his stall and saddled up one of Zarghami's geldings.

"Don't forget this," Laura said, emerging from the tack room with another orange vest. Deer-hunting season had just started.

"Are you voting next week?" she asked, as we headed away from

the stables. She had dispensed with my outburst the moment my
crying had stopped. I felt grateful for this politeness, her moving on
from emotion rather than dwelling and dissecting.

"I'm not eighteen," I said. "I'm not even seventeen till December."

"Well, that's good," she said. "You have another year to get to
Nationals."

I felt my cheeks warm from pink to red. Everyone knew about my
humiliation in Harrisburg.

"I sent in an absentee ballot," she said. I didn't bother asking
whom she'd voted for. I hadn't yet met a student who was rooting
for Reagan. Not that we discussed politics that afternoon. We just
rode up into the hills, horse hooves crunching over frozen mud. Our
faces becoming white from the deep, deep chill. Laura talked about
college and horse shows.

"You'll make Nationals next year for sure," Laura said, obviously
wistful at her own ruined career. "My father saw you last year in
Halifax. He says you're the most natural jumper he's seen in years.
And he worked with Greg Morris."

There was no envy in Laura's voice, not even particular admiration. Everything about her seemed so easy, calm, and peaceful.
Wholesomeness glowed around her shiny brown braid like an au-
reole. Anorexia was a good-girl's disease. I'd never seen Laura anywhere near the drugs that were rampant at horse shows. To me, she
looked innocent as Skye used to — the distant, pixilated Skye, staring back from the television screen.

That Sunday before, returning to Esther Percy from Cape Cod,
I found myself in uncomfortable agreement with Susannah's assess-
ment of Skye, and couldn't wait to get away from her frenetic energy.
The light beneath her skin seemed to crawl and swirl, searching for

some manner of destructive escape, and I wanted to retreat before whatever tragedy befell her could be blamed on me.

By contrast, how wonderful: toes and fingers tingling near frostbite, the musky scent of a cold-sweaty horse. An activity that no one anywhere could possibly frown on and a companion who had placidly and happily followed every rule ever laid down for her. Never occurring to her that I might teach her how to break them.

LATER, FROM ACROSS the dining hall, Skye looked perplexed to see Laura and me sitting together, still wearing our matching vests. As she slid her tray across from us, Laura perked up so visibly I had to remind myself that she had liked me before I became Skye's official best friend.

"You'll never believe what Eleanor just told me," Skye said, barely glancing at Laura, who didn't seem to notice the rebuff. She leaned toward Skye right along with me. A few feet away, the Amandas held hands under their table; they stopped talking to look over at us. Skye lowered her voice to a whisper.

"Mrs. November has disappeared," Skye said. "She packed up all her things and left. Mr. November's taking the week off to search for her, but nobody's seen her since *last Friday afternoon.*"

"Oh, no," I said. "Do you think we should say something?"

"Why?" Laura said. "Did you see her?"

"I'm not going to say anything," Skye said to me, ignoring Laura. "I mean, what if she doesn't want to be found?"

"Poor Mr. November," Laura said. I noticed she hadn't touched her food and felt a slight jab of worry. I wanted to say something, to encourage her to eat. But I couldn't think how to do it without invading her privacy.

"I'm sure Mr. November didn't know what he had," Skye said. "None of them do, you know."

Laura stared at Skye, waiting for some life-illuminating pearl. Or perhaps she was just basking in the envy of the other girls, all around us, and the status granted her by sitting with Skye.

"Anyway," Skye said to me. "How's your horse?"

"He'll be okay." I felt guilty that for a moment I had forgotten Pippin. Laura excused herself to get a cup of hot chocolate and Skye leaned over the table.

"Listen," she said. "Do you think we could do the last of that cocaine tonight?"

"Why tonight?" An ordinary Wednesday, with evening chapel looming and nothing to celebrate.

"I don't know," Skye said. "I feel so bored since we've been back. It seems so weird, doesn't it, that we could have done everything we did last weekend and not be caught? Think of how we spent our time. And here we sit, in no trouble at all."

It amazed me that Skye didn't consider herself in trouble. Wasn't she nursing at least a little remorse? I wondered if she had erased the interlude with Drew from her mind or simply decided it didn't matter. Even so, it seemed like Susannah's departure ought to have made an impact. For me, in areas of disaster, losing favor with Susannah would have ranked as high as expulsion.

"I feel like Lucy," Skye said. "From the Narnia books. Dying to get back into the wardrobe. You know what I mean? I'm so tired of this lackluster pace. I need a taste of something different."

My shoulders sagged, weary at the thought of a sleepless night. Of charged intimacy and forced confessions. I told her about the pot John Paul had given me.

"You can have that, if you want it."

"By myself?" she said. "But I've never smoked it before. And I can't do anything like that in my room, in front of Eleanor. Anyway, it won't be fun without you."

"I'm so tired," I said. "All this cold, and worry about Pippin. I think I just want to sleep."

Skye blinked at me, unaccustomed to rejection. Then she picked up her fork and began eating. And I knew as I watched the settling of her shoulders — the stubborn, childlike set of her soft jaw — that she would appear in my room tonight, regardless of what I said, because she knew that those four walls weren't nearly enough to contain me. I might commit myself to them with the best intentions. But simple, studying hours would crawl by in dull light, the moon outside my window too painfully close to earth. It would shine insistently through my worn, meager shade, and at some point I would look up from a book, or open my eyes from sleep, and there Skye would be: standing over me — all gauzy smiles and invitation — for my weak and restless heart to follow.

WINTER

9

My horse recovered—his old bright and jittery spirit, an energy that no amount of exercise could contain. But something had changed, some quality in his affect toward me, as if he thought my ministrations had healed him. When I brought him an apple he would press his nose past the fruit to nuzzle my sweater. His eyes seemed to deepen; whereas before his face had seemed a blank, horsey slate, there now appeared a specific and loving character. Seeing so clearly what I had almost lost, my ambivalence settled into staunch loyalty and unadulterated love.

The temperatures fell even lower, and the elections came and went. Douglas Butterfield kept his seat in the Senate. Ms. Latham persisted in wearing her Mondale/Ferraro button, its proud perch in contrast to her dejected shoulders. She looked so blue, so personally wounded. Pouring her morning coffee in the dining hall, her eyes looked red-rimmed and hopeless. It was impossible not to pat her back whenever she stood close enough.

"We should stop by her apartment," Skye suggested. "Buy some pottery to cheer her up."

A few minutes later, we knocked on Ms. Latham's door. "I've got hand-knit scarves, too," she said, leading us inside. "Great Christmas presents."

A sad stack of pans—tinny and meager, like camping equipment—sat in the sink. We followed her into the living room, its only furniture a futon couch with a rumpled tapestry as its cover, two metal folding chairs, and a piece of plywood propped up on cinder blocks. Pottery lined the walls—chunky, heavily glazed pieces that wouldn't interest anybody in my family.

"Can I see the scarves?" I said.

Skye picked up a dark burgundy bowl and held it up to the light. "My father would love this," she said. I had a hard time picturing the bowl amid the Butterfield's collection of antique silver and porcelain. But Ms. Latham seemed pleased. She told us to make tea while she went upstairs for the scarves.

"Isn't this depressing?" Skye whispered to me, as I filled up the kettle. I didn't know if she meant the spare disorder of the apartment or the election fliers scattered across the makeshift coffee table. If it were me, I would have gotten rid of everything the Wednesday after Reagan's landslide victory. Keeping it all—wearing the button, carrying the loss like a personal injury—seemed like a terrible exercise in hopelessness.

Ms. Latham returned with a pile of silk and wool. "My father's coming to visit next weekend," Skye told her. "He's taking Catherine and me out to dinner in Great Barrington on Saturday. Maybe you'd like to come?"

I raised questioning eyebrows at Skye. I had given her the rest of John Paul's pot, which she'd taken to smoking when she had her room to herself. I couldn't think of any other motivation for this sudden magnanimity. But if Skye's state was altered, Ms. Latham didn't notice. She beamed, and an invisible string seemed to lift her—spine, facial features, spirit—a full inch.

"Dinner with Senator Butterfield?" she said, the tea kettle whistling behind her like musical accompaniment. "God, Skye, I would love that. Thank you."

After so successful an offering, Skye felt absolved from buying anything. Not to be outdone, I bought a scarf for each of my sisters, and the burgundy bowl—which Skye had abandoned—for my brother. I imagined it in his room at law school, filled with loose change and chewed-up pencils.

We deposited my purchases amid the debris on my bed, then walked down to the stand of maple trees to get high. I sat on a gnarled stump while Skye pulled the joint out of her pocket, lighting it with her new expertise. She took a hit that sucked in the hollows of her cheeks like an aging movie star and handed the joint to me without exhaling. Before I had a chance to take it, Mr. November burst out from the path between the trees, his T-shirt plastered to his chest, his breath labored from finishing up a run. Several days earlier he had returned empty-handed from his search for his wife, disappointing us all by bearing no signs of heartbreak—only a faint and perturbed squint, more angry than sorrowful.

Now, coming upon us in the woods, he looked surprised but uninvolved. His face bloomed with exertion, and from the bracing chill. The three of us froze there, a stunned and comic tableau, the gamey scent of marijuana settling around us in an incriminating envelope. Skye's arm was stretched toward me, the smoke spiraling from her fingertips. Sap shimmered, bulbous and sticky, on the bark of surrounding trees. The only noise was Mr. November's rhythmic pants, until finally Skye's lungs expelled the hit in a fit of frantic coughing.

She bent over from the waist, the back of her hand curved to her lips. I could see Mr. November's hand lift instinctively to thump Skye on the back, then return to his side. When Skye managed to right herself, she startled me by breaking into a grin as seductive as it was challenging   leveled directly at Mr. November.

She pulled the joint away from me and held it out toward him, her smile fluid and steady. He took one unsure step backward, then placed his hands on his hips and cocked his head. I could see a return smile tugging at his lips, involuntary and unavoidable.

"Hello, Mr. November," Skye said, a singsong imitation of a flirty student passing him in the hall. He lifted one hand in a halting gesture, but his body looked completely relaxed.

"Good-bye, Skye," he said, and allowed his hand to move itself into a wave. Then he strode off into the opposite stand of trees, still biting back a smile, his more wholesome exhalation trailing into the cold air.

We sat for a minute, watching him go. Skye handed the joint to me. I dropped it to the ground and snuffed it out with the toe of my sneaker.

"Do you think he'll say anything?" I said.

Skye snorted. "Are you kidding?" she said. "He would never turn me in."

With a sad surge of indignation for his escaped wife, I realized that Mr. November's partiality to Skye had nothing to do with her writing skills. It sickened me, the idea of a teacher lusting after one of us, even a girl so plainly irresistible as Skye. And despite my disapproval, I couldn't help but feel sorry for him — the impossibility of this desire ever coming to fruition.

"Let's go," Skye said, her eyes glassy. She picked the joint up off the ground and put it in her pocket, and I followed her over the path of Mr. November's retreat.

THE FOLLOWING WEEKEND, we waited for Skye's parents in her dorm room. She lived in JR, where all the upstairs rooms were built like lofts. Stairways—little more than ladders—climbed up to trapdoors in the hardwood floors. Eleanor and Skye usually kept theirs open. The day of the Butterfields' visit, Skye and I sat on her bed while Eleanor got dressed for dinner.

I watched from the corner of my eye as Eleanor carefully concealed every attribute, draping her lovely violin of a body with an oversized sweater and ankle-length skirt. Skinning her thick dark hair into a messy ponytail and hiding large dark eyes with glasses.

"We're only having dinner," Skye said to her. "Why don't you forget the glasses?"

In perfectly fitting oxford shirt and wool slacks, her hair pulled back from her forehead but spilling over her shoulders, Skye looked like a refugee from *Town and Country.*

Eleanor didn't say anything, just jammed gold hoops into pierced ears that seemed to have grown over—she struggled with the earrings, forcing them through resistant lobes. I winced as I heard the faintest pop of skin.

"She doesn't even need those glasses," Skye said. "Her eyes are barely worse than mine. She just likes the camouflage."

"That's not true," Eleanor mumbled.

Skye swore that alone with her, Eleanor could be quite talkative—with a sharp, dry sense of humor. But in my presence, she rarely offered more than glances of puppy-dog dejection, to remind me what I had stolen from her.

On the stairs, we heard the rare sound of high heels and firm male footsteps. In a moment Mrs. Butterfield's head appeared above the floor, followed by the senator. She hugged Eleanor, then turned to me.

"Catherine, dear," she said, clasping both hands around mine. "We've heard so much about you."

"Thank you," I said. She was a beautiful woman, in the perfectly turned-out mien of politician's wife. Fair and redheaded like Skye.

I'd been desperately curious about Skye's mother. Would she seem angry? Bitter? Or like a Stepford Wife — robotically devoted? But I found myself unable to focus on her at all, not with Senator Butterfield in the room.

Skye did not greet her father with the guarded disapproval I'd expected. Instead, she leapt into his arms like a five-year-old, long legs wrapped around his overcoated waist. He hugged Skye back, then gently untangled her limbs and returned her solidly to the floor.

"Hullo, Catherine," he said, reaching out his hand. His other arm draped over Skye's shoulders as she clung to his camel-hair lapel. I noticed a small, dark spattering on his collar, like coffee spilled from a take-out cup.

I willed my hand to stay firm in his grip. He looked me directly in the eye — his own lit with humor. He had the sort of sustained, direct gaze I never accepted from adults. And yet there I was, looking back at him, blossoming under his brief but complete attention. It wasn't just the broad winter sun, slanting through the skylight. Douglas Butterfield's glow seemed literal: light emanated from his handsome, just-craggy-enough skin. Moments before the dorm room had seemed spare and oversized. Now every inch of space had been inexplicably filled.

And the most amazing thing: he looked at me as if *I* were the point of interest.

I had never registered before, the way Skye relished attention, her own reflection in admiring eyes. Because her father did not accept attention; he bestowed it. He studied my face and seemed to see fascinating things, grasping my fingers like he'd waited eons to meet me and couldn't be happier that the acquaintance had finally occurred.

In the past few weeks, whenever I thought of Senator Butterfield, I had pictured his wife: standing on a dais, smiling at his side. The two of them, waving at a crowd of well-wishers, confetti flying all around. A festive bubble, floating up into the air and then bursting. My thoughts of Senator Butterfield brimmed with smashed idealism and broken promises. In addition to the wrongs he'd perpetrated on his wife and daughter, he had already announced clear-cutting in three old-growth forests—including the one right near my home in Old Lenox. At Senator Butterfield's hands, the world turned one shade of gray after another.

Still. Faced with the man, I remembered what I'd known of him before I ever met Skye. He was one of the few politicians whose platforms I could have recited. Despite everything I knew, standing in that emanating light, I couldn't help but believe in him. I couldn't help but bask in the glamour he somehow allowed me to shine back at his smiling face. And I thought, *If only he had run for president.* Forget domestic disappointments and ancient trees. The larger world rearranged itself into proper order. Needy children fed and dangerous weapons laid to rest.

We put on our coats and walked downstairs. Outside a cloud floated overhead, darkening the lawn—late enough in the day that the light would not return once it had passed. The coffee stain seemed less visible. Senator Butterfield's face glowed brave and electric in the coming twilight.

"We have to go get Ms. Latham," Skye said.

She slipped her arm through the crook of her father's elbow, the two of them striding ahead in their long wool coats. Leaving the rest of us to follow their brisk and buoyant steps across the lawn to White Cottage.

AT THE RESTAURANT, heads turned toward us as if pulled by magnetic force. The maître d' flurried and fussed. The busboys and waitresses moved at a frantic and blushing pace, clearing the table where we'd be most visible and ushering us to it. As soon as we sat down, the waiter delivered a drink for the senator, indicating a couple at a corner table. Senator Butterfield—divested of the stained coat—turned and toasted them appreciatively, splashing amber liquid onto his tie. I longed to dab a napkin at the puckered silk, the most wifely impulse I'd ever had. He placed the drink back on the table, where it remained untouched for the rest of the meal.

He ordered wine for the table but didn't pour any for Skye, Eleanor, or me. Skye sat to her father's right, and Ms. Latham—in a pleated granny dress, the Mondale pin and kerchief for once missing—sat to his left.

"So Catherine," Senator Butterfield said. "How do you like Esther Percy?"

"It's fine," I said, accustomed to allowing adults only two or three syllables at a time.

"Skye tells us you're quite an equestrian," said Mrs. Butterfield.

"Thank you," I said. I thought about asking Senator Butterfield if he rode, but Skye interrupted.

"Catherine used to go to Waverly," she said. "She got kicked out because of a boy. Parietal rules." She broke a dinner roll in half and reached for the butter, not meeting my eye. The stare I gave her was more incredulous than angry. Blindsided.

Eleanor bit back the barest bit of a smile. What was wrong with these two girls? From what planet could they hail, not knowing to obey the most basic codes of behavior? I was floored. It was one thing to watch Skye, learning to flout school rules. Quite another to see her flout our own, unspoken ones.

"I didn't get kicked out," I said, retaliating. "My father withdrew me. He thought I'd be able to concentrate better at an all-girls' school."

Skye put down her roll and looked back at me, frankly wounded. I thought of everything I could disclose, about her own behavior. I wondered how she'd feel about the disapproval she so ardently courted when it shifted from theory to fact. In the past thirty minutes, Skye had shown her father more physical affection than I'd shown mine in the last three years.

I saw Senator Butterfield register and forgive our conflict. I saw—with great relief—that his estimation of me did not seem to lessen.

"In my day," he said, "there were no coed schools. I went to Devon, of course. Best time of my life. Uniforms, school ties, chapel every morning before classes. Lights out by ten. They didn't let us make a single unscheduled move. Which is its own kind of freedom. Limits force you to be creative—teach you how to be yourself while playing by the rules. But now everything's changed."

Skye had turned back to her meal. Her mother patted her shoulder protectively. "I'm surprised you can still feel so warmly toward that school," she said, and I wondered if she didn't know about his broken promise.

"You can't erase memories," Senator Butterfield said. "I'll always love Devon. I hope Skye will send her children there."

Skye laughed—a hard, sharp rasp. I thought for a moment she would expose him as nonchalantly as she'd exposed me.

Her father lifted his wineglass and took a distracted sip. "Funny," he said, "how the mores change. When I was in school, we were allowed to smoke cigarettes. We even had a butt room. But they suspended a boy for wearing the school tie as a belt. Another boy was expelled for sending a love letter to a master's wife. I guess that wouldn't have happened if there'd been girls in attendance."

Skye and I broke our fury with each other to laugh. Eleanor stayed quiet. Senator Butterfield smiled and put his arm around the back of Skye's chair. "It took a little more imagination in those days to go wrong," he said.

"Maybe I should write a love letter to Eugene Riley," Eleanor said, not looking up from her salmon linguine. Eugene Riley was the algebra teacher's ancient husband; he had famously prodigious nose hair.

Even Ms. Latham laughed—a shrill, nervous tittering unlike anything I'd ever heard from her. When Skye had first introduced her, outside of my dorm, she had pronounced the senator a national hero. Perhaps recognizing this as overly effusive, she'd said very little since that moment.

"What do you think, Ms. Latham," Senator Butterfield said now. "Are they too easy on our children these days?"

"Oh," Ms. Latham said. "I think they focus on the wrong things. The kids should get more chances. That's what being young is, isn't it? Making mistakes? I think they should look at the individual student and whether or not she's contributing and getting good grades. That sort of thing should be taken into account."

"Yes," Senator Butterfield agreed, with a fervor that made us all sit up a little straighter. "Absolutely right. Absolutely right! Look at Skye. Why suspend her for helping someone less fortunate than herself? Why expel her for standing up for what she believes? What kind of lesson is that?"

My anger toward Skye softened. It was one thing to have to listen to this hypocrisy in sound bites. But did she have to endure it at every family meal?

"I think what they were trying to say with the suspension," Skye said, her gaze fixed on her food, "is that I wasn't actually helping him. The whole teach-a-man-to-fish thing."

"Fine," her father said. "So you know that now. You realize it."

"It does seem ridiculous," Ms. Latham said, "to ruin her life when she was just trying to do the right thing."

"My life's not ruined," Skye said, casting a dark, sideways glance at her father.

"Of course it's not," her mother soothed. "Esther Percy is a wonderful school. Eleanor's always been happy there, haven't you, Eleanor?"

Eleanor nodded, still not looking up from her food.

Ms. Latham persevered. "I'm a big believer in natural consequences," she said. "They expelled the student whose work she did, which must have made her feel badly. So why not let her learn that way? It seems more just and effective than imposing hurtful penalties."

Skye pushed a few pieces of chicken around on her plate. "I see what you're saying," she said. "Natural consequences. It's like, if a politician cheats on his wife, his wife should divorce him. But he shouldn't lose his seat."

It took every shred of composure I possessed not to look at Mrs. Butterfield. I concentrated on mirroring Eleanor's fascination with the dinner.

But Skye's father recovered quickly. Within ten seconds he broke the awkward silence, giving us all permission to look up from our plates.

"The point is," he said, with quiet reverence, "the whole world is about compromise. That's what they force you to realize as an adult. And yet, with these kids, there's no sense of compromise at all. They're dealt with in absolutes. One false move and bam: cut loose."

He turned back to Ms. Latham, patted her shoulder in a fatherly way. "I agree with you completely," he said. His eyes accomplished a fascinating twinkle—an engaging approval and acceptance. Finally, he brought the wine to his lips.

"Annie," she said quietly, weaving her hair between her fingers as though she were our age. "Please call me Annie."

She reached for her own glass and took an inexpert draft—more gulp than sip. Skye and I looked at each other—not quite forgiving but taking a moment of alarmed solidarity.

Then we looked away, remembering our slights. We passed the rest of the dinner like a furious but polite married couple, smiling at everyone else, avoiding each other's eyes, and not addressing a single direct word to each other. I was furious at Skye for exposing me, she was furious at me for my lie of omission—letting her believe all this time that I'd been expelled. The anger rankled silently, to be exploded or forgotten at a later date.

THE NEXT MORNING was Sunday. Before Skye had a chance to appear with accusations or an invitation to breakfast with her parents, I got dressed and went over to Ms. Latham's.

"My boyfriend has a soccer game at Amherst Academy," I told her, when she opened the door. "I wonder if you could please give me a ride."

She stood in her doorway, a red bandanna tied over her long blonde hair, a handmade coffee cup steaming in one hand. The Mondale/ Ferraro button had returned to its perch on her Brandeis sweatshirt. She hesitated a moment, and I could see in that indecision a careful weighing of relinquishing her Sunday against the audience with Senator Butterfield that had come about largely through me — culminating in the fact she had nothing else to do.

"This is nice," she said, when we arrived on the playing fields in Amherst. The mown grass crunched under our feet with frost, and our breath billowed out in front of us. But the sun shone down amiably, and I shoved my mittens into the pocket of my down vest. We stood on the Amherst Academy side of the field, staring across the game at my old Waverly classmates. A towheaded girl I vaguely recognized sat on a folding chair next to the water cooler, writing down stats. She wore a tailored gray overcoat that went down to her ankles, much more grown up than the average prep school girl. It looked like something Skye would wear.

"Which one's John Paul?" Ms. Latham asked, having wrested his name from me on the forty-five-minute drive from Esther Percy.

"He's the goalie." As soon as the words were out of my mouth, the green-jerseyed team converged on John Paul, who dove to the left, keeping them from scoring. At Waverly, I'd seldom attended his soccer games. Usually I had my own competitions to worry about and couldn't spare time to be a spectator. So it surprised me, how much I enjoyed watching his graceful lunges and intense focus. One sideways leap landed him on the ground, heroically speckling his face with dirt but saving another goal. I hid myself partially, standing halfway behind Ms. Latham's broad shoulder, not wanting to interrupt his concentration.

At halftime, John Paul still hadn't spotted me. He trotted across the field, waiting behind his teammates for a cup of water. The towheaded girl sat gazing at her stats with insouciant obligation.

"Are we going over to say hi?" Ms. Latham asked.

I nodded, but walked toward him slowly. I wanted this incognito observation to last a few minutes longer. Because I could tell, with a lover's radar, that the girl's attitude would change when John Paul got to the cooler. And I wanted to see what he would do.

Sure enough: as John Paul filled his Dixie cup, the girl's pencil came down. Her brilliant hair flipped back over her shoulder—inhuman in its sheen, a faint green cast from the sun's reflection. She must be on the swim team, I thought, and racked my brain for her name. Probably two years younger than me, at least, to not be instantly recognizable.

We were close enough now to see John Paul nod at something she said. He filled his cup again, then moved away from the cooler. The girl stood, grabbing his jersey at the elbow. She pulled some Kleenex from the pocket of her luxurious coat and reached out to wipe the mud from his face.

John Paul took two steps back. He smiled—a kind and apologetic expression—and wiped his face off on the inside of his sleeve.

"Good boy," Ms. Latham murmured.

John Paul turned and saw me—his face brightening several shades more brilliant than the interloper's hair. His face-encompassing smile told me he couldn't believe his luck. And I didn't have to turn toward the girl with any kind of triumphant smile. Because Ms. Latham did it for me, a beautifully practiced and schoolgirl gesture, her chin halting just short of looking back over her shoulder, her eyes half closed, her lips perfectly pursed in pleased superiority.

I loved her in that moment, as John Paul's arms wrapped around me, an embrace oblivious to the envy of every female onlooker.

10

I HAD NO CONTACT with Skye until Monday morning in English, when she slunk into class ten minutes late, wearing sunglasses and my too-small clothes.

Mr. November stopped in the middle of his *Hamlet* lecture and watched her cross the room, a palpable and uncomfortable happiness at the sight of her. Skye returned his gaze with a combination of sultriness and disdain that seemed lost on him. His eyes softened a little, and he smiled at her.

Skye ignored the empty chair next to me and sat across the table beside Laura Pogue-Smith, whose spine straightened with privilege. Mr. November waited a moment, then resumed his thoughts on the relationship between Hamlet and Ophelia. Skye did not remove her sunglasses, and his glance intermittently traveled from the bulletin board toward her shrouded eyes. With each glance, Skye seemed to become more disgusted—as if his attention were rooted in lechery rather than suspicion. She shifted dramatically in her seat and elbowed a delighted Laura.

Mr. November pretended not to notice her theatrics until she made a sarcastic show of sliding off my gauzy white shirt, revealing a peach-colored camisole that I never would have worn on its own, certainly not in this underheated classroom. He turned faintly red, and stopped looking over at her. His Adam's apple bobbed uncomfortably, and I saw that the stubble across his neck was blotchy and irritated. Even to me, he looked sadly boyish.

After a few minutes, Skye raised her hand. She had to lean forward and shake it for him to see—he'd concentrated his focus so definitely elsewhere.

"Skye," he said, querulously. Pleading with her not to speak.

"Mr. November," Skye said. "I wonder if I could be excused. Because we read all these books quite thoroughly at Devon. We read *The Catcher in the Rye,* and we read *The Great Gatsby.* We read *The Waste Land* until we wanted to slit our wrists, and E. E. Cummings until we forgot what a capital letter looks like. And we snored and snoozed our way through *Hamlet,* in English class and in the lousy student productions. Don't you people realize that Shakespeare wrote other plays? Histories? Comedies? Do you think we could branch out a little? Because otherwise, I'd really like to be excused."

She settled back in her chair, satisfied. Nobody laughed, but somebody dropped a pencil. It clattered onto the linoleum and rolled against the door, which Skye had left slightly ajar. Laura looked less certain of her newly elevated position. Mr. November's face had turned bright pink, but the nervousness had vanished. It was one thing to smile back at her among the maple trees, with only quiet and complicit me as an audience. Another to be tested in front of his class. He knew his reaction to this challenge would be piped from classroom to dining hall to dormitory.

Knitting his brows together with unaccustomed sternness, he put down his Scribner paperback and wove his fingers together.

"Skye," he said. "Why don't you take your sunglasses off so I can see your eyes."

She paused, then obeyed with a sultry air of insolence. The skin above her cheeks looked pure and dainty as lily-of-the-valley. But her irises swam red and burning.

"Since you know the work so well," Mr. November said, his voice unnaturally deep—perhaps imitating a strict schoolmaster from his past, "why don't you read the 'To be or not to be' speech?"

"The whole thing?"

"The whole thing."

"Kind of a hackneyed choice, don't you think? So many great soliloquies. Why does everyone always choose that one?"

"To be or not to be," Mr. November repeated, with an authority we hadn't known him capable of.

"I don't have my book."

"Shouldn't be a problem," Mr. November said, "to someone so well acquainted with the text."

Skye looked down at the table. Perhaps a full minute passed. The breath of twelve other girls warmed the room; the fair skin across Skye's chest looked mottled and red. When she pulled on her shirt and pushed back her chair, I thought she would march out of class.

But instead, she plucked Laura's book out of her hands and strode to the blackboard. After leafing through to the page she wanted, she closed her eyes. When she opened them, she looked remarkably clearheaded and serious.

"*There is a willow grows aslant a brook,*" she said, barely glancing at the text. "*That shows his hoar leaves in the glassy stream.*"

The other girls in the class looked to Mr. November, who sat staring at her, unmoving. Then they leafed through their texts to find her spot.

I didn't need to leaf. I had switched schools, too: we'd read *Hamlet* in English fourth form year at Waverly. I would never be the student Skye was, but I knew the play well enough to recognize this passage. My skin turned hot and clammy beneath my turtleneck.

"*Her clothes spread wide,*" Skye said. "*And, mermaid-like, awhile they bore her up.*"

She caught my eye and interrupted her performance to smile. I glared back at her. Not wanting to think I acquiesced in any way, to assisting a tragic fate.

The sound of pages turning had stopped. Skye's voice sounded haunting, commanding. No wonder Mr. November didn't interfere: despite the defiance, her performance was splendid. Every word perfect. Her hair fell loose around her face, the unseasonable shirt flapped loose at her wrists—which she lifted occasionally, floating slim fingers through the air. It doesn't make sense, in the cold weather, that a window would have been open: but I remember a breeze, dramatically shifting cloth and curls.

"... *but long it could not be / Till that her garments, heavy with their drink, / Pull'd the poor wretch from her melodious lay / To muddy death.*"

She paused a moment, letting her virtuosity resonate in the quiet room. Then she flickered her eyes back to Mr. November—daring him to rebuke her—and adjusted her stance to pedestrian teenage boredom.

"*To be or not to be,*" she said, in a flat and robotic voice. And recited the entire soliloquy—staring directly at the book, speaking with ironic lack of emotion — before flouncing back to her chair and sliding her sunglasses back into place.

Mr. November sat with his hand marking a page in his unopened text. An actor preparing to play Hamlet might have done well to look at his pale and indecisive face — equal parts awed, angry, and uncertain.

"Okay," he finally said, his voice — after Skye's — reedy and ineffectual. "Does anyone remember what I was saying?"

LEAVING CLASS, SKYE fell into step beside me — shaking her head after a minute, as if the companionship had been mere habit and my transgressions had come back to her. English was in the old part of campus, and the buildings surrounding us were the ubiquitous white clapboard, black shutters. After the Georgian brick of Waverly, Esther Percy always seemed so homey and quaint. Peaceful.

When we reached the top of the lawn — the path splitting, headed either left to my dorm or right to the more modern, brown dining hall — Skye finally spoke.

"You going to lunch?" she said.

"Sure," I said, but neither of us moved.

"I was so angry that night after dinner," she said, and I thought she meant at me — for letting her believe I'd been expelled from Waverly. Her voice didn't sound angry at all, but more contemplative, almost sedated. In class, she had fooled even me with her performance. But now I remembered: she was completely stoned.

"I guess I should have told you," I said. "That I never got kicked out."

"Oh *that*," Skye said. "You mean that's true?"

"Of course it's true."

"I just assumed you were lying. To my father, I mean."

"No," I said.

She pushed her sunglasses up on her head and narrowed her eyes. The redness made them look paler, nearly blue. "I always wondered why they kicked you out and not him. Seemed terribly sexist."

A squirrel scampered out from behind an elm. It took several steps toward us and stood on its haunches—begging for food. We both shrugged at it apologetically, and it ran up to a perch in an overhanging branch.

"Did you see that pervert?" Skye said, and for a moment I didn't know who she meant—Mr. November or her father. Or somehow the squirrel.

"Staring at me," Skye said. "I'll bet that's why Mrs. November left him. I hope she's somewhere great now. I hope she's with someone who really loves her."

We stood quietly for a moment imagining Mrs. November, laughing over drinks with a handsome and devoted stranger.

"And who knew Ms. Latham was such a slut," Skye said.

The words, their venom, made me take a step backward. Yesterday Ms. Latham had taken us to lunch in Amherst. Afterward she took a tour of the Dickinson Homestead, giving John Paul and me time to cling to each other in the gardens. I imagined the chaste poet, staring through her window at our embrace in the overgrown hemlocks. All day, for no good reason, Ms. Latham had been so accommodating and nice. I hated the ugly negligence of that word—*slut*—applied to such a kind and careful person.

"I don't know what you mean," I said.

"Didn't you see the way she acted with my dad."

"Maybe she just admires him," I said, a lame denial, shamefully lacking loyalty to either party.

"Admires him," Skye said. "Please. Did you see the way she flirted? With my mother and me right there? It was disgusting."

The only full sentences Ms. Latham had constructed during dinner had been her defense of Skye. Other than that, she'd spoken in such quiet and deferential tones, I had to lean across the table to hear her. I didn't want to admit that this had seemed its own subtle brand of flirtation.

"Oh Senator Butterfield," Skye mimicked, in a high and jeering voice. "You're my hero."

"She was really pretty quiet," I said.

"Quiet!" Skye barked a short, campy laugh. "It's not about noise, Catherine. *You* can't tell, but I've seen it my whole life. The way these women come on to him, like he doesn't have a family. Like we don't matter! My poor mother. I could have died. I can't believe I invited her."

I let a minute pass, and then another. Skye pushed her sunglasses back onto her nose.

"Listen," she said. "I'm totally starving, but I can't stand to go to the dining hall. I don't want to see Ms. Latham, and I don't want to see Mr. November. Besides which, I know how red my eyes are, and I don't think any of the usual biddies will be so lenient with me." On Mondays Mrs. Chilton and the headmistress always ate lunch in the dining hall.

"Go back to my room," I said. "I'll bring you some food."

I stood and watched her walk to White Cottage. My gauzy white shirt peeked out of her jean jacket at the cuffs and waist. In the indirect winter light, her hair looked softer—chestnut—the curls springing despite the plodding pace of her stride.

I thought of all the times Ms. Latham had turned a blind eye to our delinquent behavior. More, I thought of how awestruck she'd been on Saturday. It had seemed more touching than seditious. On our trip to Amherst she'd been calmer—like she'd had some sort of meaningful communion the night before, become an insider. Maybe she'd felt comforted by Senator Butterfield's strength and composure. Not to mention whatever she'd seen him glimpse in herself. Maybe that was part of the reason she'd given up her day to bring me to John Paul.

And what did it mean, anyway, the way Skye's father had smiled at Ms. Latham? That he wanted every young person to fulfill her own unique potential? Or did it imply something more lecherous? Should he have been more like John Paul, stepping away from the slightest contact? Or would that have been arrogant, impolitic?

I understood what Skye expected. She wanted me to participate in her bristle, condemning Ms. Latham in a knee-jerk way. And while I couldn't quite participate in this defamation, neither could I bring myself to refute it. When I returned to my room with overbaked chicken and soft pecan brownies, I said nothing to defend Ms. Latham.

The truth was, I felt too relieved to be back in Skye's good graces to risk them. I didn't want to demand an explanation for her behavior at dinner, or sing Ms. Latham's praises. As much as Skye's performance in Mr. November's class startled me, another part of me admired it more than I could say. Such fearlessness. Such disregard for any consequences, resulting in no consequences at all. If I'd been the sort of person to gossip, or tell stories, I would have phoned

Susannah and told her what had happened in the most minute detail. Instead I kept it inside, like everything between Skye and me. So that it swelled with importance, sometimes feeling like sanctity, other times feeling like peril.

"So you really didn't get kicked out," Skye said, ripping a chicken leg from the thigh with savage purpose.

"No," I admitted. "But it was still pretty bad."

She shook her head. "You're lucky," she said. "You don't know what it feels like."

Despite the preface of solace, the words had the effect she meant. Before, she thought I'd done for love what she'd done for peace and egalitarianism. Now I felt excluded. Apart from and less than her.

The afternoon bells chimed, one lovely and dismal note. AP French class for me. AP history for Skye.

"Let's not go," I said suddenly.

Skye looked up from her food, bemused at the novelty of this idea. As if skipping class were far more radical than showing up stoned out of her mind.

We snuck back out to Percy Hill Road—hunching low when we walked past our classroom buildings—and headed down toward the orchard. Skye came back to life once we were off school grounds: as though every surface not belonging to the school belonged to her. She seemed to grow two inches taller. Her shoulders lifted and evened.

"Oh Catherine, my Catherine," Skye said, pirouetting down the dusty road. "I forgot to get you high. I've hoarded all your drugs for myself. So rude of me."

"I'm okay," I said.

But watching her featherlight stride, feeling responsible for her, I wished for the same energizing numbness. To feel the visible breath through my lips a little more sharply, smell the air's pine and wood smoke a little more wholly. I longed to be Skye, and I longed to escape her. I looked forward to my birthday and solstice. The coming Christmas break and all the time Susannah and I would spend together, with Skye in DC and me in Old Lenox: enforced exile my only chance of breaking her spell.

11

SUSANNAH HAD ALREADY told me everything about her first visit to Venezuela, but at home for winter break, as plans for our trip seemed to become more real, she told me again. This time she started with the birds. To her, they were what mattered most. Not the streets of Caracas, with its hand-painted storefronts. Not the umbrella-shaded tables at the hotel in Ciudad Bolívar, or the stilt cabins at the biological station on the Orinoco Delta. Not her father's absentminded attention — wandering off, taking his field notes, consulting with the other ornithologists. Not even her anger at him, for abandoning his family.

Peter Pan, Susannah used to call her father, deriding his tropical estrangement.

But that was before she visited him there. Before she saw the anhingas, with their prehistoric poses — still as statues in the cover of the mangroves. Exploding into parachutes of wingspan when she took a step closer. The scarlet ibises and the toucanets.

Susannah always swore her great-grandfather was a full-blood Apache. She and her older brother backed up this claim with a spattering of dark freckles across their noses and an almost Asian slant to the eyes. Slight builds and heavy black hair. The Venezuelans took them both for natives, until they spoke their high school Spanish.

SPOON-FED EVERY LAST bit of information, I can see Susannah's trip to Venezuela almost more clearly than she—who had only her own internal view. Whereas I know exactly what she must have looked like on that puddle jumper from Caracas, the pilot insisting she leave her brother in back and sit next to him. I can see her making her way from the back of the plane, pushing her hair behind her ears. Gorgeous teardrop of a girl, men forever imploring her to smile.

"Smile," the pilot said, with a flash of crooked white teeth. "The view will be beautiful."

And Susannah, resting her hand on the copilot's yoke, took in her breath at the great, green fecundity—the snaking rivers and swooping frigate birds.

Stepping off the plane, she would have felt torn in a hundred different directions. After weeks of refusing this trip, this consolation prize of a visit, she had acquiesced only with the greatest reluctance, terrified she'd encounter a more ominous reason—the real reason—her father had left.

Now he stood waiting for them on the tarmac. His fair, thinning hair and sunburned brow nothing like hers or her brother's. Charlie gave their father a hug, but Susannah refused to greet him with any kind of warmth, frowning at his new beard. She regarded his female assistant with suspicion and surprise: chubby and pimpled, the woman presented an unlikely temptation. Susannah refused to frown at her. Accomplished at the silent lording of her own beauty, she simply offered her hand, along with the sort of smile that would let the woman know every imperfection had been registered.

Susannah's father used to be an investment banker. He used to coach her brother's baseball team: clean shaven, pacing the dugout. *Mr. Twining,* the kids called him, never dreaming he might have a first name.

On weekends and vacations, he walked local nature trails with his binoculars. He hung bird feeders in the backyard. There was never any warning of his own impending flight. Susannah had felt sure, despite his protests, that a woman had lured him away. She was not convinced that a place could have that kind of power until she arrived there herself.

Those two weeks in Venezuela, she waged war with her own melancholy: the deep, damp buzz of the jungle. An uncomfortable and primal love, not only of the surroundings, but of her father—whom she'd determined to despise, not only for leaving them. For bringing them here, showing it to them. Excluding their poor mother and allowing them in for just this barest moment. Never thinking to ask them to stay.

Susannah felt outmatched, unloved. And dizzy with ineffable desires.

He invited her to check the mist nets—the two of them walking out by the river toward twilight. Her brother still fishing with Eduardo, the cook's husband. Susannah followed him through the cahoon palms and watched him unravel a yellow warbler, its bright wings flapping in useless protest—brief liberation—before he stuffed it into a tiny burlap sack.

"Hush," he whispered to the bird, holding the bag next to his face. It wriggled and pulsed like a slapstick kidnap victim. "We'll let you go soon."

"I'm sure that's very comforting," Susannah said.

Her father sighed and leaned against a palm tree, the shade of tropical leaves fanning out in banana-shaped spikes at their feet. Skin flaked off his nose, exposing new pink skin—freckled and vulnerable.

"Susannah," he said. "My girl. When are you going to understand I still love you."

"Is that what you think this is about?"

She'd braided her hair too tightly. Her temples ached with the pull against her scalp. She had expected there would be less of him—that he would have grown thin and gaunt, living on mangoes and love. Instead there was a new paunch, a strange and incriminating testimony to contentment.

"I hate the way you act like you know things," Susannah said. "What's going on in my head. You ran off. You left us. You love this place more than us."

And I understand why, she wanted to say. She waited for him to deny the accusation, but he just took off his baseball cap and bunched it up in his hands. An old man's nervous and supplicating gesture.

"You think you still get to be this authority," Susannah said. "It's smug. It's hypocritical."

She stepped out of the shade. The sun assaulted her eyes, sharp white light, obfuscating her view of him. She could hear the bird, the intermittent and melancholy flap of its wings sounding like dismal surrender.

"That assistant," Susannah accused. "That girl at the airport. Is that who you're with now?"

"Of course not," he said. His voice strained with a world-weary plea, the sort Susannah used to hear when he argued with her mother. "It isn't about that kind of thing. Not at all."

"You expect me to follow the rules," she said. "To get good grades and listen to what you say. Remember how mad you got, when you found pot in the basement? And that was nothing. That was nothing compared to this."

"I got mad at you," he said. "But I didn't stop loving you."

She squinted through the sunlight. This bald plea struck her as flatly pathetic. She wanted him to talk about something else, something unemotional. The bird's wings flapped their feeble protest. It wasn't like her father, not to give her the name of the bird, tell her the species. She put her hands over her ears.

"What are you doing, Susannah?"

He stepped forward and put his hands on her wrists, gently trying to pull them away. She kept them clasped firmly. He had done this on purpose—cornered her alone, away from the conspiratorial glances of her brother.

"I don't want to know," she said. "I don't want to know."

She pulled herself out of his grasp and ran down the path to camp.

THAT NIGHT, AN HOUR or two into her sleep, Charlie shook Susannah awake. She blinked in the darkness, the form and scent of her brother instantly familiar but everything else strange. Wooden walls the wrong texture, mosquitoes flying effortlessly through their slats and knots. The moving leaf shadows nothing like those cast in her room at home. The brine off the river smelled primal and fetid— like gallons of mulch and seaweed. *So weird and wrong,* she wrote to me later. *Like one of those dreams where you keep waking into another dream, except this waking was real. It felt like opening my eyes and finding myself in a past life, or another dimension. It didn't feel like the right century. I felt like I'd left myself behind.*

"Dad's doing lines in the dining hall," Charlie said.

"Of coke?" Susannah said. Her voice sounded small and un-formed. She watched her brother nod. His black hair swayed above narrow shoulders. Above his head, the river cast prismic shadows onto exposed rafters. "It's like being on a boat," she said, and he cocked his head, assessing her — not sure if she were still dreaming.

They walked together through the palm and cocoa trees. Susannah had hurriedly donned khaki shorts and a too-big oxford shirt but had forgotten shoes. She stepped gingerly in the leaf litter, afraid to feel snakes slithering beneath her bare feet. "Is he with a woman?" she asked Charlie.

"No, he's with the cook's husband."

"Eduardo," Susannah said, annoyed that Charlie didn't know. "His name's Eduardo."

They climbed the wooden stairs to the dining hall, one low lamp burning behind the mesh windows. They could see their father sit-ting at the head of the table, Eduardo to his right, the two men taking turns gesticulating. They spoke Spanish; Susannah was sur-prised that the foreign language didn't slow her father down, his words tumbling and effusive. A small round hand mirror — powder blue, like something a woman from the fifties would carry in her purse — lay between them, neat rows of white lines on top of it.

Outside, just above the porch's eaves, a flurry of dark birds darted in circles through the dim light's shadows. Susannah reached out and grabbed the hem of Charlie's T-shirt as he pushed the door open.

Their father stopped midsentence and stared toward them. A quick glance down at the coke, as if he thought he might have time to hide it.

"Children," Susannah said, in a stern, mocking voice. "I can explain."

Her father stared past Charlie, at Susannah. The room looked smaller than it did at mealtimes, without the students and biologists to give it mass and volume. A few wooden picnic tables with long benches. Low bookshelves under the windows, sparsely packed with field guides and board games. Susannah imagined the missing pieces inside those tattered American boxes, the mismatched dice, and crunching Scotch tape holding the boards together. She glanced across the narrow counter that separated the dining hall from the tiny kitchen. Tin pots and pans hung from the ceiling. Utilitarian white plates, just like the ones at school, stacked in neat piles of varying size.

The restless drugs had filled her father with unfamiliar intensity. She remembered him leaving her house every weekday morning of her childhood—coat and tie, briefcase in hand. When had he become this errant camp counselor? No doubt her father saw this question staring back at him. I imagine Susannah's ethereal form surrounding the unapologetic scorn in her eyes. And I can't help but feel a sharp pang of sympathy for her father—realizing, perhaps for the first time, the formidability of his own daughter.

Susannah felt a faint ache in her palm and realized she was still clutching Charlie's shirt, her fingernails digging through the worn fabric. She let go, reaching from behind her brother, and held out her hand toward the coke. Waiting for her father to hand the straw to her.

I see the moment clearly as if I'd been there myself, standing beside them in the close remove of night. In the tropical country—so far from Old Lenox and the family they had believed themselves to be. Their mother so many miles north, pacing the rooms of their house in abandoned bewilderment and growing bitterness.

Susannah stepped around Charlie and sat down on the bench across from Eduardo. He smiled at her, one gold square where a cuspid should have been. She smiled back, the warmth an intentional affront to her father.

"This coke," her father said, in a hoarse voice. "You can't believe how good it is, how little it costs. We're living like kings here."

Susannah glanced around the shabby dining hall and laughed. Outside, one of the dark birds fluttered down, a sideways flicker, its wing scraping against the mesh window. Hearing a high sonar screech, she realized they were not birds at all but bats.

Charlie walked into the kitchen and grabbed four beers from the refrigerator. He handed one to Susannah. Condensation melted luxuriously beneath her fingers as she gripped the bottle. The beer tasted bitter and watery. Fantastically cold.

"Like kings," she repeated wryly. Her father handed her the straw.

Susannah knew as she bent over the mirror, that this night would last well into morning. That her father would feel closer to them than he ever had before. That he would disclose all manner of motive and inner workings: laying bare his new life, his new self. And she didn't need to hear a word of it. This hour of night, this wooden room. She hadn't come to her father's world. He had come to hers. There was nothing here that he could tell her.

Let him confess, she told me later. There was only one piece of information she wanted now. The rest could drift through the mosquito netting into the night air, to dart and flutter with the bats and bugs.

SEVERAL NIGHTS LATER, while Susannah and Charlie bought the coke behind the Laundromat in Ciudad Guayana, an oropendola trilled its otherworldly cry from the branches of a trumpet tree. Susannah walked away from the transaction, away from the Venezuelan men in American T shirts. Too dark to see the dirt beneath her Adidas, but it felt red, sandy. The night pressed into her chest the way only the warmest, closest climates can. And she listened to the *oohwaleo-oohwaleo* of the bird echo through the dense sky, closing her eyes to the forgiving pulse of the tropics.

"I guess I should have been scared," she wrote to me. "But the two men, Rico and Alan, were so nice. They invited us back to Rico's house for dinner, but we had to meet my dad at the restaurant in Bolívar. Not that he would have cared if we never showed up at all, but of course Charlie was stressed about getting caught, because Dad would have died if he knew we were using his connection. So we said no, and Rico gave us a loaf of banana bread his wife had baked and told us if we ever came back we could stay with him. The money we paid is nothing to what it would cost here, but I think it will support his family for a long time."

They bought three ounces, which Susannah zipped in the inside pocket of her jacket and carried onto the plane. Through the window, she watched her father wave good-bye from the tarmac. He looked so forlorn and hopeful. It made her think of that story by Truman Capote, "A Christmas Memory," and for a moment she expected him to run forward and board the plane—demanding to know whether she and Charlie loved him. This vision, too painful to consider very long, gave way to her own incarceration. She imagined him visiting her in jail, dropping his head into his hands and blaming himself.

Burn this letter, Susannah wrote at the bottom.

But of course I didn't. I jammed it into the hanging wall file where I kept all my friends' letters. I still have it somewhere, tumbled in an old steamer trunk in my mother's attic, its crumbly spiral edges turned to yellow.

ONE MORNING IN JANUARY, I told Susannah about the dream I'd had on Skye's beach. The same landscape that haunted all my postnuclear visions: a scorched earth, branches burnt bare, white fallout flurrying through the air like deadly snow. In the dream I had ridden Bloom to the top of a ruined hillside and discovered body after lifeless human body, all laid out in neat and endless rows.

"Was I there?" Susannah asked.

We stood in the tack room, returning our saddles after an afternoon ride. Two scraggly barn cats mewed, pressing themselves against Susannah's legs. She knelt and picked up the smaller one, holding it to her chest. I wiped a green stain from the bit of Bloom's bridle, not able to remember if Susannah had been among the lifeless forms.

"You were," I said, knowing she'd be upset if I said I wasn't sure. "Everyone was there."

Skye, and my mom and dad. John Paul. Eyes closed, empty faces toward the sky. I stooped to touch their shoulders, to see if they'd wake.

"And then I woke up, for real. Alone on the beach."

"Poor Catherina," Susannah said. "All by herself at the edge of the world."

Through the barn windows, the sky had gone dark in the brief time it had taken us to unsaddle our horses. I poured Cat Chow into the crusty cereal bowls by the door. We each took a sugar cube from the jar my mother kept by the grain barrels and walked back to the stalls.

"Do you want to stay for dinner?" I asked Susannah, as Bloom licked my hand in search of more sweets.

Susannah's mother had a new boyfriend in residence. "Bald and Boring," Susannah had pronounced him. "It's weird," she'd said. "This new guy is like the person my dad should have grown into, if it weren't for the birds and the coke."

I wondered if this meant she preferred the less-traveled path her father had taken, but she still referenced him with curt dismissal. He was coming in a few days, to stay at the Old Lenox Inn. I was invited to go out to dinner with him, Susannah, and Charlie.

"You'll be my force field," Susannah said. These days, she wanted little as possible to do with her family, even Charlie. Except for Christmas, she had eaten dinner at my house every night since we'd been home.

We fell in step beside each other, our boots crunching through the snow as we walked back to the house. School had been out two weeks. For me, the two things that felt most like home were spending time with Susannah and riding Bloom. My brother and sisters had all been back for my birthday, and the holidays, and then returned to their various lives in the week after Christmas. Strange, being the youngest of four: growing up in so much chaos, safe under the radar while longing for attention, until one by one they all left. When my sister Claire went to Waverly, three years ahead of me, I wandered through the big, empty rooms. The most startling aspect of only childhood was finding myself alone with my parents' marriage—the icy realm that had seemed an incidental matter of course suddenly

the uncomfortable and unavoidable everywhere. Whereas before my
siblings had been my primary objects of allegiance, I found myself
shifting loyalty toward my mother. The two of us against him, our
calm and sunny countenance against his perpetual scowl.

Susannah and I walked into the kitchen, where my mother stood
at the counter pounding chicken fillets — an apron tied over her pink
silk blouse. She employed a maid to clean up after her and serve but
insisted on doing the cooking herself, disliking American shortcuts.
Claude, her Australian cattle dog, sat at her feet, staring intently
up at the meat. Susannah always said my mother seemed as if she
should have fancy, little dogs. But my mother would laugh this off,
saying that the thick mottled creatures she preferred did far better
on trail rides than the average bichon frise or Cavalier King Charles
spaniel.

"Susannah," my mother said now. "Would you like to spend the
night? You can come with us early, to see Catherine ride. I'm sure she
told you, it's a very important event." She cut a small piece of chicken
and dropped it into Claude's mouth. He swallowed it without chewing, barely registering the morsel before resuming his concentrated
begging stance.

Susannah and I sat down at the kitchen table and poured wine
from the bottle my mother had opened.

"Sure," Susannah said. "I love to watch Catherine win." When
we were younger, we'd both ridden in Short Stirrup classes, but she
had long since given up horse shows in favor of field hockey and
lacrosse.

My father opened the door to the kitchen, which my mother always kept closed — hating to have cooking odors permeate the house.
In his usual armor of coat and tie, he bustled in with a newspaper

under his arm. He almost never made an appearance before dinner was served, and Susannah put her wine down, startled. In contrast to his youthful wife, my father's breath always seemed to labor slightly. Standing next to her, he looked gray and meaty, a stern and coarse laborer beside a sleek and lenient aristocrat.

My mother waved her mallet in his direction—a vague sort of greeting—and then went back to her work. He placed the local paper on the table in front of me.

"Look," he said, tapping his forefinger on a black-and-white picture of Douglas Butterfield. "Isn't that your friend's father?"

Susannah leaned forward. "He's so handsome," she said. And he was, broad shouldered and beautifully tailored. Susannah pointed at his boyish shock of hair, curling unbecomingly to the left. The text below the photograph explained that clear-cutting would begin in a few days.

"Ha," my father said, as if he had proved irrevocably the flimsiness of my beliefs, my friends, myself. "So much for your hero," he said.

"He's not my hero." My voice equaled his in disdain and topped it in venom.

"Right," my father said, for all he knew devastating all my deepest-held illusions. He didn't care a whit for the real weight this development carried—the other promises that could tumble in its wake, the effect that would have on the river basins and Boston Harbor, on the winter sky: clear, star filled, and—only for the moment— impervious to mushroom clouds.

THAT NIGHT, I LEFT my wine in the kitchen, untouched. Late the next day, I thought perhaps I would never have wine again, or any other mind-altering substance. Because it was so much better, winning every class. It made me feel invincible, not in the faux and fleeting way of coke or alcohol but as if I could conjure a very real power from somewhere inside myself.

And something new had developed between Pippin and me. In the old days, on Bloom, the horse had been like a part of myself. She had understood me so well—responded to me so innately that I'd barely needed to communicate commands. With Pippin there was something different. Instead of his becoming me, I myself was erased, the mechanics of what needed to be done so intrinsic that my mind became immaterial. Courses lay bare and obvious before us. My seat became a streamlined melding into Pippin's high-strung and gorgeous lines.

We trotted into the ring, my post unthinking. From somewhere in another world, the voice over the speaker, announcing: *Catherine Morrow on Corner of the Sky.* The polite silence of the audience. The sweet smell of hay, manure, dry dust. Spotlights the color of termite-ridden rafters. And then a gallop, the most wonderful speed of my own making. A soar and post that seemed completely divorced from my muscles Pippin's sinew, Pippin's movement, and yet I could feel it in my heart and marrow, owning it just the same. Clearing every jump by miles, my body effortlessly achieving the posture that riding instructors had been shouting at me my entire life—heels down, hands up, eyes forward. Natural and unthinking as breath.

And then the applause. The subsequent and lesser performance of my opponents. Followed by the best part: returning to the ring, my heart pounding and my brain divided into foggy pixels, until my name was called, and I could ease Pippin forward to accept our roses.

• • •

ON THE WAY HOME, Susannah and I reclined together—legs crossed over each other's—in the backseat. The multicolored championship ribbon hung from the rearview mirror, my trophy clanking in the way back. My mother at the wheel, we could see the back of her slender neck flushed pink with pride and satisfaction. "It's only January," she kept saying. Muttering the words again and again. So that I could see her thoughts clearly as if they'd been screened on the back of her head: Catherine earning enough points to qualify by early summer. Catherine finishing in the top ten at Regional Finals, so that DC and Harrisburg would hardly matter.

This new incarnation—Pippin and me no longer horse and girl but centaur. It was unbeatable: functioning not in concert but as a single creature.

"You're going to Madison Square Garden," Susannah said. "You're going to be on television."

I imagined the greater hush, the larger pounding. Winning, just by virtue of being there. All my father's ideas about me proved wrong or invalid. Worthy, finally, of an attention bestowed. Impervious and consumed by focus and intent.

In the dark, leaf-shadowed backseat, I watched Susannah's face. I imagined journeying with her, just the two of us, along dirt roads lined by tropical forest. In that moment, the idea of the trip to Venezuela felt ominous and unappealing. Already, Susannah had collected enough money for plane tickets from other students at Waverly. But we never discussed the venture in financial terms. What did money mean to us? An endless and preexisting net, somewhere far below, while we walked the tightrope wire of our lives.

Susannah loved the idea of profit, the way it lent savvy to our wayward intentions. But when we spoke about Venezuela, it wasn't the money or the drugs but the rainforest and the Mayan ruins, the birds and the green Carribean.

Still. That night after the horse show, I crawled into bed—the rhythm of Pippin's stride still undulating beneath me. I retraced every step and jump in my head. Like a math problem, the spots still open for improvement. The future and all its possibility.

Excellence. Championship. No unauthorized adventure could have been more exhilarating, and there was nothing in the world I wanted more.

12

OVER THE BREAK, we boarded Pippin at a stable in Stockbridge so I could train mornings in its indoor ring. The goal of making Nationals had captured my mother's imagination far more than college admissions, and she woke me up every day at seven, café au lait in one hand and my riding boots in the other. But the day after my championship, she let me sleep late and forgo training, allowing Pippin and me to rest. So it was well past noon when I found Skye hiding in our barn. As I entered the tack room she bounded out from behind the hay bales like jumping out of a cake at a bachelor party, her hands raised high over her head.

"Skye," I said. I wore my wool woodsman coat, and my ears burned with cold from the short walk. Skye had on nothing but jeans and a long-sleeved Indian print T-shirt that seemed to actually fit her. I tried to remember if it belonged to me.

"You must be freezing," I said.

She burst out laughing. "Is that all you're going to say?" she asked. "Aren't you surprised?"

I sat down on a hay bale. My head felt groggy from the long sleep and my own triumph. Over the past weeks, Skye had receded in the face of the familiar: Susannah. Bloom. The snowy trek between my parents' house and the barn.

She walked over and sat down next to me. A barn cat she had clearly befriended jumped into her lap, purring. Skye stroked it with one cold, unmittened hand and placed the other over my warm leather glove. "You aren't happy to see me." A statement, calm, no hint of rebuke. Too confident to believe such a thing could possibly be true.

"No," I said. "I am."

Not a lie, exactly. It only seemed that she didn't belong here—more parallel universes colliding. I closed my fingers around hers and asked if she wanted my coat.

"Let's go back to the house," I said, as she shrugged into my too-narrow shoulders and too-short sleeves. "You can warm up and meet my mom."

"No," Skye said, as I stood up. "You can't tell them I'm here."

I heard the sound of Susannah's car crackling up the driveway—the '72 Beetle she had no business driving in the snow—and felt a churning mixture of curiosity and dread. Susannah's father arrived in town this afternoon; our dinner was tonight. Though I wasn't yet sure of Skye's circumstances, I couldn't quite picture her joining us.

Bloom whinnied from her stall and pawed at the door, impatient for her sugar cube. "Susannah's coming," I told Skye. "We're going for a ride."

"Fine," Skye said. "I'll go, too."

It was the first I'd heard of Skye riding. An instant rule broken: someone my mother hadn't seen ride going out on one of her horses. But I didn't have any notion of how to tell her no. So I grabbed a down vest off a hook. I zipped it to my chin as Susannah walked into the barn. At the sight of Skye, her face rearranged itself from placid to perturbed.

"Skye," she said, less as a greeting than an accusation of me. "Did you know she was coming?"

"Well, hello to you too," Skye said.

THE THREE OF US rode four miles of dirt roads, out to the old-growth forest. I put Skye on Petunia, my sister Beatrice's ancient pony, and her head bobbed beside our shoulders. Petunia was stubborn and sleepy—irritated at being brought out of retirement on such a chilly day. Skye had to give her periodic kicks to make her keep up, close enough so that she could tell us her story.

"They say a good man can't get elected," Skye said, digging her heels into the pony's side. "But I can't believe it's true. My father was a good man when he first took office. He just hasn't fought hard enough to stay good."

I listened to her with my new wry cynicism, the result of seeing Skye's father through her eyes. And I realized that my ability to wholly believe—in anything—had been permanently tempered. I remembered the sky on the day I'd met Senator Butterfield, opening up in clean and looming safety. I'd understood that the senator had already proved untrustworthy. The world becoming dangerous again came as no surprise—but still, somehow, as a grave disappointment.

"He's very down right now," Skye said. Our horses walked off the road, under a canopy of oak, beech, birch, and maple. "The weird thing is, nobody loves the outdoors more than he does. He would weep to see these trees come down. Do you know how many acres of land he's bought on the Cape, just to turn around and hand them back to the Conservation Trust?"

"I read about that," Susannah said. "Wasn't that after a lot of flack for adding on to that huge house?"

Skye stopped short, and Petunia stepped back a few steps.

"That's not true," Skye said. "He didn't make those promises in any hollow kind of way. He meant every word. He cares about the environment. He cares about poor people. He gives money to Greenpeace. To the ACLU. He supports all of that in the Senate. He cares about keeping us safe."

We walked on quietly for a while, horse hooves cracking into the snow as we left the path to wend through the trees, breaking our own trail.

"Anyway," Skye said. "He's wrong about this. He knows he's wrong. He feels like he's up against a wall."

"He's just barely back in office," Susannah said, "and he turns around and breaks one of his major campaign promises."

"Well," I said, trying to sound light and worldly. "That's politics."

When Skye told us her plans for the next day, Susannah didn't mince words. "You're crazy," she said. But the derisive sentence was spoken in a reverent tone, and I saw that she could not help feeling the tiniest bit impressed. And I felt a remote twinge of pride, at my ownership.

"Somebody has to do something," Skye said. "I'm not trying to hurt him. I'm trying to save him. And also the trees."

When we returned to the road, Petunia broke into a fat-bellied gallop, tearing back toward the barn. Susannah and I watched the pony's unaccustomed and awkward pace, while Skye clung to the pommel of the saddle, her long legs seesawing on either ungainly side.

"So what are you going to do with her," Susannah asked, "when you come to dinner with us?"

I remembered dinner with Susannah's dad and brother. Much as I wanted to be there for Susannah, the thought of leaving Skye alone in my barn made me panic. I couldn't trust her not to frighten a horse, or start a fire, or fall to a sudden paroxysm of virtue and expose me as her accessory. It seemed imperative to stay within running distance. "I don't know," I said. "Maybe I should join you guys tomorrow night instead. Stay with Skye this one time."

Susannah turned her head, her eyes narrowed toward Skye, who had let Petunia stop abruptly to graze on dandelion spoores that peeked out of the snow by the side of the road.

"I don't have to," I said quickly, though I could tell the damage was done. "If you really need me."

"No, it's fine," Susannah said, in the flat, shut-down tone I'd heard her use often with others but seldom with me. "It's totally fine. I'll see you tomorrow."

She gave her horse a quick, gentle kick and trotted ahead—her measured post the graceful antithesis of Skye's awkward retreat.

AFTER SUSANNAH LEFT, I told my mother I'd be eating at home after all. "The Twinings need some family time," I lied, as my mother carefully chopped long sprigs of fennel.

We had just sat down to dinner when Mrs. Butterfield phoned.

"I'm sorry," the maid apologized, calling me from the table. "But it's Mrs. Douglas Butterfield. She says it's very important."

My mother followed me into the kitchen, Claude click-clacking loyally at her feet. I pressed my ear tightly to the receiver to keep her from hearing.

"Hello, Catherine," Mrs. Butterfield said, as if she phoned every day. "How are you enjoying your holiday?"

"Fine, thank you," I said. And then, inanely, "I won the championship ribbon at Fox Hill Farms."

For some reason, this disclosure upset the adults. My mother frowned. Even before Mrs. Butterfield spoke, I could hear her vocal cords tightening. With the non sequitur, I had managed to tip my hand.

"Catherine," she said. "I wonder if you've heard from Skye today?"

"I haven't," I said. "I got a postcard from her last week, of the Lincoln Memorial."

"Because she told us she was spending the night at Eleanor's house, but when we tried to reach her there they said they hadn't seen her."

"Are you sure?" I said. "That's not like Skye."

"No," said Mrs. Butterfield. "That's why we're so very concerned."

"I'm sorry," I said. "But maybe it's just a misunderstanding?"

"No," she said again. I could hear her mother's agitation, simmering beneath her polite presentation. "I drove her there myself. I watched her walk around to the back door. And then when I called tonight, Eleanor said they'd never had plans."

I was amazed that Skye wouldn't have filled Eleanor in on what she was doing. And that Eleanor wouldn't have thought to cover for her.

Mrs. Butterfield paused for a moment, and said, "Eleanor thought *you* might know where she was."

A distinctly accusatory stress on that personal pronoun. I wondered what else Eleanor had told her. Obviously incriminating enough to assuage the Butterfields' fears of kidnappers.

"We're getting ready to call the police," Mrs. Butterfield said. "But if she's just being rebellious, if she's just being a teenager and it's another situation like Chanticleer, we'd rather not get any kind of officials involved."

Of course, I knew that Skye sat snug and unharmed in our barn, camped out in my sleeping bag with a pile of books, a flashlight, and my warmest knit hat. Still I bristled, that they would take time to worry about officials, or publicity, when Skye's safety might be compromised. I pictured the headline: SENATOR BUTTERFIELD'S ONLY CHILD MISSING. At the same time, I felt sorry for them. My deepest nature was obedient, and I would have liked to tell Mrs. Butterfield that Skye hid—safe but chilly—in the trophy room of my mother's barn. But my obedience had already been pledged elsewhere. Even if Skye's life had been at stake, I wouldn't have divulged her whereabouts.

"I'm sorry, Mrs. Butterfield," I said. The niceties we'd been taught to use with adults made lying ridiculously easy. "I promise I'll call you the very second I hear from her, if I do."

"I hope you would tell us, Catherine, if you knew where she was."

"Of course I would," I said. And then added, a contrite offering, "I'm sure she's all right."

"Why are you sure of that?"

The conversational equivalent of a hopeful double take. I hated to shoot her down.

"Just because," I said.

"I hope you're right," Mrs. Butterfield said, and I thought I heard the faintest hint of warning.

"What was that," my mother said, when I hung up. She followed me back to the dinner table. "Her child is missing?"

I didn't say anything, just took my seat.

"Whose child is missing?" my father said.

"The senator's," my mother said. Ordinarily she tried not to engage him, but the subject matter was too interesting to deflect conversation.

My father snorted. "I'm surprised he even noticed she was gone," he said. "He's so busy breaking campaign promises."

I knew that my father, who always voted Republican, would relish Senator Butterfield's turnabout. I also knew that it would have taken him days or weeks to notice if I myself were missing. And I thought that even with Senator Butterfield's glory tainted, I would have preferred him to my own gray, disapproving, and distant father. For a brief second I imagined stealing out of the house and heading not to our barn, but to the Butterfield house in Georgetown — as if small, blonde me could ever occupy the gaping and charismatic space that Skye had left behind.

"He might not have noticed," I said, the closest thing to defiance I could muster. "It was her mother who called."

"What was it like, *chérie*?" my mother said. "Their house."

And I gave them a little gift, describing the rambling vastness of the Butterfields' Cape house, the old hotel and the new ballroom, the screening room and the caretaker's house next door. My mother had grown up in what she considered genteel poverty. One of her rare points of commonality with my father was an outsider's fascination with wealth — even equal or less than their own.

"Where does he get all this money?" my mother said. "Surely not from politics."

My father snorted again. "His father was a bootlegger," he said, and went back to his beef bourguignonne.

And despite the absolute falseness of that remark, I immediately incorporated it into what I knew about Skye's family fortune. The more plausible things she'd told me about banks and investments and television stations flew out the window of my transient awareness. No matter how I disdained all my father's attitudes and opinions, whenever I heard him make a statement like that, I always archived it in my mind as fact, even as I rolled my eyes and pushed my plate away, refusing to eat in his company.

The food tasted better cold, anyway—hours later, out in the barn with Skye, where we lit candles despite the bales of hay, the stacks of straw, the roving tails of curious cats. Agreeing on the danger, we hesitated before continuing with our meal.

"But it's so beautiful," Skye said. "Flickering against these wood walls, with all the snow outside."

And there went our worries, with the undeniable beauty of the flame-cast shadows.

HERE IS WHERE police in three states searched for Skye: on the deserted campus of Esther Percy, in her dorm room and in mine. On Cape Cod, through the cavernous rooms of the Butterfield house, and just in case, through the caretaker's house. They searched the campus of Devon, and they searched every room in Eleanor's house and the outbuildings at Dumbarton Oaks. They didn't arrive at my house until midmorning. By then, I had done an impressive job eliminating all traces of Skye from the barn and was occupied across town, jumping with Pippin in the indoor ring.

The two police officers who came to our house barely began interviewing our startled maid when they were radioed by comrades attending a protest. Senator Butterfield's daughter had been found, protesting with a local branch of Greenpeace. Chained to a northern red oak, purportedly the oldest tree in the state.

"I HAD TO WEAR DEPENDS," she told me later. "The woman who organized the whole thing, Angela, went to get the box of chains and stuff from her car. I went along to help her, and when I saw that package of Depends I turned away, all embarrassed, thinking I'd invaded her privacy. Then it hit me: they were mine! I almost backed out then and there. All I could think about was peeing in those diapers."

Fear of the diapers occupied the bulk of her hours chained to the tree. She didn't worry about her parents—whether they might be searching for her, or worried. She didn't worry about forthcoming consequences.

"All I worried about was when I would have to pee. If I'd thought about it, I wouldn't have had any fluids at all that morning, but for some stupid reason it never occurred to me. So I stood there waiting to have to pee, and when I did have to pee I thought about how if I held it too long, when I really had to pee I would probably have to pee twice. You know how that happens? And then I worried about the police, and how I would smell when they came to arrest me. I wondered if they would report it on the news, that Senator Butterfield's daughter was arrested wearing a wet diaper."

The papers never had time to report Skye's disappearance. Instead it was her protest. A television crew arrived to film Skye's mother, stepping up to the tree and whispering fiercely. Skye still wore my woodsman coat—red and black checked. The actual woodsmen—waiting with their chainsaws—wore thick yellow slickers. Skye's breath billowed out in excited puffs as she loudly insisted she would not unchain herself from the tree until her father himself arrived, to listen to her plea for the ancient forest.

Susannah and I rode through the woods to watch the spectacle. In the swirl of the excitement, she couldn't help but forgive my treachery, even though dinner with her father had been strange and stilted. "He wouldn't talk about the coke at all. Like he wanted to pretend it hadn't happened. But then after dinner the three of us went to the playground and smoked a joint. We sat on that rickety merry-go-round and lit up. It was the weirdest moment of my life."

"Did he bring any coke back?" I said.

"I asked him," Susannah said, "and he obviously thought I was insane." She threw her voice far down into her diaphragm, mock deep. "Do you know what they do to drug smugglers in South America?" Returning to her normal voice, she looked sideways at me from under her velvet helmet and said, "Pussy."

We laughed, then rode quietly for a few minutes. "I'm sorry I didn't come with you last night," I said. "Skye can be very distracting."

Susannah shrugged, a more petulant gesture than she'd probably intended. And I knew that whatever anger she harbored was not directed at me, but at Skye.

"This is the second time I've met Skye," she said, as we urged the horses over the crisscross of fallen tree trunks. "First time, big drama. Second time, big drama. A lot of drama with this girl."

"Keeps things interesting," I said.

"I could do without that kind of interest."

"Skye's all right," I said. "She's just going through some intense things right now."

From up above, hidden in a tall oak, came a mournful kind of cooing, loud and resonant. We both looked up.

"Sounds like an owl," she said, "but it's a mourning dove."

We listened a minute, then pressed on, leaving the toneful music behind.

"That's the one thing I still love about my dad," Susannah said. "Because of him, I know things like that. Birdcalls."

"Maybe we should visit him when we're in Venezuela," I said, suddenly wanting to see his transformation for myself.

She shook her head. "No way. He's this unknown quantity now. It's not like when he was an investment banker who collected field guides. Now he's this professional bird-watcher specializing in midlife crisis. I wouldn't trust him not to make a pass at you or something."

My mind reeled at this concept.

"It was fun to get high with him," she said, impervious to the deep creepiness of her suggestion. "But only in a trippy kind of way. I enjoy thinking about how much shit he'd be in if he were caught."

Through the next stand of trees, we could see the yellow coats of the wood crew and the bright lights of the television cameras.

"Some people can't help but pull you into their messes," Susannah said, quietly—perhaps worried a broadcast microphone would pick up her voice.

For some reason I thought of Drew and Skye on Cape Cod Bay. And I swear I would have told Susannah, if I didn't think on some level she already knew. That the information would not surprise her in any useful way but just confirm her already dubious assumptions—about Skye, and Drew, and her father. About human nature and all its traitorous inclinations. It was true that I wanted to protect Skye from the maelstrom she might inspire in Susannah. But I also wanted to protect Susannah from the same dangerous vortex.

We bent our heads to duck under low-hanging branches, squinting at the crowd as if traveling from night into day.

Senator Butterfield arrived shortly after we did, late in the afternoon. Camera lights flashed and multiplied as he hiked through the snow, wearing khakis and his sleek camel-hair coat, looking years older and inches shorter than the day I'd met him. I couldn't identify his trademark imperfection—the stain had been lifted from his coat's collar. Minus a specific flaw, he somehow managed to emit a strong impression of disarray. He kept his eyes on the ground until he greeted his wife—a quick hand to her elbow, like they were polite acquaintances with a shared grief. Then he walked toward Skye. From where we stood, it was difficult to hear what he said. My mother told me that the TV microphones picked it up perfectly, but I never had the heart to watch the footage, which was rebroadcast throughout the state, over and over during the next few days. What Susannah and I saw was Skye's face as her father approached: triumphant and proud of herself. Waiting to witness the miraculous change. And her father, a study in realist defeat, his shoulders hunched. Skye shook her head as he spoke, at one point raising her hands to cover her ears.

"I won't," she said, her voice sharp and rising like a child's. "I won't until you can promise this entire crowd that those saws will never touch this tree."

Senator Butterfield stepped closer. He pulled her hands down from her ears, and spoke to her in a furious whisper. The only words Susannah and I could make out were, "Listen, little girl."

But we didn't need to hear the words. His contorted face—all that approving light gone—told us everything we needed to know. And Skye, defiance melting as she turned a shade paler, her chin quivering with the recognition that nothing she did would make a difference. The tree would fall, along with those around it. Her father would not be converted—only exposed. She bid her chains unlocked and was loosed. I felt disappointed that she would cave so quickly. Her father took a deep breath and put his arm around her shoulders as if helping her up after an injury, holding her to him closely. The brief anger disappeared—replaced by relief, I suppose at her safety as well as her relinquishment. Her mother fell into step behind them as they walked through the woods. If Skye knew Susannah and I were there, she didn't give any indication, just kept her eyes to the ground in synch with her father.

Susannah and I trotted ahead to the road. We found the limo parked illegally, precariously perched astride a small snowbank. We rode into the trees and waited there, watching. By the time they arrived, Skye was crying.

"I'm sorry," we heard her say. "I'm so sorry."

Her father didn't reply, just shielded her head as they ducked together into the backseat, the film crew close on their heels.

The luxurious car wheels sputtered in the snow—a whir like the chainsaws, curiously silent in the distance—and then lurched onto the barely plowed road.

"That's the saddest thing I've ever seen," Susannah said, as they drove away. And I knew she didn't mean Skye, her tears, or her apology, but Senator Butterfield, whose every aspect—his shoulders, his brow, his hair—looked wilted. Even his footprints looked deep and broken, gathering behind him in the snow.

Dense air, matte light. It felt like another winter storm, brewing its way above the trees. The limo rolled out of sight, on its way to the city where Ronald Reagan presided, his old man hands trembling above the red button that would annihilate us all. From somewhere out in the world, whispers of a disease called AIDS had risen to audible volume, no one absolutely sure what it was or how it could be communicated. And who was there to protect us? Not Senator Douglas Butterfield, who had acquired what Susannah and I recognized as the unmistakable air of a great man ruined.

We understood that nobody would save the world. It would have to find a way to survive on its own.

13

I TOLD MY MOTHER students were expected back at Esther Percy on Saturday, and for some reason she believed me. First thing in the morning she put me on a bus going north. I got off at the next stop and bought a ticket for Connecticut. John Paul drove his cousin's battered Buick to Chester and picked me up; then we drove back to his house in Saw River.

John Paul lived with his mother on one of the narrower stretches of the Connecticut River, in a modest white ranch house—aluminum siding, the lawn unseeded. His mother's job waitressing in Essex left her with little time or energy for cleaning. She had equally little energy for policing her son and friends, making her home a likely destination whenever a place to ourselves could not be procured.

We pulled into his narrow driveway in the late morning. The storms that left drifts of snow in western Massachusetts and Vermont had provided the barest sift of frost and white in Connecticut. The sun shone brightly on Susannah, who stood on the porch wearing Laura Ashley overalls and a white shirt with billowy sleeves. Her dark hair was piled on top of her head, and she raised a blue goblet in greeting as if she hadn't spent nearly every day of the past three weeks with me. When I stepped onto the porch, she stood on tiptoe and threw her arms around my neck.

"Catherine," she said, her grip tight and urgent like a little girl's. "We're so glad, so very, very, very glad that you're here. At last, at last."

"Ah," John Paul said, carrying my overnight bag through the front door. "I guess you two went ahead without us."

NONE OF US were addictive personalities. We could go days, weeks, months without altering our states in the slightest. The drugs themselves—the chemical effects—were not what we keened to-ward so much as the dark and fascinating world their obtainment opened up to us. The illegality of the drugs made them feel like a vacation, leaving behind the endless rules we wove ourselves into and out of on a daily basis. Empty a gram of coke onto a mirror, blow a bong hit into a rolled-up towel, and suddenly—no question—we had broken free. Whatever happened next happened in our own land, on our own time, following the laws we had constructed for ourselves.

Not that the drugs weren't fun. I liked the sinking ease of alcohol and the foggy mindlessness of marijuana. The coke Susannah bought in Venezuela was pure and electric; it could change ordinary evenings—ordinary selves—into an endless awakening, our nerves open and exposed. The interminable New England winter trans-formed into the unceasing brightness of an Alaskan summer.

But the only drugs I ever truly loved were the hallucinogens. That breathtaking whorl and swirl, like someone had opened the pages of a storybook and allowed me to step inside. Not only watching aurora borealis but invited to dance with the lights themselves. Everything intensified and expanded into the rolling white water of disassembled brain waves.

"Here," John Paul said, ripping a hit of acid in half and placing it on my tongue. He ate a whole hit plus my other half. "You're a lightweight," he said, to my protests.

Then the four of us—he, Drew, Susannah, and me—went down to prowl the mud banks of the river.

"Here's the thing," Susannah said.

We had taken off our coats. The sun rose high overhead, and it seemed to be feeding us intravenously. We could scarcely stand the heat. Our bare feet squished into the muddy snowmelt. We twined our hands together, and her fingertips merged through mine, tingling velvet.

"When you're in South America," she said, "you always have to check your shoes before you put them on. You can't just crawl into bed, you have to pull back all the sheets and blankets, to make sure nothing else has crawled in there with you. And then you get home to the States, and it seems like the best relief, to just stuff your feet into your shoes without looking. To just slide into bed feetfirst. Do you see what I'm saying?"

Susannah's face had an unlikely construction for such a tiny girl—apple cheeks that brushed the lowest fringe of her eyelashes. Her grandmother's neck was waddled with the most prodigious folds of flesh. It amazed me now, staring at Susannah, that the expanse of skin beneath her eyes would one day gather beneath her chin. I reached out a finger and touched the taut, fine smoothness at her clavicle.

"I see what you're saying," I said. "You're talking about Skye."

"Yes!" Her voice echoed over the water, amazed and elated at my understanding.

From somewhere above, along a tangled path of brush and bramble, Drew called to us. "What are you two doing down there?"

Susannah didn't answer but lowered her voice to a whisper.

"You think I'm jealous of her," Susannah said. "But that's not it. Because no one could ever come between us, between you and me. Even if you think you love someone more than me, I'll know in my heart that you never will."

Straggled phragmites rose up behind her, sickly and wilted, their clean wheat hue inexplicably beautiful as they keened toward the river, Susannah's words so intrinsically correct, there was no need for confirmation.

"You want to protect me," I said.

"Yes," she said, more quietly this time. "I don't want you to have to live like that, all cautious and worried. I want you to be able to put on your shoes without looking. You saw what she did to her father. Think what she could do to you. I want you to be with me. The person you can trust."

"You think Skye's the poisonous thing in my shoe," I said, and Susannah and I melted into hysterical laughter. We sank to our knees, hers flower-print corduroy and mine denim. Pellets of ice disintegrated through our clothes and into our skin.

"But if she were here," I said, when our laughter had ended, and we gathered our breath, leaning against each other. "You wouldn't care about trusting her. She would just be the most beautiful thing you ever saw. And you would love her."

There was quiet all around us. Susannah tightened her fingers through mine, a squeeze of reverent thanks for telling this secret. She shivered a little, and I remembered our coats, discarded somewhere, probably soaked through.

"That's why I don't want her here," she said.

The dark freckles across her face fluttered and shimmered. One of them grew wings and flew away. It crossed the short stretch of air between us and landed just above my right eyebrow, planting itself there, where it's remained—I swear—until this very day.

"Not here."

John Paul held me by the shoulders. My hands had sunk deep into his jeans, his back pressed against the red bark of an eastern cedar.

"It's too cold," he said again.

His breath burrowed into my ear. He always seemed this way—stoic, scarcely affected by the drugs, amused by those of us who were. I let him lead me up the path to his house, to his sewing closet of a bedroom. Where we passed hour upon pulsing hour, the light outside fading and returning until it dwindled into nothing, Pretty Girl squawking jealously from the next room. Through the many gloamings of that afternoon—true and artificial—a reel played in my head. I had no doubt that John Paul saw into my brain and watched along with me, seeing himself when he'd first arrived at Waverly in the fall of my fifth-form year.

"There's a gorgeous newie," Susannah had said, to me and some other girls. "But we might as well forget about him, since Catherine will get him no matter what we do." Susannah knew better than anyone, the radar beautiful people followed to get to me. She, after all, was the original scout from their home planet.

Someone else had agreed John Paul was not only gorgeous but *cool,* and then pointed him out to me, there on the green behind Umpleby Hall, his hair curling just above his collar. Kicking a Hacky Sack to the art teacher's dog, scooping it high in the air while the dog hurtled through the grass.

The next day in chapel John Paul had walked down the aisle and slid into the seat next to mine. He had leaned in and offered his hand in a mock-formal handshake. And of course I had taken it — firm, calloused grip — and laughed. Susannah elbowed my ribs hard enough to make me quiet, and John Paul had been mine ever since. Though as the other girls no doubt whispered, I'd never done a thing to deserve him.

There was between us, always, the special connection of a reticent pair, each one understanding the other's desire not to disclose, along with the inevitable distance from admitting so little. But that afternoon at his house — laboratory chemicals surfing the waves of our blood — we passed through each other with an intimacy that was almost painful, our fear and admiration of what the other contained mitigated by quivering delight in our suddenly shared skins.

Then night arrived in his window, and the drugs waned — objects in the room still moving like shadows, but the hurricane of intensity beginning to dilute. John Paul lifted my hand from underneath the covers and interlaced our fingers as Susannah had done earlier. I felt disappointed at the lack of merging. Just ordinary skin, stopping at its own fingertips.

"Look," he said, the first word in hours. "It's us. You and me."

"Yes," I agreed.

"Will it always be this?" he said. "The two of us together?"

"No," I said instantly. "Of course it won't be."

He let go of my hand and moved over an inch—his skin disengaging from mine like velcro. "Why not?" he said. "Why couldn't it be?"

"I don't know," I said. But of course I did know—that I would go to college, and the next year he would. There would only be more time apart from each other, changing into different people, these brief meetings insufficient to sustain everything we had become to each other.

"We could take a year off," he said. "Go to France together."

I understood immediately—his wish to present me to Monsieur Filage. The image of himself beside me—a fresh-faced girl from a good family, speaking French like a native. I saw John Paul's love for me, strong enough to boomerang toward his father and back to himself, strong enough to right the rejections of his past. But something in my brain and nerves—the pulsing drugs—misfired, and I laughed, a quick and airless trill. John Paul frowned, then brought his hand up to shade his eyes. As if my laughter had instigated tears.

"Don't," I said, pulling his hand away and pressing my lips to his salty eyelashes. "It's all going to be okay."

And then we were both crying, new reels in our heads, this time of each other's future: college and the struggling years beyond. The marriages and the children and the deaths and the divorces and the growth and the gaining and the decay. I saw the countless women who would love John Paul, so many of them never glimpsing the steady kindness behind his ridiculous good looks. I saw the father he would be, digging in the sand and pushing swings. I saw him suit-coated and gray at the temples, the monogram on his briefcase faded and chipping. All of it—these thousands of minutes that constituted his life—ticking forward without me.

We got out of bed. John Paul went into his mother's room and

released Pretty Girl from her cage; the bird fluttered behind us spas-
tically as we hobbled down the stairs, limping and leaning into each
other like we'd been crippled. Susannah sat kneeling over Drew—
who lay on the floor, curled up in a fetal position.

"Parents," Drew muttered, his teeth clenched and eyes closed.
"Parents, parents, parents."

Susannah looked up at us, her pupils so huge her irises had disappeared. "He's been like this for over an hour," she said.

I sat down next to Susannah and touched Drew's forehead,
beaded with tiny drops of perspiration. We had all heard the stories:
someone's second cousin once removed, who had tripped on acid
and never come home. I pictured a middle-aged Drew wandering
the halls of a mental ward—white haired, potbellied, arms crossed.
Muttering away: Parents, parents, parents.

John Paul went to the kitchen and returned with four cans of
beer. He pried Drew into a sitting position, pulling his legs and arms
straight as if yanking them from rigor mortis. Then he pushed an
open beer into his hand.

"Parents," Drew said, but he took a tentative sip. Then a deeper
one. "Parents," he said, and then fell quiet, leaning into Susannah
until they became a cuddled heap on the floor.

John Paul and I settled beside them, drinking our beer and staring out the sliding glass doors. Pretty Girl alighted on his shoulder, preening against him with one rivalrous eye on me, disgruntled
white feathers on either side of that terrible bare neck. I remembered
the cannibalism she'd endured and forgave her disdain for me.

"That's the second time you've done that," John Paul said, pressing his forehead against the bird's wing. "Laughed at me. You never
would have done that before you met Skye."

He didn't sound angry, just contemplative. I slipped my arm through his, squeezing hard enough to convey my plea for forgiveness. Pretty Girl squawked in protest. I pointed to Drew, expecting John Paul to realize—the way he realized everything—that my laughing had nothing to do with Skye, but only the LSD, the chemicals: playing games with my synapses.

"I'm sorry," I said. "I'd like to go to France with you."

This time he laughed, a hard sound, not like him at all. He brought the beer to his lips, not looking at me. I wished the bird would fly away so I could rest my head against his shoulder without being pecked. I squeezed his arm again, reminding myself not to become frantic—lest the drug run away with that emotion and I wind up curled into a ball like Drew.

Outside, violent green reeds shot up through what remained of the snow. A horrible strip of red-brown mud—diseased and contaminated—lay between the end of the snow and the beginning of the river. There was a vast, silver stretch of water, teeming with red and orange glow, and beyond, a smoky overhang of color. The very spectrum lapping at the sky, eternal and combustive on the water's other side.

"What are you kids doing?"

John Paul's mother came through the front door with a weary voice, her shoes in her hands after a long day on her feet.

"We're watching the fire," John Paul said, tonelessly.

She padded over to the door and looked for a minute, dutifully searching the horizon.

"I don't know what you kids have been smoking," she said, "but there's no fire out there."

And then she disappeared into the kitchen, to fix herself a drink.

14

News of Skye's protest had made headlines in New England — all the papers and the local news. And, as she told me herself, in some broader venues: a small article in the *New York Times,* a brief mention on the national news. Except for a promise to save the oldest tree — the one she had chained herself to — there was no talk about stopping or even delaying the logging. In fact, more trees were scheduled to come down in Shutesbury. All Skye had done, aside from rescuing a single oak tree, was bring more light to her father's broken promise. His unreliability. Shamed him in a way he couldn't talk his way out of, or use to his advantage.

"But he's not mad," Skye said. "Because he knows I'm right."

She had come back to school not cowed, but restless and full of plans. Her father had bought her a BMX mountain bike, and she rode it all over campus, her lanky frame hunched over it like a springboard, her bottom never touching the seat as she tore up and down the snowy hills. This afternoon she had ridden it out to the stables, and reclined languorously on a clean pile of straw while I mucked out Pippin's stall.

"Maybe I'll go to Shutesbury," Skye said. "I won't even bother with Greenpeace. I'll just chain myself to one of those trees. Maybe I'll even set up camp and live in it. And I won't let anyone talk me down. They can mow the whole place down around me, but I'm going to at least save one more tree."

"Your poor father," I said, pitching a shovelful of manure into a wheelbarrow.

"My poor father," she said, "can handle it. He should be glad someone's willing to fight, for the sake of what's right."

I didn't answer but rolled the wheelbarrow out of the stall. I had been in a terrible way since coming back to school. It had taken me almost a week to realize that John Paul and I had broken up. I hadn't understood it that Sunday, when we went out to breakfast with Drew and Susannah. She had announced our trip to Venezuela, and Drew of course protested that he should accompany her instead of me. I'd sat a person's width away from John Paul. Overdosed on intimacy from the day before, I didn't register his palpable melancholy or his inability to eat. Susannah fenced halfheartedly with Drew, tossing her hair in unconvincing argument.

I understood immediately that Drew would replace me as Susannah's accomplice in Venezuela. I saw the rain forest, but not John Paul, slip away from me.

I hadn't realized it when he kissed me good-bye at the station—on the cheek instead of the lips—and gave me the fiercest, longest hug before I boarded, waving to me as the bus pulled away. It only began to sink in back at school, when I opened my suitcase to discover a plastic bag filled with psilocybin mushrooms. He had included a strip of paper, like a fortune cookie, and written in his slanting scrawl, *I'll always love you*. Not the sentiment, but its expression, so out of character as to seem startlingly final.

As the days went by with no word from him, and I replayed those gauzy hours in my head, I realized that our shared, trippy mourning had been the real thing. We hadn't been grieving the future end, but the actual one.

"John Paul," I said, when I finally reached him by phone. "I've been thinking about the whole France thing and how we might be able to do it. After my freshman year, after you graduate."

"It's all right, Catherine," he said. "We don't have to talk about it."

I pressed my face against the receiver, wanting to ask him to come see me, but not sure how I would navigate Skye — how I would tell her she needed to stay away for a night or two. On the other end of the phone, John Paul stayed quiet. And I could hear in that silence his inability to say aloud but his need for me to understand: the two of us were finished.

"Good-bye, John Paul," I said, praying I was wrong.

I waited for him to call me or to send a letter. I composed my own letter, scratching out sentences as soon as they were formed, not able to put into words what I needed to say to him. The one draft of that letter knew a hundred incarnations, finally crumpled and jammed into a desk drawer. Sometimes, while my days unfolded as usual, I would forget. Then, in a perfectly normal and happy moment — standing in my stirrups for a two-rail jump, picking out a fresh piece of apple pie at the orchard — the loss would come back to me, a terrifying swirl through the middle of my gut.

What had I done, what had I done?

SKYE SHOOK HER HAIR, fishing out stray bits of straw. She followed me outside to the steaming compost heap behind the barn.

Since the day I'd met her, it seemed that she had been unfurling a series of tests. *What if I take cocaine. What if I disappear on the ocean. What if I go to class stoned. What if I run away. What if I chain myself to a tree.* The answer to each of these *what ifs* consistently disappointed her with apparent *nothings,* instigating a more and more urgent need for some form of spectacular repercussion.

"I could come by your room tonight," she said, "with those bottles of wine." Along with the BMX, Skye had returned to Esther Percy with three bottles of her father's vintage Château Margaux, hidden in her duffel bag.

I shrugged. The next day, Friday, I was traveling with Zarghami to a weekend horse show in Dover, New Hampshire. I told Skye I couldn't drink, that I was in training.

"Training," she said. "Since when?"

"Since this is my last year to get to the National Horse Show riding Medal Maclay."

Skye tilted her head quizzically, as if she didn't understand the need to achieve. I drew in a frustrated breath. The Skye from a year ago—the girl on the podium—was nothing but a figment of my imagination. I guessed I'd be able to explain myself to that girl. This one didn't seem to know anything beyond thrill seeking.

"It's exciting to me," I said. "Being able to win. It's important. I've been working toward this my whole life, and I always manage to blow it in the eleventh hour. I'd really like the opportunity to prove to myself that I can do it."

"Of course you can do it," Skye said. Her voice sounded resolute and certain, not placating at all. As if she believed me truly capable of anything I wanted to do.

"Thank you," I said, flattered, but also annoyed at her persistent ability to draw me out of annoyance with her.

She threw a long leg over the seat of her BMX, straddling it like a little boy would. "Okay," she said. "You focus on your training. Maybe Eleanor will join me."

"Eleanor! I thought she was a teetotaler."

"Well. If I can change, why can't she? Don't underestimate how persuasive I can be."

She winked at me — a failed gesture, incongruously awkward. I balked for a moment till she laughed at herself, rescued from borderline dorkiness.

"You don't know her," Skye said. "She seems like she's all about books, but she's full of desires and secret longing. I think a little vino might be just the thing for her."

And she rode off, leaving me with my empty wheelbarrow, staring after her as jealously as she'd intended.

"Catherine." One of the Amandas poked her head into the bathroom as I showered off the barn smell before dinner. "Phone call in the student lounge!"

My hopes skyrocketed as I grabbed my bathrobe and jogged across the lawn without rinsing the shampoo out of my hair. Less than two minutes' travel, by the time I picked up the phone my hair was frozen enough to crunch against the receiver. I could almost hear the sound of John Paul's voice — filled with reassurance, and amazement at my presumptions.

But it wasn't him. "Why didn't you tell me about John Paul?" Susannah said.

"I didn't know," I moaned, too crushed with the weight of confirmed dread to notice her curt tone. "I wasn't sure."

"Like you weren't sure about Drew and Skye dry-humping at Sandy Neck?"

I froze at the uncharacteristic vulgarity; my misery fled under the interrogative beam of her voice. Behind me, the wall clock jumped forward, then back. Its strained, mechanical click barely out-ticked the beating of my heart.

"Aren't you going to say something?" Susannah said. "Or are you sticking to your policy of full nondisclosure?"

"I'm sorry," I whispered, my hand curved over the receiver. "But I really wasn't sure it was true. And I didn't want to hurt you."

I could see Susannah exactly. I knew the tapestry covering her bed at Waverly, its periwinkle camels marching around the rim. A Jim Morrison poster identical to mine, in the same position at the head of her bed. The stuffed elephant—patched and worn—she'd had since before we'd met. She would be lying on her stomach, wearing her red Adidas sweat suit, her thick hair skinned back into a ponytail. The phone cradled under her chin, and her hands around the beloved elephant's neck in a fierce but ginger grip. Her eyes would soften the slightest bit, sensing my anguish.

I wanted to ask her what John Paul had said about us. I wanted to ask why Drew had told her about Skye and if they had broken up. I hated myself for liking this last idea, the commiseration that might overcome Susannah's anger. And I kept quiet one more minute, knowing she wouldn't be able to stand the silence and would offer me something just to end it.

For once, I had the lounge to myself. The air felt close and moldy, thick with overbrewed coffee and damp tea bags. The clock jumped again. Twelve minutes till dinner—the warning bells would chime any minute. I longed for the comfort of their tremolos echo.

"Listen, Catherine," Susannah said quietly. "I'm not some guy you've known a year. I'd never break up with you. But you should have told me about Drew and Skye. If it had been reversed, I would have told you. That's what friends do. They tell each other things."

This last, a scathing indictment. I wrapped the phone cord around my finger and pulled it tightly enough to cut off circulation.

"I'm sorry," I said.

"I don't care about Drew," she said. "Boys will be boys, right? But I do care about you choosing Skye over me."

"That would never happen," I said, not sure this was true. Feeling, as Susannah did, that in ways I had already chosen Skye, and would do it again. Not understanding myself why Skye persistently proved so irresistible a force, only doubting my own ability to not succumb to her.

Susannah laughed, the same derisive snort when talking about her dad. I unwound the telephone cord, seizing on something I could offer her.

"Maybe I can still go to Venezuela with you," I said, "if you don't want Drew. I'd really like to go."

"Never mind," Susannah said. "He's coming. It's probably safer, with a guy. Even an asshole like Drew."

I nodded into the phone. A deep, red mark circled my index finger.

"Don't just nod," Susannah said. "You have to speak, Catherine."

I nodded again, this time accompanied by a little sob. For the loss of John Paul and the forgiveness of Susannah—evident in the exasperation in her smoky voice, the same tones I'd been listening to all of my short, protected life. Susannah would understand that my inability to speak was only that, and not a refusal. But I could sense her patience finally running low and couldn't think of a way to help her replenish it.

"I'll talk to you later?" I said, my voice sounding husky as hers.

"Sure," she said, crisp but not without compassion. "Later."

And we hung up, both of us leaving our hands on the receiver a moment, as if we could will the unfinished strands of our conversation resolved.

THAT NIGHT AS I nursed my wounds alone in my room, Eleanor and Skye drank together, less than two glasses before Eleanor dissolved into tears and then passed out. Which left Skye with two more smuggled bottles and a buzz that had just barely begun to work its lightening, exhilarating magic.

She sat on her narrow bed, watching Eleanor sleep, feeling lonesome and melancholy. "I wanted to come to you," she said, the next evening. "But you needed to rest, for the horse show."

She said this matter-of-factly, even respectfully. I had just returned from Dover with three blue ribbons, which I stacked on top of my dresser.

"You should hang these up," Skye said, leafing through them.

I shook my head. At home my room was filled with photographs and prizes and Breyer horses. But displaying the ribbons in my dorm room would have felt not only boastful but too revealing.

Skye shrugged her shoulders and went on with her story. In the face of sleeping Eleanor and sequestered me, Skye had sought out the only other person at Esther Percy she felt close to, Mr. November.

"Mr. November?"

"Sure," Skye said, with flat irony. "He's my faculty adviser."

He didn't even live on campus. She had put on my woodsman coat—her wrists freezing in the too-short sleeves. After a while the blood left her hands and she could no longer carry the wine. She stashed the bottles behind a tree. When we went back for them the next day, they'd frozen to burst—the red wine laced with white frost, the green glass shattered across the snow.

Skye told me she'd trudged two miles into town, arriving at his door well past midnight.

"But you hate him!" I said. "I thought you hated him."

"I do, kind of." She shrugged again. "The truth is, I'd respect him more if he'd put me in his car and driven me to Mrs. Chilton's. But of course he didn't."

Mr. November had opened his front door, the look on his face shifting from groggy irritation to palpable delight. The unexpected boon of her: beautiful, shivering, and shimmering girl.

Skye walked into the warm, messy house—dishes piled high in the sink. Dirty laundry draped over chairs. He picked up a flannel shirt from the couch and put it on over his T-shirt.

"Are you cold?" he asked. "Do you want me to turn up the heat?"

"Sure," Skye said. She let her eyes fall on the ash-filled fireplace. "Or a fire might be nice."

He immediately began stacking kindling in the shape of a teepee. Pulled newspaper off the coffee table and shredded it into strips. While he worked, Skye walked around the house, looking for remnants of his escaped wife. She searched the bookshelves and mantel for photographs. She peered into the bedroom closet for clothes, searched the bathroom sink for scented soap. The only remains were empty hangers and the art deco rings, which she found in a small ceramic dish—possibly one of Ms. Latham's creations—on the cluttered bureau. She slipped the rings onto her finger and walked back into the living room. Mrs. November had strong, wide hands. The diamonds slid around to Skye's palm.

"So," Skye said. "You're alone."

"Why wouldn't I be?" He carefully placed a log on the modest blaze. They both stared a while as the flames lapped upward and then caught. "I'm always alone these days."

Skye ignored the plea for sympathy. "My dad says fires are the original television," she said. "You can't help but stare at them, zoning out. Mesmerized."

"It's true," said Mr. November. "I haven't built one for a while. It seems like too much work, I guess, for one person."

He had fine, sandy hair that probably turned blond in summer. Skye wished there were a wedding photograph. She wanted to see his hair streaked with gold. She wanted to see Mrs. November's fierce, handsome face smiling out from behind a veil.

"Do you want something to drink?" he asked. "Cocoa? Tea? Glass of wine?" A change of tone on this last item, the offer of alcohol confirming the unspoken nature of her appearance. Confirming his willingness to be complicit.

"Sure. Wine would be good."

He banged around the kitchen for a minute, returned with two juice glasses filled with red wine.

"Jane took all the wineglasses," he said.

Skye sat down on the couch, still wearing her coat. He sat in an easy chair across from her.

"Jane," Skye said, testing the first name. "Jane November."

"Used to be Jane Sniegowski. Sometimes I think she married me just for the name. Apparently it's the only thing she's keeping."

"That and the wineglasses," Skye said.

Mr. November smiled, wry and bitter. "When you put it that way, I guess she's keeping quite a few things."

Skye noted the edge in his voice, a hard sound that hadn't been there in the early months of fall. It made him seem older. More appealing. As if the loss of Jane Sniegowski had changed him irrevocably. Skye reached out her hand. He paused for a moment, then took it. He squeezed, and felt the diamonds on the inside of her palm. Turned her hand over and frowned at them.

"I'm sorry," Skye said. "I wasn't stealing them. I just saw them in your room and wanted to try them on."

He ran his fingers across the setting, back and forth, like scratching an itch. "She gave them back to me," he said, "when I went to find her. She was at her grandparents' cabin in Maine, on Sabego Lake. She seemed surprised to see me. Like she didn't think I would come looking for her."

"Why did she leave?" Skye asked.

He dropped her hand and grimaced, a condescending and bitter expression.

"Why did she leave?" he repeated. "Why did you come here? Why are you wearing her rings? My rings. Why does anybody do the things they do?"

"Usually for a reason," Skye said. "Some sort of reason. Like, why did you let me in?"

"Because I don't care anymore," he said. And then—knowing she was seventeen and would only kiss him if he said it out loud— "Because you're beautiful."

Skye smiled. He leaned forward to kiss her and she pulled away. Reclining into the sofa and drinking the wine—which tasted like sour grape juice, after the Château Margaux. Mr. November leaned back in his chair, watching her, satisfied, understanding that her refusal to kiss him tonight meant there would be other nights.

He held his hand out, palm up, and she handed over the rings. He put them on the cluttered table behind him, and as they talked through the night Skye worried the delicate jewelry would be lost among papers and coffee cups, eventually rolling to the floor and consumed by the vacuum cleaner. When they finished their wine, Skye stood up and plunked the rings into an empty shot glass on the mantel. By now strands of light cut through the gray outside his window.

"I better drive you back," he said.

He dropped her off at the end of the school's long driveway. Gave her his gloves for the walk back to JR, but didn't try to kiss her again.

I tried to imagine next English class, how I'd be able to look from one to the other. I wondered if Mr. November would be able to contain his attentions toward her or if they would just seem like his usual favoritism.

"I'm going back there tonight," Skye said.

"Really." I wondered what else would happen between them. I wondered what I would do, how I would distract myself, if night after night Skye crept out to Mr. November instead of to me. "I don't think that's a good idea," I said. "He doesn't seem like an honorable person."

"Honorable," Skye said, finding the word ridiculous. "Like John Paul is honorable?"

I stared back at her, flummoxed. To me John Paul's honor shone

bright and inarguable as the blue of his eyes. That Skye should be
blind to this astounded me. If she were willing to insinuate otherwise
while believing us still together, what would she say if she knew we'd
broken up? I couldn't bear to grant her that license.

"He is honorable," I said, never managing to tell her anything else
about John Paul and me.

WHEN I WENT TO take my predinner shower, Amanda and
Amanda were in one of the stalls together. I heard a giggle and then
a moan, and I turned on the hot water with an intentionally loud
creak. The dark-haired Amanda poked her head from behind the
curtain.

"It's just Catherine," she said, and they returned unabashedly to
their affections. I closed my eyes under the cascade of water, wishing for earplugs and wondering if *It's just Catherine* referred to my
trustworthiness or my insignificance.

On the way to the dining hall I stopped in the student lounge to
call Susannah. Her voice sounded breezy and not quite right—a
poor mimicry of our usual rapport.

"Hey," she said. "I never got a chance to ask you about Skye and
what happened after the protest."

I paused, not only because of personal loyalties and inclinations
(hearing the edge in Susannah's voice, her hunger for dirt on Skye)
but because of the half-dozen girls, who over vacation had seen the
news reports and boasted about knowing Skye (inflating, of course,
their connection to her). Girls who whispered whenever Skye strode
past, once she was safely out of hearing range, but who would never
dare ask her for particulars. I was their only chance.

"Forget it," Susannah said. "You don't have to tell me anything."

"No, it's not that," I said. "There are just . . . you know. People."

"Whatever," Susannah said. "Aren't you going to ask about John Paul? Because I haven't really seen him much."

How could that be? When the four of us had lived every minute, every meal, together.

"He's been studying a lot," she said. "It's an important term for him."

"Do other people know?" I said. I glanced back at the other girls, their pricked ears. "About me?" That last word, the barest whisper. Susannah couldn't possibly have heard it.

She paused on the other line, understanding her witness to the thing I feared most—the sudden rush of girls, the silky ponytails and tanned limbs. Matching Fair Isle sweaters and turtlenecks. All the girls who had been just waiting for this moment, to pounce with their superior charms.

"I think they might," she said. I imagined, unkindly, a vindictive pleasure in her voice—at hurting me with disclosure the way I'd hurt her with silence. "But try not to worry."

Walking across the lawn from the old part of campus to the new, my legs felt leaden. My heart a bitter, shriveled acorn. And I felt a barely contained rage at Susannah. How easy it would have been for her—to tell me nobody knew and let me rest a little lighter.

I GAVE SKYE my stiletto, to protect herself on her nightly forays down the road to Mr. November's. I could no longer stand the sight of him, his scrawny neck and hardened voice, his inexpert shave and chalk-stained fingers. The undeserved confidence in his

stride, and the wry, canary-eating smile. A perpetual look of vindica-
tion, as if he relished contrasting his estranged wife with his teenage
mistress.

In real life, Mr. November never could have come near a woman
like Skye, certainly not one his own age. Only the circumstance of
being one young man among two hundred girls allowed him access
to someone so beautiful and illustrious. He could give himself no
personal credit beyond a willingness to exploit his status as teacher,
and I found his new outlaw swagger distasteful and pathetic.

In my mind, there were three worlds. The world outside—lofty
and compelling, the whisper of destruction and glamour. The world
inside—where rules were made for us to follow, a comforting but
cumbersome straitjacket. And the world in between: a no-man's-land
where my friends and I could build camp and call our own. It had
no past, no future, and no consequences. Mr. November was past
the age for access to that no-man's-land. Out of college, and gain-
fully employed, he should not only have been following the rules
but upholding them. It sickened me, the way he looked away from
Skye in class, a barely suppressed smile that dangerously resembled
smugness.

"You okay, Catherine?" he asked one morning after class, as I
sidled past him.

"Fine," I said, narrowing my eyes and then casting them aside. I
hoped he realized I knew everything.

Because of course I did. Skye dogged me at meals and in between classes. She rode her BMX in circles around me as I walked
to the barn in the afternoon. She told me every article of clothing, every tongue, every finger. Every compliment and glass of wine.
Every last, most minute detail: like she were preparing me to testify

against them at trial. Toward Mr. November she expressed mostly contempt. But the adventure itself exhilarated her, and she pursued it with amazed and electric fervor.

"He's dying to have sex," she said, and I wondered if she considered this unexpected.

"You should just do it," I said. "What's the big deal?"

We stared at each other, wordless. Me daring her, to take this experiment to its irrevocable conclusion. Her silent refusal tipping her hand, that my ways were too sullied and sordid for the likes of her.

It infuriated me. I loved John Paul. Having sex with him was more noble, more honest, than any of her illicit acrobatics with Mr. November. At the same time I felt sickeningly jealous of Skye, for having such a seamy and absorbing escape, and of Mr. November, for stealing Skye away from me.

So I DID WHAT I should have done, when I first came to Esther Percy and needed a way to occupy myself in the absence of John Paul. I rode my horse.

Zarghami did his best to set up different jumping courses, working with picket planks and cavalletti. He would stand in the middle of the ring, calling out formations while I practiced dressage. Sometimes he would offer to just send me off by myself, on a quiet trail ride. But I always declined. Working in the saddle — making myself one with Pippin, the two of us sailing over jumps or perfecting figure eights — was the only thing that quelled the jammering of my brain. The icy disappointment of the winter that would turn to spring, when college acceptances and rejections would arrive.

If I could collect enough points at the shows, I could forget about everything else. I could forget about John Paul, and Skye and Mr.

November. I could forget about Susannah, transferring the plane ticket she'd bought for me into Drew's name with barely a word of apology or regret. I could forget about graduation—the first leap toward the real world. There would only be a summer of riding and horse shows, a stack of blue and championship ribbons too big for my dresser drawer. And next fall the National Horse Show.

And if I won there. For the rest of my life, whenever I walked by, they would whisper behind me everything I had accomplished.

MEANWHILE, AT MR. NOVEMBER'S, pictures of his wife began to reappear. Not the wedding photo Skye had originally searched for but a snapshot taped to the refrigerator door of Mrs. November playing guitar at an assembly. A framed picture on his dresser, of the two of them on a mountaintop picnic.

"Why did you put pictures of your wife back up?" Skye asked. She lay on the bed with him, both of them naked from the waist up. On his bedside table was a small hand mirror with a few lines of coke he'd bought from a friend.

"I didn't put pictures back up," he said. "I never took them down."

Impossible: they would never have escaped Skye's careful rummaging. She gazed over his shoulder at his wife, who smiled back at her from happier times. Clearly, the reappearance of these pictures had something to do with Skye. Perhaps his relationship with her had made him nostalgic for his wife. Or else she had restored his confidence enough that the photos no longer brought him grief.

"I'll put them away," he offered. "If they bother you."

She lay back against the pillow. It disappointed Skye, the idea that he'd use the pictures to gain leverage, displaying them so their removal could constitute a nod of respect to her feelings. His face hovered over her, expectant, and she peered back—trying to ascertain whether he believed he'd fooled her.

"The pictures don't bother me," she said. "I like them. I like looking at her."

"You like looking at my wife?" he said.

"Sure. Why wouldn't I?"

He stared back for a long, quizzical moment before leaning in for a kiss. A few minutes passed before he reached inside her jeans. Skye let him unzip them but stopped him firmly when he reached for his own buttons.

He sat up and shook his head, feeling, no doubt, as if he'd traveled backward in time—to the frustrating make-out sessions of junior high.

"Here," he said, reaching for the mirror. "Do you want another line?"

"No thanks," Skye said. "I don't like that cocaine. It makes me nervous, jittery. It's nothing like Catherine's."

"Catherine's," he echoed, with a forceful jolt of surprise.

And I can see the picture of me in his head: sitting in his class, quiet and fidgety and looking younger than seventeen. Crossing campus in my jodhpurs and helmet, my cheeks rosy from the cold—the shyest and most unlikely of drug runners.

"I CAN'T BELIEVE you told him."

We sat on Skye's bed, studying French—the one subject I could actually help her with. I whispered my rebuke fiercely, not just because of Mr. November but because Eleanor sat at her desk, woolsweatered shoulders hunched over a book. Skye followed my startled gaze.

"Don't worry about Eleanor," she said. "She won't tell."

"What did Mr. November say?" I whispered. I had yet to hear Skye refer to him by his first name, which I think was Stuart. For all I knew, even in the throes of their everything-but-intercourse gym nastics, she persisted in the student–teacher nomenclature.

"He said he wants you to get some for him," she said. "He's not going to turn us in. Don't worry."

"There is no more coke," I said.

"Well," she said. "They'll get more, right?"

I thought about the multihued birds and the green, green jungle. The wind in from Africa and the evening storms drumming percussive concerts on tin roofs. At the biological station where Susannah's father worked, they collected rainwater in great cisterns. To bathe, they pulled a string that released the sun-warmed rain through a nozzle. Sometimes, Susannah found jaguar prints in the soapy mud her shower had left behind. Not so many years later I would travel to South America myself, carrying a backpack that contained two pairs of shorts, two T-shirts, an extra pair of Teva sandals, and a raincoat. Plenty of insect repellent. And I would be amazed at how exactly Susannah had bestowed the place to me, in all its heat and color.

Esther Percy and Waverly had their breaks on the opposite sides of Easter. So it worked out well that Susannah had chosen Drew to accompany her instead of me. Still, I sustained that original slight, especially since she'd discovered his faithlessness. The image of Venezuela lingered in my mind as a personal belonging, something Drew had been allowed to usurp.

"There might be more coke," I said to Skye. "But not till after Easter vacation."

"Maybe we can all meet at the Cape house again," she said, oblivious to Susannah's feelings toward her. "Or you and I can go down to Waverly."

I thought how livid Susannah would be if she could hear us — talking about her coke in conjunction with a teacher. Eleanor listening away while she pretended to study. And of course I realized that Susannah was right, that Skye was hell-bent on a trajectory of destruction. She embarked on every possible avenue toward an ignominious expulsion and didn't care who she took down with her.

Still too young to believe in my own instincts — let alone the potential for my own tragedy — I dismissed the realization like a midnight fear of burglars or ghosts.

Mid-February, Zarghami declared the cross-country course free enough of snow. Laura and I took turns on the outdoor jumps. A crisp day, gentle green hills rolled for miles across the sky, a watercolor backdrop. Pippin was never great on cross-country, the open air and successive jumps a little too much stimulation for his high-strung disposition. I worked with him by following two jumps behind Laura; the lead of her older, calmer horse seemed to mellow him. Afterward, we rode through the woods and down toward school. The warm weather had brought everyone outside. Girls sat on the stoops of the dormitories and walked together toward the damp dirt road that led away from campus.

Laura suggested riding to the orchard to see if Mrs. Gray had made pie, and we followed the exodus of girls in their down coats and sneakers. As we reached the road, I heard the sound of bicycle wheels. It was Skye, racing to catch up on her BMX. I squeezed the reins and turned Pippin around, so she wouldn't take him by surprise.

She barreled down the hill and came to a sideways halt, mud spraying up at us. Both horses startled a little, Pippin especially, and Laura frowned—less prepared than I was for Skye's entrance, righting herself awkwardly in the saddle.

"You going down to the orchard?" she said. "Let's race."

Pippin pawed the ground, uncertain of the little bike and its lanky rider. The breath from his nostrils looked like the agitated steam of a cartoon animal.

"That's not a good idea," Laura said, giving her horse a kick and heading out onto Percy Hill Road. I was impressed that adherence to safety rules could override her longing for Skye's approval. I shrugged an apology to Skye and followed Laura. Skye stood up over her seat and pedaled after us.

"Don't be so prim," Skye said. Her face looked drawn and mottled from lack of sleep, the nights with Mr. November finally wearing her down. She had the restless, uncontainable air of an overstimulated child.

"She's not being prim," I said. Apology lingered in my tone, but my horse's quivering withers gave me the rare ability to assert myself. "We're on top of large, high-strung animals here. Pippin's not some gentle pony."

"Oh, come on, Catherine," Skye said. "I thought you were an expert." She maneuvered the bike too close to Pippin, who backed away from her with a sideways canter. Skye laughed.

"Hey," Laura said. She laughed in a stilted, ingratiating way—clearly wounded at the earlier rebuke. "You really do have to be careful," she pleaded. "These horses spook easily."

Maybe it had been too long since I'd allowed my state to be altered. Maybe some sort of dullness had crept into the clear, sunny day, and I liked the idea of Pippin at a gallop, the reins slack in my hands, standing in my stirrups the way Skye stood over the seat of her bike. Maybe I preferred Skye's daring to Laura's caution. Who wanted to be oppressed by rules, the endless dos and don'ts of safety? Who could help longing for high speed, the full-blown racing gallop? Certainly not me, in kinship with Skye even as she goaded me, even as I scolded her.

Laura wore dainty metal spurs on her riding boots, blunt silver rectangles to prod into her horse. But I'd never needed anything of the sort with Pippin. Just the slightest touch of my heels and the barest easing out of the saddle. And we were off, that wonderful immediate advance, a moment where it seemed I'd left my body behind and dissolved into mist through horse-induced wind. As we headed downhill, the other girls on their way to the orchard shrilled objections to the mud and dirt raised by Pippin's hooves. His mad clip-clop thundered through the calm day, and Skye couldn't possibly catch us.

Pippin tore past the orchard. I wondered if he could have had a career in racing. The trees galloped backward in a gray and green blur. I sat back in my seat and whispered, "Whoa, whoa Pippin." He slowed to a trot, too smooth for my seat to bounce on the saddle, and then a walk. We turned around and I could see Skye, waiting for us by the orchard's driveway, sitting sideways on her bike seat, defeated.

I recognized Pippin's pace as calm and exhausted. I let my feet dangle out of the stirrups and relaxed the reins completely, so they hung in two wide half circles. A light steam rose off his neck, and I leaned forward and combed my fingers through his coarse black mane, still crimped from our last show's braids. So that I saw Skye too late, back on her bike and heading toward us. I remember that she held her legs out to the side, away from the pedals. I remember her hair streaming behind her like some kind of crazed Amazon warrior.

And of course I remember Pippin: rearing up and then racing forward. I flew out of the saddle for a moment, then heaved forward and grabbed the pommel as he galloped up the hill, toward the barn and safety. Skye stopped short as we passed from the opposite direction, her brakes letting out a mud-soaked screech. Pippin started sideways before I had a chance to right myself. So that I flew off of him, my foot catching in the reins like a lassoed calf, and then landed on the road at Skye's feet, mud geysering up around us, my arm cracking audibly as it broke in two places.

While my horse thundered away, the clattering of his hooves still heard as he rounded the corner and ran, riderless, out of sight.

15

MY PARENTS DID NOT arrive in Brattleboro until after my arm had been set. I don't know how long I'd been asleep — drifting in a blissful haze of Demerol — when I woke up and saw my father sitting in a chair beside my bed. I instantly closed my eyes again, hoping he hadn't seen me stir.

Once, when I was about seven years old, I hurt myself jumping rocks in the stream behind my elementary school. For some reason they hadn't been able to reach my mother, and my father came to bring me to the pediatrician. While the doctor had stitched up my knee, a nurse had comforted me — holding me in her arms and muttering soothing, motherly words. My father stood far to the side, hands in his pockets, wincing.

"Catherine," he said now, the gruff voice never familiar as it ought to have been.

I opened my eyes reluctantly. His face was drawn with concern, but to me he looked stern and admonishing. For some reason his hair always seemed especially white when it had just been cut. He smelled like cigars and rich coffee.

"Where's Mom?" I said.

She bustled into the room the second I'd finished the sentence, smelling of Diorissimo and seeming in contrast like all the youth and light in the world.

"*Ma pauvre*," she said. She ran her fingers through my hair, her pinky snagging awkwardly on a tangle. "You close your eyes and worry about nothing," she said. "Your horse is just fine, safe in his stall. Your arm, it will heal."

I glanced down to my left, where a thick plaster cast bent my elbow into a stiff ell. Three days until a winter equitation in Connecticut.

"The Nationals," I whispered, looking straight into my mother's dark eyes, hoping she would say something breezy and comforting. That she'd spoken to the doctor, and the arm would be healed in a month, maybe two. There was still plenty of time to amass the points I needed in time for the August qualification date.

She paused for a moment, then laid a cool hand on my stringy blonde head.

"You still have the college team," she said, disappointment evident in her softest and most forgiving tone.

I SPENT A WEEK recuperating at my parents' house. When I returned to school, the first thing I did was walk out to the stables. Because I had begged—and because his board was paid through the end of the year—Pippin was staying at Esther Percy. Even though I couldn't ride him, I felt the need to have him close by. In his stall I fed him an apple, then knelt to examine his legs. I ran my hand disbelievingly over each perfect fetlock, certain I should find an injury comparable to my own. But the only discernible change in him was a strangely calmer demeanor, as if the accident and my ensuing absence had not traumatized him but made him wiser.

Afterward, on the way to the dining hall, I stopped to check my mail. A postcard from John Paul waited in the little wooden slot. On the front was a picture of Wallace Hall, the library at Waverly. Laura stood a few feet away from me, checking her own mail. The only communication from John Paul that I didn't save, I remember what he wrote verbatim.

Dear Catherine,

Bummer about your arm. Here the snow has melted but it still doesn't feel like Spring. Mostly I've been studying. Anyway, I seem to be running out of space. I hope you're feeling better.

Your friend, J. P.

We had never been the sorts, either of us, to gush romantic poetry. There had been no carving our initials in trees, no *T*s, *L*s, and 4s connected in a true-love-forever diagram. But there had been a tacit language, full of short syllables and ellipses, a whispered rustling of spiral notebook paper that bore its own testament to everything that occurred between us. And now: *Your friend, J. P.* The name that squirmy third-form boys used, calling across the game field in hopeful admiration. The wooden configuration of mail slots blurred before my eyes, less with tears than fury. I made an instinctive motion with my left hand to rip the postcard in half and was reminded of my debilitating injury by a sharp and frantic pain in the fractured bone below my elbow. I put the card between my teeth and ripped at it with my right hand.

"Here," Laura said, stepping toward me. She took the postcard gently from my mouth, as if retrieving a dollar bill from the jaws of a puppy. Without a glance at what John Paul had written, she tore it neatly in half, then quarters, then eighths. She walked across the room to the garbage can, deposited the pieces, and returned to me.

"Thank you," I said.

"You're welcome."

Most other girls would have asked me who the card was from. Laura just slipped her arm through my good elbow, and I felt a swell of affinity.

"Can I sign your cast?" she said.

"No," I told her. "I want to keep it clean." I didn't want anything cheerful about this injury—colorful markers and glib sentiments insinuating that what had happened was just fine.

"I understand," Laura said, and we walked into the dining hall together.

Skye sat at a table across the room, with Mr. November and Eleanor. I averted my eyes in the awkward, obvious way of teenagers, but could feel her unmoving stare as Laura went to load a tray with both our lunches. When I couldn't help but look back, Skye's face looked drained and white, like the sight of me was frankly shocking. As if I were a ghost and hadn't been meant to return.

Laura returned with the tray, giving me an excuse to look away. I busied myself with my one-handed dining.

"She's staring at you," Laura said, so that the other girls at our table turned to look, Skye as usual managing to suck any vortex of attention toward her. I looked, too, and saw that she didn't blush or glance away. Just kept watching me, in a way that conferred all of her discomfort, her disquiet, her sorrow, her guilt. While Eleanor looked inordinately pleased to have her back—evident in the triumphant rhythm of the rise and fall of her soupspoon. Apparently sharing

Skye with Mr. November was more amenable to Eleanor than sharing her with me.

You're both welcome to her, I thought.

Those first few days at home, I'd sat in the barn with Bloom. Every afternoon, I would haul myself onto the horse's bare back, lying back against her haunches, staring up at the post-and-beam ceiling. And thinking that it should have been Skye, not only because her life would have been minimally altered by a broken arm but because of the misalignment of stars. A mistake had been made. Skye was doomed. Not me.

Many times during our association, I had feared being held responsible for the terrible fate that awaited her. But until I got hurt, it never occurred to me that the bullet meant for her might strike me instead.

"Now do you see?" Susannah said, on the phone from Waverly, scarcely able to contain her victory. "Skye's on this mission," she said. "She doesn't care who else takes a fall. If breaking your arm will hurt her father, then she's perfectly happy to break your arm."

I didn't point out that Susannah seemed perfectly happy to have my arm broken, as long as it meant the end of my friendship with Skye. Still, she didn't suggest that I tell the headmistress what had really happened. Even Laura Pogue-Smith understood: we never turned each other in. Besides, getting Skye in any kind of trouble would have felt more like reward than punishment.

While I was home, Skye called every night at five forty-five—just before the dinner bell at Esther Percy. I would listen to my mother or the maid explain again that I was not available for conversation, and I would imagine Skye standing in the student lounge, her finger looped over the pay phone's cord. Incapable of accepting rejection, she would replace the receiver gently, resolute to try again tomorrow.

The girls at my table turned back to their meals with brief, apologetic glances thrown my way. With my good hand, I pushed my plate away and walked out of the dining hall, followed by a collective sigh.

It was 1985. The term *anorexia nervosa* had joined the common vocabulary with the same filmy glamour as cocaine. As my deserted dinner companion knew all too well, loss of appetite was as enviable as the swirl of drama that now surrounded me.

SAD FOR THEM, those curious girls in the dining hall, that they didn't see Skye racing after me as I crossed the road to the old part of campus.

"Catherine," she called. New snow last night, and I could hear the moronic squishing of her sneakers. I pictured the neat row of warm winter shoes and boots in the closet of her dorm room. *Why don't you wear the right shoes?* I wanted to scream at her. *What will frostbite accomplish? Why can't* anything *be normal with you?*

I picked up my pace, refusing to look back.

"Catherine, wait," she said again, impassioned as Stanley Kowalski. White Cottage had come comfortingly into view, but of course there was nothing to stop Skye from following me inside.

"Leave me alone," I said, not looking back at her. My pace was fast, but her legs were longer. I could hear her closing in.

"I can't," she said, remorse rendering her anguished. "Catherine, please."

I turned around and there she stood, closer than I expected. Our noses almost bumped, and I took a step back. She reached out and laid her fingers on my cast.

"I can't tell you," she whispered, "how sorry I am."

I could see Mr. November, walking briskly across the lawn, trying hard to look like a concerned teacher rather than a worried boyfriend. I wanted to scream at him to go back to the dining hall and mind his own business.

Instead I turned on Skye. "Sorry doesn't change anything," I said, the very words I had hated my father for saying, after Waverly. Still, I went on.

"Sorry doesn't let me ride Pippin," I said. "Sorry doesn't give me my championships. Sorry doesn't get me to the National Horse Show, which I've only worked for my entire life."

She just stood there, looking down at me. Blameworthy and forgivable as Guinevere. I had started prep school at thirteen. Rich, wild girls — the ones who couldn't contain their outlaw yearnings — were dazzling and commonplace as New England snow. But Skye was a newborn rebel, with a vengeful and mercurial heart. At any moment she might repent, or head for a cliff, not caring who else got hurt.

"Sorry," I said, "doesn't do one single thing."

Not a twitch, not a word.

"Does it?" I said, wanting an answer of some kind, even a denial.

She fell to her knees. Ms. Latham had come to her door and stood on her stoop, watching us. Behind Skye, Mr. November stopped in his tracks. Girls had begun to appear on the hill, finished with lunch and heading to dorm rooms or the library before afternoon classes. He frowned and stared at his feet, hands stuffed in his pockets, impotent.

I stuffed my good hand in my pocket—liking the looks of that stance, its refusal of further involvement.

"I am covered in shame," Skye said, like she'd read my mind, and wanted to stick to a medieval script. She reached out to throw her arms around my legs and I took a step backward, letting her pitch forward into the snow. Because the drama wasn't for me: it was for Skye. Feeding and living off these scenes, the swirl and the crash of them. The sight of her there, curls spread out on the ground, her quivering face when she raised it up toward me. The uncontainable mess of her—thoughts and emotions and needs and neuroses, all spilling out over their corporeal lines. It was as thrilling as Pippin's gallop and frightening as my fall. I couldn't take it anymore. I didn't want it.

At the doorway to White Cottage, I looked back. Mr. November was heading back to the dining hall, hands still in his pockets, while Ms. Latham went to help Skye to her feet.

"Leave me alone," Skye said, yanking away her elbow and standing. Her voice was a precise imitation of my own—not just the words but the tone and modulation. The slight edge of tears.

You wouldn't think it would be so hard—running with just one arm. I clambered awkwardly upstairs and stayed there until the afternoon bells.

THAT NIGHT, I TOOK the last of my Percodan and crawled into bed. About fifteen minutes later, nearly sunken into the blissfully dreamless sleep only prescription medication can provide, I heard footsteps coming up the worn wooden steps. They sounded too light and fervent to be an Amanda returning from the bathroom. I let my eyes flutter open, blinking at the ceiling.

She paused outside my door for a long time, impressively still. I could almost see her hair, its motionless disarray, catching the muted light of the hallway's dim, bare bulb. The floorboards didn't emit the barest whisper of a creak. I thought about getting out of bed and opening the door, shouting her back down the stairs. But my body felt glued to the sheets, my voice muted by the persistent impulse to protect her.

Finally, an envelope scraped through the crack beneath my door, and Skye's footsteps retreated. I could hear her taking the stairs three at a time, a weightless and endearing scuttle. Her letter lay on the floor, a neon swatch of white in dark shadows. I stared at it, barely seconds, before my eyelids pasted themselves together and let me forget her until morning, when I slid the letter—unopened—back into her mailbox outside the dining hall.

A few hours later, in English, Skye's seat was empty. Ms. Latham sat at the head of the table. She told us that Mr. November's father had died suddenly, of a heart attack, and he was taking a brief leave of absence. I found myself wondering if the story were true or if he and Skye had been found out. Perhaps the rejected letter had not been an apology or plea for forgiveness, but a farewell. I felt a lonesome scratch at the base of my throat, at another person gone.

But Skye hadn't gone anywhere. I saw her at lunch, sitting next to Eleanor, the unopened white envelope on the table beside her soup bowl. *Dear Catherine.* Skye's pretty, schoolgirl script called to me from across the long, noisy room. So that when the next letter came—later this time, after I'd fallen asleep—its floating scrape woke me, and I threw my covers aside. I gave her enough time to leave the dorm, not wanting her to hear me cross my room and pick up the envelope. This time she hadn't sealed it, an irresistible concession

that allowed me to open the letter and pore over it, before putting it
back in her mailbox, to pretend I hadn't read a word.

Dear Catherine,

It hardly seems worth it, telling you how sorry I am. I know that
sorry isn't enough, because you think I don't get it. You think I don't
know how much Nationals meant to you, or else you think I don't
care. But I do know, and I do care, more than I can ever find a way to
say. If I could somehow go back, and keep myself from riding down
that hill toward you, I would. If I could take a hammer to my arm, if
that would heal you and let you compete again, I would.

But I don't suppose that helps. Maybe you'd rather hear how much
I miss you. When you were gone, I waited and waited for you to come
back to school. Even though you wouldn't take my calls, it never occurred to me that we wouldn't be friends anymore. Because to me, our
friendship is just fact. Ever since last year, the world has been divided
into two eras. I think of the time before and the time after. Obviously
the time before was better, everything seemed clear and in a way
very pure. I remember once when I was twelve or so, driving somewhere late at night with my parents, some town I'd never seen during
the day. And I fell in love with this house that had two screened-in
porches and a funny breezeway. It was near a lake, and the lights were
on inside and it just looked so merry and cheerful. Then the next
day we drove by the same house in the daylight, and it was so measly
and ill repaired, with this tacky aluminum siding. Did that make
the house I'd seen the night before, the one I'd loved, any less real?
Does this make any sense? Of course it doesn't. The only thing that's
made any sense since I left Devon is my friendship with you. I can't

tell you how I hate that I've managed to ruin things between us, and especially that I've hurt you. Hurt you, literally! My God, Catherine, I broke your arm. You must know that never in my life could I ever have thought myself capable of causing that sort of harm.

But at the same time, I think there's a place for you and me, still, and that we'll find it again. I know you've heard about Mr. November, how his father died. He asked me to come to Newton with him, to the funeral. I told him he couldn't show up at his father's funeral with a teenage girlfriend. He said we didn't have to tell anyone I was a teenager, as if I look anything like an adult, as if my face hasn't been plastered all over the newspapers since the day I was born. Meanwhile the pictures of Mrs. November are multiplying—he must have gone out and bought new frames. There are pictures of her rowing a canoe and pictures of her at the beach in a red bathing suit. She has beautiful legs, they're very long and strong. I wanted to tell him to call her, to call his wife, to bring her to the funeral. He seems very wrecked and shaky, and I can't come close to managing his emotions. After I saw him today the only thing I wanted was to come to you and tell you everything.

So now you're rolling your eyes, and you're thinking that I'm impossibly selfish, and all that I want is an audience. But that's not true. I don't want to defend myself, or pretend I'm not a terrible person, because obviously in so many ways I am. But what I'm trying to say, what it really boils down to, is that I miss you. I miss you, Catherine, and I love you, and I still am and will remain your friend whether you want me to or not.

> With all my guilt and love and hope,
> Skye Butterfield

There was much in that letter, and the succession of letters that followed, that wooed me back. At the same time, there was much that repelled me, enough that despite my genuine sympathy for her, and a growing return of the love she professed for me, I did not approach Skye. I only returned the letters to her box, newly sealed, my careful reading evident in the creases and folds of the delicate paper. Once, across the table in English class, in response to her intent stare I allowed her the smallest smile, a fraction of a hint at forgiveness. Her return smile seemed so infused with victory that I quickly looked away, not wanting to see her satisfaction or disappointment. Knowing now that it was just a matter of time before I gave in—to both our relief—and allowed our friendship to continue.

I didn't hear from John Paul, and I didn't hear from Susannah. But the letters from Skye persisted, as she traveled across campus almost every night, her own determined mailman.

IT WASN'T ENOUGH for her, those midnight deliveries. With Mr. November still in Newton, Skye felt lonely and restless in her spotless dorm room. She would watch Eleanor's head bent over books and try to throw herself into her own studies to forget what had happened—to forget what she had done to me. *But that only makes me feel guiltier,* she wrote. *It's not fair at all, that I can still do what I'm best at, while you have to sit on the sidelines because of me.*

Skye writhed miserably beneath the weight of this new remorse. Since her expulsion from Devon, nothing had caused her serious regret. The expulsion itself and her civil disobedience at the old-growth forest—both were tinged with an odd sort of heroism. As for the drugs and Mr. November she had yet to be caught. Such late-night transgressions, without the rebuke of authority, took the form of dream occurrences: blameless and unaccountable, like the twelve dancing princesses and their ruined slippers. *But the snap of your arm and your body tumbling through the air will stay with me till the day I die. The sound and the sight are with me every day and every night, so that I can't sit still. I can't sleep.*

Late on a Friday night, she shook poor Eleanor awake. Without glasses, with her hair loose, Eleanor looked like a startled fairy queen. She blinked through the dark at Skye, alarmed and uncertain. Reading Skye's letter, I imagined Eleanor had begun to feel it, too: the foreshadowing of Skye's doom and the fear that at the pivotal moment, fate would decide to leave Skye—in all her shining and dangerous *life*—and take her instead.

Still, Eleanor followed Skye's directions like an indentured servant, putting on her warmest clothes. Skye watched her transform herself from magical creature to dumpy girl. When Eleanor started to wrap her hair into its usual messy knot, Skye braided it for her. "And no glasses," Skye said. "You don't need them."

Eleanor stuffed them hastily into the pocket of her down coat.

March, and still the snow. They trudged down the dirt path to Percy Hill Road. No cars that time of night in the sleepy village. By the time they got to the main road—trucks and occasional sedans kicking mud into the breakdown lane—the cuffs of their pants were soaked and their knuckles (Eleanor's under her mittens, Skye's bare) chapped and red.

"Where are we going?" Eleanor asked Skye, when she woke up enough to think.

"To Waverly. To buy coke from Catherine's boyfriend."

Catherine's boyfriend. The scholarship student. Skye couldn't bother with names. I sometimes wonder how she would have reacted if she'd met my father, with his furrowed brow and townie accent. Of course she persisted in believing the coke came from John Paul regardless of what I said. As if coke that pure could have emerged from the banks of Saw River.

I imagine Skye arriving on campus in the gray predawn. Completely at home, stealing between silver evergreens and redbrick buildings. Like the native she was, she would be able to differentiate between halls and dorms. When she rapped on a random window, the sleepy student who answered would recognize her as one of his own and direct her to John Paul's window.

In deference to me, John Paul would have invited Skye and Eleanor to sleep on his floor. I imagine Eleanor's face, waking in the morning to see John Paul tangled in the covers, the gorgeous, sleeping wonder of him. He would have brought them breakfast from the dining hall and sent them home to me empty-handed.

But they never got to Waverly. *This man picked us up, college age but not college type. He said his name was Van.* Van was headed to Ince, Massachusetts, just south of the Vermont border. Not much progress, but enough to get them started. Eleanor climbed into the passenger seat. Skye sat in back.

"You girls go to college?" he asked.

Eleanor said no, they went to the Esther Percy School for Girls. Skye kicked the back of her seat, and Van laughed. He looked at Skye in the rearview mirror, his eyes off the road too long. He was young, probably in his early twenties, and might have been handsome but for some unnameable and unsettling air.

"What's wrong, Red?" he said. "You worry I'll show up at high tea?"

"Not at all," Skye said. "We have excellent security."

"Can't be too excellent, with the two of you out wandering at this hour."

"We have permission," Skye said, and he laughed again.

There was a television movie we had all seen, it may have been an after-school special. *Diary of a Teenage Hitchhiker,* starring Charlene Tilton. In it, a serial rapist drove a battered Japanese sports car, black and tinny. *That's exactly what Van's car looked like,* Skye wrote. *I should have known not to get inside.*

They drove past the sign WELCOME TO MASSACHUSETTS. MICHAEL DUKAKIS, GOVERNOR. Skye and her parents had eaten dinner with him and his wife in Boston. She rolled down the window and sipped the dark, frigid air, wondering if Van recognized her.

Van took the first exit. Eleanor sat up straighter in her seat. Skye could see the crown of her head, the glossy brown braid. She wanted to stroke it—comfort her and apologize.

"You don't need to get off the highway," Skye said. "We'll keep going from here."

He didn't answer but drove through a dimly lit strip of gas, food, lodging. Then continued on down the road—the streetlights blinking yellow and spaced farther and farther apart. He drummed his fingers on the steering wheel—an effort to appear cool or an inability to contain jitters.

"Where are you going?" Skye said.

I imagine her voice still bright enough to engage him, but he didn't answer. Just glanced into the rearview mirror, only slightly less nervous than his captives. *I watched Eleanor's head,* Skye wrote. *I could tell she wanted to turn around and look at me, but she was too scared. And I knew this whole thing was all my fault, and on top of everything else now I'd put Eleanor in danger.* Skye put her hand in her coat pocket—my Black Watch plaid—and closed her fist around the handle of my stiletto. She wondered if she should just lean forward and slit Van's throat before he had a chance to hurt them. I imagine blood spurting onto the steering wheel. Poor, helpless Eleanor, and the car skidding off the road. The senator's daughter, climbing into her victim's lap to take the wheel and save them all, and pleading self-defense in the morning newspapers.

Van turned onto a winding dirt road. Civilization disappeared behind them. The car bumped uncomfortably over pebbles and potholes. Skye felt the end of a dull spring, breaking through the Naugahyde upholstery. She pictured herself and Eleanor, murdered in a ditch, and worried that on top of everything else poor Mr. November would somehow be blamed. In the rearview mirror, she could see the headlights of another car, following them. For a moment she felt a surge of relief, thinking they'd been rescued. But then she saw Van look in the mirror again and his slight nod of recognition. The blood in her chest turned to ice. *I killed Eleanor,* she thought, and closed her hand more tightly around my knife.

The road rambled to a dead end, and Van pulled the car off to the side. The other car stopped behind them. Skye saw two men get out of the car. Doors slammed. Van tapped the steering wheel. Broad footsteps in the snow, walking toward them.

Eleanor screamed. Skye released the blade of her knife but kept it hidden by her side. Van touched his keys, about to turn off the ignition. And then changed his mind. Pressed his foot to the gas. Turned the car around and headed back up the road. Skye and

Eleanor turned around in their seats, watching the faceless men recede. One of them raised his arms in a wide, angry question.

They rambled back out to Main Street. Skye rolled the window down, so that the three of them shivered—breath escaping in thick, visible gusts—by the time the car slowed down, and Van pulled into Ince's all-night Texaco. Both girls waited until he'd come to a full stop before fumbling for the door handles.

"Thank you very much," Eleanor said, as if he were somebody's father—driving them home after a sleepover. Then she climbed out of the car.

Skye waited the barest second, allowing herself to catch his eye. He had nice blue eyes and a Roman nose. Some angry-looking acne across his jaw.

"What just happened?" she said.

Van shrugged. He seemed shaken and relieved. Then he jutted his chin toward the rearview mirror, and Skye knew he was indicating her knife.

"That wouldn't have helped," he said, and she scrambled out of the car fast as she could.

The neon lights from the gas station bathed the parking lot in a dull yellow glow. Skye and Eleanor clung to each other a moment, their bodies trembling. Then Eleanor pushed Skye away.

"I hate you," she said. She raised her heavily gloved hand and swatted the side of Skye's face. Skye lifted up her arms to deflect the next two lame and frazzled blows.

A thirty-something woman walked out of the Texaco and pulled Eleanor away. Listened to their story and drove them back to school.

I WAS INUNDATED with mail. On a snowy Saturday, I received a thick letter from Susannah, which I slit open immediately. I peered in to see one folded piece of notebook paper, and a small plastic bag filled with coke.

I took out the letter so I could read it at the lunch table, and shoved the coke into the pocket of my down coat. I began reading as I crossed the dining hall and knew before I sat down that another meal would go uneaten. Because this letter didn't narrate Susannah's life. It narrated my own.

Susannah explained in the most thorough detail: John Paul's new relationship with Regan Mercer, a platinum blonde fourth-former from Manhattan, who was planning her sweet sixteen party at Regine's. And I knew instantly: the scorekeeper, in her fancy gray coat.

I'm only telling you because if it were me, I would want to know.

She must have known how incriminating these words sounded but wasn't conflicted enough to strike them out. Instead, she followed her punishments (of accusation and information) with offerings: *It's been a sad ending to a difficult winter. I am sending you the last of my private stash, which even Drew doesn't know about, because I think you could use it more than me. If it's any consolation, I don't think he loves Regan, at least not close to the way he loved you.*

Regan. Regan! The name gloamed above my life, like the Black Thing from *A Wrinkle in Time*. An oppressive and ominous overhang, presaging destruction, ruin, and all the gullible frailty of human nature.

Of course John Paul would have a new girlfriend. How could he not? Waverly had been teeming with his suitors — like Penelope in reverse — since the school year started without me. He would have to give in to one eventually, if only to deflect the others. I folded the letter carefully and stowed it in my pocket with the coke. For some reason, probably reflex, I scanned the dining hall for Skye but didn't see her. Eleanor sat hunched alone over her Brunswick stew, still red-eyed and pale from her ordeal.

Bummer about your arm. Your friend, J. P.

It made sense in a way that almost made me feel better. Good, stalwart John Paul. He would never allow himself anything other than the most polite communication to a woman other than his girlfriend. So easy, for someone like him, to lead a girl on. He had learned through hard experience to tread carefully.

Back in White Cottage, I considered throwing Susannah's letter away but couldn't bring myself to do it. Instead I filed the envelope in my box and hid the coke beneath my underwear. Someone knocked at the door—an assertive and male retort—and my heart bolted with the illogical expectance of John Paul.

"Come in," I said, sliding the drawer shut.

He opened the door but didn't come in. So tall, it seemed his head almost grazed the top of the nineteenth-century doorway. Wearing jeans, a ski jacket, and an itchy wool scarf. Faint scratches just below his right cheekbone—from feline or female fingernails. The wound looked strangely tinted, as if he'd tried to cover it up with powder.

"Hello, Mr. Butterfield," I said. Though I thought of him as senator, using that title seemed rude—calling unnecessary attention to his celebrity.

"Hullo, Catherine," he said. "Do you have a minute?"

I looked around the room. Since my injury, Ms. Latham had been helping me clean up. Minus the dining-hall plates, with two days' worth of dirty clothes instead of five, it still looked fairly wrecked. Especially compared to Skye's. But of course he wouldn't stay, any- way—not wanting to be alone in a girl's dorm room. Grabbing my sweater, I hoped his intent on leaving kept him from noting the mess. We walked downstairs to the tiny common room.

The Amandas were downstairs—thankfully sitting across from each other, playing cribbage. They gathered up their cards and fled, leaving us to take their places. Skye's father settled into a rocking chair and I perched on the very edge of the couch.

"How's your arm?" he said.

"It's bad," I said. "Broken in two places. I'll be wearing this cast till the end of the summer."

"I'm sorry,"he said. "Skye told me what happened. She feels com- pletely responsible."

"That's because she is," I said, surprising us both. "I won't be able to compete at all this year. This was my last chance riding Medal Maclay."

Senator Butterfield paused for a moment, then allowed me a sympathetic smile. He looked younger than when I'd last seen him, escorting Skye out of the woods. An ease that hadn't been there pre- viously—like he'd just let out a long breath.

"I took Skye out to lunch," he said. "She doesn't know I'm here talking to you. She feels terrible about everything."

For a strange moment, I thought he was going to make me an offer. Money or admittance to college, in exchange for becoming Skye's friend again. But he did nothing so dramatic, only settled more deeply into the wicker chair. Accustomed to the slight weight of teenage girls, it creaked in protest.

"I feel bad, too," I admitted, wondering what else Skye had told him.

He rubbed his hands together and looked directly at me. I didn't turn my eyes away. He still had his lovely way of regarding—as if he had assessed me entirely and was pleased with what he saw. Never mind how deeply he had sunk into mortal status. I still found myself wishing that he were my father.

"Skye doesn't make friends easily," he said. "I've never understood that. She's so special. So lively and smart. And pretty. Don't you think she's pretty?"

I nodded.

"Maybe too pretty," he said. "Maybe that's it. People are intimidated. Or jealous."

I didn't say anything. Whatever Skye's problem, it wasn't her looks.

"At any rate," he said. "She hurt me, too. With that protest. A god-awful mess."

"She just meant to do what was right."

"If only it were that simple," he said, with a deep and worldly sigh.

"Some things are that simple," I said, not sure I still believed it.

He smiled at me like I had announced the sky was purple, a mistake equally adorable and incorrect.

"You hid her that night," he said. "Didn't you."

I didn't answer, and he smiled again.

"You're a good egg, Catherine," he said. "I hate to see Skye lose you."

I raised my eyebrows. I almost felt more comfortable talking to Senator Butterfield than to Skye. A man who appreciated the necessary precautions when taking wayward paths. A man who knew how to cover his tracks—or at least understood the imperative of trying, even if he hadn't always been successful.

A faint pelting against the window pane. More snow. I felt a little sinking inside, at the endless March weather and the conviction that spring would never come.

"She probably hasn't lost me," I admitted.

He clapped his hands together. This was what he'd come for.

"Good," he said. He stood up. Pulled a gold Cross pen from his pocket. "May I sign your cast?" he said.

"Sure."

I stepped forward. He didn't seem to notice the bare expanse. Just signed below my elbow, in broad, bold letters that I couldn't see without standing in front of a mirror.

I could hear his footsteps receding—still confident in the sway of his own audience and the effect it would have on the future.

SPRING

16

Spring started slowly the last semester of our sixth-form year—not so much mudluscious as mudterrible. Rivulets of mud, cakes of mud. Mud tracked through the dormitory. The bathroom floor had a permanent film, wet and whirling. Hilary Knudsen slipped in JR and broke her wrist, which somehow bode well for forgiveness: accidents happen.

After Senator Butterfield's visit, I walked across campus to JR. The door to Skye and Eleanor's loft was open, as usual, but when I poked my head up through the floor the room was empty. I thought about crossing to Skye's desk and leaving a note, but my shoes were caked with dirt. The beds were so neatly made and the floor so spotless. And in truth, I was almost, but not quite, ready to see her. The pristine, empty room felt like a reprieve, however brief.

The next few days lagged on, empty and dim. I could have studied, but it seemed so pointless—college acceptances were already en route and would land in our mailboxes any day. I let Laura ride Pippin, trying to coach her, but that also seemed pointless. Laura was good, passable. But her hands were way too busy for my horse's soft mouth; he repeatedly tossed his head, trying to loose the reins from her hands, and if it hadn't have been for my voice nearby I was sure he would certainly have thrown her. Besides, Laura had already aged out of Medal Maclay, where she'd seldom won anything other than yellow and green ribbons.

The hideous limbo of the seasons, poised in this brown wasteland between white winter and the green shoots of spring, created a restless and uneasy depression. At night my dreams alternated between nuclear waste and horseback. Pippin and I would gallop through high grass, jumping fences, the mud splashing behind us in sickly, neon tidal waves. Sometimes John Paul would appear, on the opposite side of a riverbank or barely visible through a haze of mist. I would wake up breathless, desperate for something more.

One night I woke from such a dream and immediately got out of bed. Wriggled into a pair of blue jeans, another impossible one-handed task. Got Susannah's coke from my dresser drawer and put it in my pocket.

I snapped up a window shade, trying to assess the night, but it lay outside in utter darkness. And I felt the happiest surge—the first positive emotion since my accident. Just the act of stepping out of that room, and crossing the unlit campus, all at once the mud *would* be luscious, as I squished my illegal way through it. I opened the door to my room, and there was Skye, about to slip tonight's letter under my door. We stood for a moment, blinking at each other. Then we burst out laughing, clapping hands over our mouths to silence ourselves.

"Come outside," Skye whispered. "It's wonderful."

AND OF COURSE it was: the filthy chunks of ice, stubbornly clinging to the side of the road. The drooling puddles rainbowed by gasoline. The starless, cloud-covered night and the two of us bundled underneath it, walking across the road and over the hill toward the dining hall. We jumped over the divots in the lacrosse field and settled on the metal bleachers.

"My dad says you two spoke," Skye said.

"I thought that was supposed to be a secret."

She shrugged and said, "The real secret is that he's resigning his seat in August. That's what he came up here to tell me."

"Because of you?" I asked.

"He says not." She looked past me, intent on the field, as if a game were going on. "He says I was right, on some level. That being a politician means compromising and fudging. That the system is corrupt, and he can't change it without being a part of it, and that means bending to some of the corruption. He says that I made him remember what it was like to see things on purer terms. He says he's tired of championing the gray areas. Tired of being a gray area himself."

This sounded unlikely to me, even then. I wondered if Skye's father had been caught doing something illegal, or if he couldn't stand the idea of losing his next campaign. Skye leaned forward, hands between her knees. A vertical line formed above the bridge of her nose, and I saw that one day it would be there permanently. I looked out at the field and imagined girls from years ago, cradling their wooden sticks, running against each other in the night; attempting their blocks, checks, and goals. Skye stared in the same direction, intent on that ghostly game.

"Do you remember that day Mrs. November gave us a ride?" she said.

"Of course." I pictured the glossy dark hair. The beak of a nose that was fascinating as it was disappointing.

"I knew she was leaving him."

"You did?" I said. "How?"

"I had a bad feeling about Mr. November from the first day of school. The way he always looked at me. Did you ever notice the way he used to look at me?"

I reminded her that I did.

"So then I saw him and Ms. Latham, one night when I was coming across campus to your room. They were just over there, under the elm tree. Kissing."

I remembered Mrs. November strumming the strings of her guitar, singing "And the Band Played Waltzing Matilda" in her cool contralto. I pictured her at home, sitting on their battered couch in the semidark, waiting for her husband to come home.

"Did they see you?" I asked.

Skye shook her head. "No. But I wrote a letter, an anonymous letter. To Mrs. November. I sent it just a few days before we saw her. Then when we got into her car, and I saw all that stuff piled in back, I knew."

"Does Mr. November know?" I said.

"No. But I may tell him, just because I need a way to get rid of him."

"That should do it," I said.

"I did feel bad," she said. "I felt both ways. Like I'd done something terrible to all three of them. But then I felt like I'd set Mrs. November free. And Mr. November was wrong, right? Somebody had to tell her. You know? So it seemed like the right thing. But then it also seemed cruel. What do you think?"

I didn't know. Mr. November and Ms. Latham clearly weren't together now. This seemed to indicate that whatever had been between them hadn't amounted to much. With the letter to Mrs. November, Skye had managed to insert herself exactly where she didn't belong—in their marriage—becoming more of an obstacle to their union than Ms. Latham might ever have been. Still, Mr. November and Ms. Latham had both broken the most serious rules of the heart. Mrs. November deserved better, and I felt glad she'd got away.

"But Skye," I said. "Why did you want to go to Ms. Latham's house and buy pottery? Why did you invite her to come to dinner with us?"

"Because there's something wrong with me," Skye said.

Months ago, coming from Susannah, this same pronouncement had made me bristle. But coming from Skye, the words sounded ominous, frightening. For a moment I wished I'd stayed in my room.

"Ms. Latham looks a little like my dad's girlfriend. I think there may have been more than just the one. I think it might be a part of the reason he's resigning." Skye said. "He doesn't want anything to come out publicly, and humiliate my mother. He says he's tired of living in dread of the press and the next bad newspaper story."

She dropped her head onto her knees. Her hair fell forward, grazing the mud below our feet. "I knew my protest would put my father in a bad spot. Because how could he say anything, after he supported the whole Chanticleer thing? It must have been like seeing himself, in a way, some part of his insides, speaking out publicly against himself. But in my mind, I couldn't see how protecting a tree would be bad."

She sat back up and looked into my face, as if begging me to believe in her lack of self-awareness.

"Letting it get chopped down seemed like the bad thing," she said. "I thought I was being noble. Brave. But now I'm confused. I see my father's face, and I see him leaving everything he's worked so hard for. And I just feel terrible."

She sat back up. Our shoulders rested close, nearly touching; despite the disturbing nature of the information, and my passing wish to flee, it felt completely natural to be with her. Skye and I had been like that—comfortable—within hours of first meeting. I guessed that we could be separated over a span of years, decades, and all it would take was one hello before just *knowing* each other again. Despite any misgivings, faced with Skye herself there was nowhere else for me to go. I wanted to be with her, simple as that. Sitting there on the bleachers, hearing her confessions and soaking up her reflected glow, I came to life again.

"It sounds like your father's grateful, in a way," I said. "Maybe you saved him?"

We both breathed in, slightly shuddery. If the likes of Douglas Butterfield needed saving, where did that leave the rest of us?

"Well," she said. "Whatever the case, I feel positively shitty about it. And about you. About everything."

"Oh," I said, as if these past weeks had never occurred. "Don't feel shitty."

"I do," she said. "I feel like some sort of toxic slime, oozing out of a nuclear power plant and into a pristine river."

I thought how much Susannah would like that analogy.

"You're being too hard on yourself," I said. "It's all okay now."

She laughed. "What is? The destruction of my father's lifelong goals? Or your broken arm and your riding career."

I thought for a minute and came up with an answer that I knew to be exactly true. "You're giving yourself too much credit," I said. "Your father must have been wanting to resign for a long time. You probably just gave him that last push he needed. That he wanted. And for me, as far as the horse shows."

Not sure of how to mitigate this loss, I stopped talking. I could have comforted Skye with everything I might accomplish as a college equestrian. I could have announced new plans to become professional and the ways I would surmount my spotty performance riding Medal Maclay. But reaching that far ahead proved impossible. That night Skye and I sat on the familiar grounds of an athletic field amid the New England scents of pine and wood smoke, the springtime brewing of forsythia edging its way into the air. A year from now, who knew? I would be eighteen, finally. When I tried to think to that girl (woman!) about to finish her freshman year in college, I had no inkling as to her identity. I didn't know what she liked or wanted, what the shape of her life would be. It was a little like contemplating death: that endless, forthcoming void. Suddenly nothing seemed to matter. Not even the loss of John Paul, which I had ascribed at least in part to Skye's influence.

"You can't tell anyone about my dad," Skye said. "Not a living soul."

"You know I won't."

We heard a creak from across the way and turned our heads to see an adult form leaving the dining hall. We dove under the bleachers as the floodlights turned on.

It was Mrs. Riley, the algebra teacher. A midnight snack? An escape from her gruesome husband? Either way, she was no Ms. Latham or Mr. November. She had been teaching at Esther Percy since Armistice Day and had been one of the strongest opponents of abandoning school uniforms. If she saw us she would not turn her head the other way, but take chase.

"Hush," Skye whispered, and we stifled laughter at the unnecessary warning. We crawled away from the field, to where the grass grew deeper. Skye slithered like a snake, but I had to push up on my knees, sidling awkwardly like a fiddler crab. At the Assembly Hall, we pressed our backs against the wall and skulked around the other side.

Our shirtfronts were covered in mud. Brown streaked across Skye's face, and little drops hung from her hair. Even in the poor light, I could see my cast had turned soggy and brown.

We crept along the wall and waited, till Mrs. Riley's sad steps had receded. Then we clasped hands and ran toward White Cottage. It was easier to run, with Skye's weight balancing me on the other side. The air felt light and blooming.

I didn't need to ride Pippin. I didn't need ribbons and trophies and the National Horse show. I didn't need John Paul. I barely even needed Susannah. Not as long as I had this.

And I don't know if it occurred to me, that in fact Skye had rendered me exactly as she wanted. Forgiving, unencumbered by loftier goals — my broken arm limiting all concentration to her.

But I am fairly certain it didn't occur to Skye. Otherwise, I think, she would have told me.

BACK IN MY ROOM, I unveiled the coke. We pulled out the toaster oven and found my razor blade. Because of my arm, the work was all Skye's. She cut and fanned and told me that Eleanor had moved into another dorm, taking over the room of a third-form girl who'd been sent home for cheating on midterms.

"She won't even talk to me," Skye said. "Like it's my fault that guy was a psycho."

She filled me in on Mr. November, whom she'd stopped visiting. "He's too broken up about his dad's dying," she said. "It's made him crazy. He thinks he's in love with me, which is the last thing I wanted. And of course he's still dying to have *intercourse.* So I blew him off, and now he keeps showing up at my dorm room. He throws rocks at the window, like he thinks he's Romeo. Sooner or later somebody's going to hear him."

I sat on my bed, tapping my feet in a clear, sweet rhythm.

"I'm so glad I'm here tonight," Skye said. "I've got to get away from him. He's really nuts. And I can't turn him in, because think of where that would leave me. That's the last thing my dad needs, right?"

My feet stopped tapping. A droplet of the old chill returned.

"Mr. November knows about the coke," I reminded her.

She held up the toaster oven, offered me another line. I took the straw and inhaled, as if it would make my thinking clearer.

"He knows about it," I said, "and Eleanor knows."

"Oh, Eleanor. The last thing I'd worry about is that mouse. And let me tell you, Mr. November would get in a lot more trouble than us if anything about this came out."

I nodded. We, after all, were the golden treasures — entrusted to Esther Percy's care and woe to them if any harm befell us, especially at the hands of their faculty. Mr. November would have done better to rob Fort Knox than put his hands on Skye.

So I swept my trepidation aside. Why think about repercussions? When I felt so purely invincible — the good drugs back in my body, and my friendship with Skye restored.

17

MR. NOVEMBER LOOKED on the brink of disintegration. Skye would sit resolutely in her seat, chewing the end of her pencil and staring at the table. She stopped raising her hand, leaving too much silence in the room. The knot of Mr. November's tie always looked wrinkled at the edges, pulled too small and tight. His face rebelled against shaving with screaming red dots, matching his bloodshot eyes. His hands had acquired a little tremor, and he gave up writing on the board altogether.

I couldn't help it. I felt sorry for him. At the same time I felt indignant on behalf of Mrs. November, that he hadn't exhibited nearly this level of heartbreak on her behalf.

He would pause in the middle of lectures and stare hopelessly across the table at Skye, his chin quivering like he might start crying. She would frown and tap her pencil, refusing to look up. The other girls couldn't possibly have missed it.

"Mr. November," Laura prodded one morning, when his silence had gone on too long. "You were saying?"

"Right, right." He fanned miserably through his text, searching for his lost thought, then slammed the book shut and dismissed us early.

"Let's go to town for lunch," Skye said, closing the door to the English building.

She had foresworn hitchhiking, but the early dismissal gave us time to walk. After a series of rainstorms, the weather had finally turned fair. Slits of color quivered under blossoms and white flowers opened in clover patches.

At the foot of Percy Hill Road, I opened the door to the general store, its collection of cowbells clanging.

"No, no," Skye said, shaking her head. "Let's go there." She pointed across the street, to the Sheepshead Tavern.

"I don't think I have enough money," I said, assuming I'd have to pay for both of us.

"My treat," she said. I raised my eyebrows, and Skye laughed. "Seriously," she said. "Come on. You're nothing but skin and bones."

We ate rare burgers with bleu cheese, and thick cottage fries. I used my sister Claire's old student ID to order a beer and a shot of vodka. I poured the latter into Skye's Pepsi.

"You don't look anything like her," Skye said, studying the card. "Does your other sister have blonde hair?"

"No," I said. "Nobody but me and my father. He did, anyway, when he was younger."

"How old is he?"

"I don't know," I said. "Old. Sixty something."

Skye whistled. She looked at Claire's picture again. "Is this what your mother looks like?" she said.

"Sure," I said. "A little bit. My mom's prettier, I think. And older, obviously."

"Tell me something about her," Skye said.

"I'm her favorite," I said, surprising myself.

Skye laughed.

"No, really," I said. "Everybody knows. They joke about it all the time."

Skye's only child sensibility was horrified and fascinated.

"Come on," she said. "Don't stop there. Tell me something else."

"I had another brother," I said. "He had blond hair, like me. At least when he was little. He died before I was born. He was four."

The waitress brought the bill, sliding the faux leather bill holder onto the table. Skye watched me, her hands on either side of her plate.

"How did he die?" Skye said.

"He drowned at a birthday party. A pool party. My mother went to pick him up and they were trying to resuscitate him. But he was dead. My sister told me my mom refused to leave or let them move him. They had to sedate her before they could take him away."

"God," Skye said. "That's very intense. What was his name?"

"Marc."

"And you never even met him," Skye said. "That's so weird."

I didn't want to continue. I wished I hadn't told her. It was too hard to talk about, too personal and complicated. The information was so intrinsic, and yet so strangely unemotional. Pressed for information, I didn't know what else to say.

"Does Susannah know?" Skye said.

"Of course. She's been in my house a million times. There are pictures, all that."

"But you didn't tell her."

"Not expressly, I guess."

"What about John Paul?"

"I think Susannah told him. He does know. Maybe I told him."

I knew that I hadn't. Susannah always imparted this information for me. And what did it matter? I'd never known Marc. He hardly had anything to do with me. I wished I hadn't said anything.

Skye put her hand over mine. "I'm glad you told me," she said. She picked up the check folder and slipped a credit card inside.

"Hey," I said. "What's that?"

I pulled it toward myself, and Skye slapped her hand down on top of it.

"Nothing," she said.

"Your father gave you a credit card?"

"Not exactly."

The waitress came by and asked if we were ready. Skye handed her the bill.

"We better hurry," Skye said, looking at her watch. "We're going to be late."

I stayed quiet on the walk back up to school, my head foggy as if I'd drunk four beers instead of one — the illuminated pre-hangover glow, from the unaccustomed rush of information. Which had buoyed Skye so much that I myself felt weightless. I wondered why I had told her. Not because I trusted her, necessarily. More because I had wanted to give her a gift. And even though I didn't particularly like the way she had received it, I felt an odd sort of philanthropy. Like I had given her something she desperately needed at my own expense. I reminded myself to remember this feeling — its pros and cons — if the need to confide, to anyone, ever gripped me again.

The two of us walked up the hill, past the very spot where I'd broken my arm. If the site still haunted Skye she gave no signs, picking up her pace as the bells tolled class, and we both breathed in the thin and fragrant spring air.

• • •

Susannah's letters and phone calls had tapered off. I imagined her preoccupied with the coming trip to Venezuela, the danger and the excitement, gathering contributions from fellow students. I imagined meals in the dining hall at Waverly: her and Drew, John Paul and his new girlfriend. The four of them laughing and full of secrets. I pictured Susannah and Regan, friends now. The spirit of our foursome retained—one of its members easily replaced. Susannah using Skye to justify her own shift in allegiance.

My own Easter break loomed dismally, the first school vacation of my life that would not revolve around horses. And then Skye invited me to spend the week on Cape Cod. I knew my father would say no. On the rare occasions he trained his radar on my friends and me, his natural pessimism struck with precision accuracy. He had enough information on Skye to want me far away from her. What I didn't expect was for my mother to agree with him.

"Your arm, *chérie,*" she objected, when I called to ask. "You need to be at home, where we can take care of you. Make sure that you heal properly."

I reported the bad news to Skye.

"I'll have my father call," she said. She'd just received a package from L.L. Bean and sat on Eleanor's stripped bed, cutting open the box with an X-Acto blade. I watched as she sorted through piles of plastic wrapped sweaters and turtlenecks, flannel pajamas and duck boots.

A few days later, a girl ran up to my room, breathless, pounding on my door.

"Call for you in the student lounge."

I ran down the stairs and across the lawn. While the pay phone's receiver dangled off its hook, my mother waited patiently—staring through the window at our newly blossoming apple trees.

I picked up the phone, too breathless to speak. My mother didn't wait for me to gather my breath before granting permission. "We'll tell your father you've gone on holiday with Susannah and her mother," she said.

I waited for her to add some sort of endearment—her usual signal that acting as my accomplice caused her no trouble. Instead I heard her sigh, slightly weary. And then she said, because she knew I was waiting: "Have fun, *chérie*. I'll miss you."

"Thanks," I said, pushing the discomfort far, far down. So that guilt could in no way interfere with the coming week, its promised adventures necessary as air.

18

EASTER WEEK OF 1985, in Sesuit on Cape Cod. That rarity of rarities — early spring in New England.

I could have had my own room, but that would have kept us too far apart. We slept together in Skye's wide bed under the eaves, a world away from her parents, whom we saw only in passing — glints of their hands, waving good-bye as we sped through the house on our way into each day's halcyon light.

The sun went easy on us. Temperatures that forbade chill, even when we tied a plastic bag around my arm and dove into the frigid water, screaming as we ran back out. We paddled kayaks to Sandy Neck, looking for whales. We smuggled good wine up to Skye's room, then crept back out, riding our bikes to Maushop Lake. We tried to skinny-dip under a full silver moon, but the still water was nearly as cold as the ocean, and we bundled back into our damp clothes, shivering. We had brought the coke along, and sprinkled it like salt onto the sides of our thumbs, snorting it off damp skin. Then sat on the pier, talking at warp speed, our sentences tumbling out and crashing together, blending. My cast already ruined, fetid and violently itchy.

We brought our tape player down to the bluff, blasting "Sugar Magnolia" and dancing on the sand in mad, whirling circles.

"Did you call my name?" she asked. "That night I was missing?"

"No," I said. "We didn't think you'd hear."

"Don't you know how sound carries across the water?"

She cupped her hands around her mouth and called her own name across the wide, black bay.

"You see?" she said, turning back to me. "They heard that all the way over in Ireland."

We threw off our shoes and ran into the waves—freezing water washing over our knees.

"Skye," we shouted, the music blaring behind our voices. "Skye!"

The word reverberated out into the night, as we waited with illogical expectancy for some manner of reply.

THE NEXT MORNING I introduced Skye to John Paul's mushrooms—spreading them into thick peanut butter sandwiches, which we choked down with determined grimaces—before we bicycled all the way to Provincetown.

The world spun by in threads of gray, blue, green: swirls of treetops, cloud formations, and passing cars. We stashed our bikes in the dunes and made our way down Commercial Street. The good weather and Easter weekend had only barely wakened the town from its winter hibernation. A scattered collection of tourists, cross-dressers, and scowling old Yankees made their way down the sidewalk, blinking into the sunlight. We saw three little girls eating ice-cream cones and realized we were starving. Up a flight of warped wooden stairs we found ourselves on a rooftop, eating fried clams and french fries under a green umbrella, the sea assaulting all five senses no matter which way we turned. From across the table, Skye looked as if she'd been spun from seaweed—rippling mermaid hair and eyes the color of algae. As the waiter presented the check we dissolved into uncontrollable laughter, at the preposterous notion of his accepting mere paper in exchange for our fried feast.

Afterward, we wandered back out to the street and found the source of the ice cream. Skye ordered a strawberry cone, I ordered chocolate. We traded halfway through.

"Nothing has ever tasted this good," Skye said. "Nothing will ever taste this good again."

"Don't think like that," I said, and grasped her hand. She nodded obediently, her chin tilted into the breeze. Her face solemn but entirely open. Eager to drink up whatever moments came next.

Fewer people now. The sky began to pulse from purple to blue. We walked out to the lighthouse and dared each other to dive off Cape Cod's fingertips—that easternmost point on the continental United States. With the sun gone, we both shivered slightly, and to my surprise even Skye backed down. At some point boys appeared, also on Easter vacation—presumed handsome because of the way their skin reflected moonlight, but never clearly seen. Our hands held bottles of beer, the world calmed to thrilling perfection. We each retired to a different length of sand, a different stranger's cold bare hands beneath our T-shirts. I willed myself not to long for John Paul and lost myself in the salty skin of another tribesman.

Then Skye tickled my feet, and I rolled the boy off of me. We said our good-byes and made our escape, traveling back to the bicycles, wobbling back over hours and hours, sneaking into the palatial house as dawn crept over the windowsills. Pretending when we woke—the sun high and bright over the ocean—that we'd returned, as promised, before midnight.

I suppose there's no way to explain. That all of this—in its own odd and natural way—seemed magical and wholesome as the Hundred Acre Wood.

THE SAME DAY Susannah and Drew boarded their flight to Venezuela, Skye and I returned to Esther Percy. Letters from colleges had arrived. I got into Amherst, Bryn Mawr, and Middlebury and was wait-listed at Dartmouth and Cornell. I opened the letters one at a time, surprised at my lack of excitement or disappointment. Any future of my own still seemed such an abstraction; I barely considered these choices or imagined myself at any of these schools.

Skye got into Harvard, Yale, Stanford, and Oxford. "Merit scholarships," she said. We stood in line for milk lunch, the graham crackers and boxes of milk served at a dining-hall window every morning at ten. "I wonder if I'll be allowed to use them. I just want to feel like I'm paying my own way."

I understood this. But still it seemed a terrible waste—when tuition to private universities would be such a painless expense for the Butterfields. I hoped Skye's money would fund someone more financially deserving—someone like John Paul. But I didn't say anything.

"It would be nice to go to Oxford," Skye said. "Somewhere far away where I could start over. Where nobody knows who my father is."

"Or who you are," I said, imagining her exotic status. Even without the preexisting renown, she would become instantly famous: the redheaded American girl who quoted Shakespeare.

"But Harvard's a good school, too," she said, and we laughed.

The weather had turned cold again. Skye wore her old, tailored wool coat, abandoning my groovier clothes in favor of a more familiar, preppy look. It was a surprising relief to see her in garments that actually fit.

We carried our snacks to a low stone wall. "I want to get serious when I start college," Skye said. "No more drugs. It's been fun. Especially the Cape. But soon I want to get serious. I want to accomplish things."

She brushed graham cracker crumbs off her lap and sipped some milk. Wiped the mustache away with the back of her palm. I thought how similarly I'd felt starting Esther Percy, and wondered if while walking by the Thames or the Charles, Skye would encounter someone like herself, brimming with temptations. But I knew as soon as the idea formed, should such a person appear, Skye would resist easily.

"All this time, I've wanted to get back at my father," she said. "But maybe the best revenge—the most productive revenge—would be to make him proud. Who knows? Maybe I'll grow up to be the person he couldn't be."

I imagined Skye under the waterfall of confetti. Possessing all the unvarnished idealism her father pretended to. Forests saved. Disarmament treaties signed.

"I got rid of Mr. November," Skye said. "Next I'm giving up the drugs and alcohol. I'm going back to my original self. Only better. Wiser." She peered into my face, the admonishing look of a disappointed analyst, and I wondered if this were her way of breaking off our friendship.

"You should think about it, too," she said. "Cleaning up."

I stared back at her, amazed at her oblivion to thwarting my plans to do exactly that. I thought about saying something, but before I had a chance she said, "I think you should give me the rest of the cocaine. For safekeeping."

"I wouldn't do it alone," I said. "Besides. Why not just flush it? If you want to keep us from doing it again."

"Well, just in case. We don't want to be purists, Catherine."

She plucked a cracker from my untouched stack and bit into it, scattering cinnamon and crumbs.

LATER THAT AFTERNOON I found Ms. Latham on her hands and knees in the White Cottage common room, searching under the furniture.

"What are you looking for?" I asked.

"My American Express card," she said. "I can't find it anywhere, and I'm always leaving my coat in here. I think it might have fallen out of my pocket."

"When did you lose it?" I asked.

"Who knows? I never use the damn thing."

I knew instantly how Skye had been paying for expensive lunches and new clothes. I felt a rush of guilt. My mother had probably spent more on my Vogel boots than Ms. Latham had on her entire wardrobe. I wondered if Skye planned to give up Ms. Latham's credit card along with drugs and Mr. November.

"You should cancel it." I peeked under the sofa cushion in a lame imitation of assistance. She stood and wiped dust from the knees of her jeans.

"I guess I'm not going to find it here," Ms. Latham said.

"I guess not."

"It'll turn up," she said, shrugging.

"My mother lost her card once," I said quickly, as she started to turn away. "They charged nearly five thousand dollars."

"But I haven't had it anywhere besides school," she said. "I can't imagine anyone here would steal it."

Her trust made the veins in my neck ache.

"How's your arm?" Ms. Latham asked.

It had just been reset. The cast now came up to below my elbow, so I didn't have to wear a sling. The mud-stained cast with Senator Butterfield's signature had been sawed apart and thrown away. I wished I'd thought to save it for Ms. Latham.

"It itches," I said, and she smiled.

"You and Skye are friends again," she said. "I'm glad."

She was the first and only person to express this sentiment, at least on my behalf. I smiled back at her, sad that Skye would never know how to appreciate her good wishes.

She reached out as if to ruffle my hair, then changed her mind. She patted my shoulder instead, and I felt disappointed by the less affectionate gesture. I noticed that the Mondale/Ferraro button was finally gone, a delayed but final acceptance of defeat. And I knew that I should hate her—on behalf of Skye and Mrs. November— but couldn't bring myself to do it. Instead I admired her small kindnesses, not the least of which was her determination to overlook Skye's dislike of her. I resolved to find her credit card in Skye's belongings and cut it to shreds. But that plan became just one more thing that I didn't do.

Susannah's college acceptances waited for her back at Waverly, locked and lulled during Easter break. About this time, she and Drew floated along the Orinoco Delta, her father only a few miles away, with no idea of her proximity.

Before Venezuela, Susannah's father had never taken her out of the country. But when she was a child, he had brought Charlie and her on weekend birding trips. They had visited osprey colonies on the Westport River. They had looked for brown-headed nuthatches in the woods of North Carolina. And while they'd never been unusually close — not in the way Skye and her father were — since his defection, Susannah had noticed a marked difference in her feelings toward him. As a child she had taken him for granted in the way of imperatives: bone marrow, oxygen, her father in the next room. Now she couldn't help her own refusal to accept or respect him. His leaving had forged a chasm that no amount of late-night confession or shared coke could bridge. The more overt his attempts to reach her on her own level, the greater the sense that this new South American father had replaced the old one — the one she'd believed would be around forever.

With Drew it was different. Later she told me about floating down the river while she pointed out everything her father had taught her about the region. It struck Susannah that since she'd found out about Skye — once her anger had dissipated — her feelings remained more or less the same. Drew never seemed like a new person. She didn't trust him less. She didn't love him less. The discovery had not affected her feelings toward him so much as clarified them.

And she wished it were anybody else, sitting in the boat beside her, floating down the murky green river, swatting away the mosquitoes and flies. She found herself formulating plans that would allow me to accompany her instead of Drew, as if the trip weren't already well under way.

"Look," she said to Drew, pointing to a ragged osprey nest. She heard a hoarse catch in her smoky voice as she recited what her father had told her—information she'd pretended not to hear. She told Drew that the young ospreys would spend a year in warmer climates before beginning the migration whose rhythm would dominate their entire lives. She didn't tell him because she thought he'd care but because the knowledge her brain contained longed to escape, to be shared with the person closest to her, even if closeness referred to mere proximity.

She told Drew the birds she knew. She told him about the trogons and the blind oilbirds. The yellow-shouldered parrots. "Look," she said, again and again, pointing toward the amazing colors, the prehistoric silhouettes, the shocking wingspans. The curassows, quetzals, and parakeets. Susannah could recognize and identify them all.

"You're amazing," Drew said, sincere and regretful.

"No," she said gently. "It's not me. It's this place." *It's my father,* she wanted to add, almost wanted, but not quite enough. Still, the thought echoed in her head: *It's my father and everything he's taught me.*

Their boat puttered toward a white puddle duck, who suddenly disappeared in an explosion of feathers. Susannah and Drew let out simultaneous shrieks as a caiman's eyes rose and then sunk beneath the surface. Then they laughed—sad, horrified, and exhilarated. Susannah climbed back onto the bench beside Drew, and he put his arm around her shoulders.

Everything moved more slowly in the sticky climate. Along the riverbanks, clotheslines held faded garments, ruffling in the warm breeze. Even with his fingers pressing against her smooth, bare clavicle, Drew couldn't help staring at the pretty brown-skinned girls, unpinning dry shirts and dresses. Susannah looked away, knowing for the hundredth time that she was finished with him. She saw an ocelot crouching behind a tree, its predator's glare fixed on a small, hapless iguana.

It was all so beautiful and scary and strange, she wrote to me, from her shabby hotel room in Caracas. *And I missed everybody. I missed my mom and my brother and my dad and the family we used to be. I missed you, of course. I even missed Skye, and Drew—though he was sitting right beside me.*

At the same time she felt happy. If she'd gone back to school that very day, her schoolmates' money still bundled in her backpack, the connection with Rico and Alan never made, she would have felt her journey had been complete.

It was raining in Ciudad Guayana. Susannah and Drew lunched on steak and rum in a small café. The rain danced and drummed on the tin roof. Susannah listened to its music and watched Drew with increasing dispassion. She appreciated the rare opportunity to assess a person who would soon be exiting her life. To look at him and think about the things she liked, the things she would miss. She waited for a bittersweet twinge in her chest but felt mostly the gentle buzz of the rum. The meat thick and knotted in her unaccustomed stomach.

She looked at her watch. "Why don't you finish," she said to Drew. "I should probably meet Rico alone, anyway, since I'm the one he knows."

Drew put down his glass and pushed the hair out of his eyes. Susannah reached out and smoothed one strand behind his ear.

"You're handsome, you know." She realized as she spoke the words that she'd never told him before.

"Is it safe?" he said. "To walk around here by yourself?" Susannah nodded, and he left his protest at that.

Outside, the hood of her slicker pulled up over her head, her Guatemalan sundress brushing her knees, Susannah thought she was probably safer than most Americans. Black hair and sun-browned knees, so little besides her freedom at one o'clock in the afternoon to differentiate her from the local schoolgirls. She stopped to pet one of the pointy-eared dogs, crouching under the porch of the general store. The animal cowered and then closed its eyes, its bulging rib cage trembling blissfully. Stepping away, Susannah held her hands out under the rain, letting the water gather in her palms. Scrubbed them together as she walked up the stairs to the store.

She saw Rico immediately, unloading a case of Fanta onto the sparsely stocked shelves. She reached out and touched his elbow. He turned and looked at her blankly, waiting for her to ask a tourist's question.

"Remember me?" Susannah said. She pulled back her hood. Shook her hair. "My name's Susannah. My father is Señor Twining, from the Orinoco Delta."

Rico pushed the box of soda aside with his foot. He let his eyes travel up and down Susannah, registering her form more than leering at it. His face eased into a wide, white-toothed smile, and Susannah realized that the compliment she'd given earlier to Drew really belonged to him.

Because afterward at the café, where Drew sat slumped beside the near-empty bottle of rum, he didn't look handsome at all, only disheveled and young. Susannah imagined his mother in a department store, picking out his polo shirt and khaki shorts. Sewing printed name tags inside.

"Did you get it?" Drew asked, as she walked up to the table. Susannah thought that John Paul would never have let a girl wander off alone in a foreign city, in the rain. Not even her brother, or her father, would have done that.

"We're going to his house for dinner tonight," Susannah said. "We'll get it there."

RICO'S WIFE, MARIA, was even smaller than Susannah— sharp elbows and knees, dark braid, childlike feet in flat leather sandals. Impossible to think of her carrying the five children who gathered quietly together in doorways, staring at Susannah and Drew.

The house was low and sad and cozy—green stucco walls and endless stacks of laundry. Susannah emptied her and Drew's backpacks of everything: Levi's and American T-shirts. Mosquito repellant and Adidas. Her raincoat. The two of them could go home in the clothes they were wearing.

Alan arrived, and they all sat down for dinner—beef and sausage and rice and rum. They laughed and toasted. One of the little girls sat in Susannah's lap while she ate, stealing sips of her coconut milk.

It was civilized, Susannah wrote me in her letter. *It was beautiful.*

After dinner, Rico took Susannah onto the cement patio that constituted his backyard. More clotheslines, tiny dresses fluttering in the damp night air. When she zipped the coke into her empty backpack, he bent down and kissed her on the lips. She could hear his family's laughter through the open windows, feel the dim red lights shining behind her. The oropendola again, from a tree nearby. She couldn't help wondering if it were the same bird that trilled the first night they met. And she kissed him back, because he was handsome and because the air was fragrant with sauteed spice and mariposa. And because she didn't love Drew but forgave him: understanding moments like this, arising in a split second of opportunity. Beautiful, lawless, and ephemeral. She tried to transfer this generous exoneration to her father but found the moment trading its softness for hard and jagged edges. So she dispensed with the idea immediately, that his abandonment would ever be excusable.

"You can never tell my father I was here," Susannah whispered to Rico.

And Rico answered, as if he knew everything, "Of course."

Inside, everyone hugged good-bye. Susannah carried Rico's name and address in the pouch of her backpack, so that she could send dresses and T-shirts to the children when she returned to the States.

19

THOUSANDS OF MILES away from dinner at Rico's, Skye woke up after midnight. Mr. November perched at the edge of her bed, staring down at her. She sat up abruptly and threatened to scream.

"Don't," he begged. "Please don't."

"Don't scream?" Skye said.

"Don't leave me."

She sighed, raising her eyes toward the skylight. In jeans and a T-shirt, with his hair too long and in disarray, Mr. November looked like one of the boys who snuck cigarettes behind the dining hall at Devon. Skye felt older than him, beyond and above. How to say this nicely, to anyone—let alone a jilted English teacher.

He pulled her hand from under the covers and placed the twin diamond rings into her palm. She stared down at them, unbelieving.

"Not for an engagement," Mr. November said. "I understand that would be preposterous. I just want you to have them. I know how much you like them."

"Don't you see," Skye said. "I like them because I like *her*. Your wife."

His face readjusted to anger, distance. The same qualities that had earned him his fleeting moments of appeal. "I don't have a wife," he said.

"Look," Skye handed him back the rings. "Pretty soon I'm leaving anyway. For the Cape and then college."

"Cambridge isn't far," he said.

She felt a creeping panic, that for the next four years he would know exactly where she lived. In that moment, she decided definitely: Oxford over Harvard.

"Mr. November," she said, trying to sound gentle. "You need to go."

She pulled the blankets up to her chin and instantly regretted the movement—betraying a certain level of fear and shifting the power.

"You don't need to cover yourself up," he said. "Not in front of me."

"You've got to get yourself together," Skye said. "I'm sorry, but it's over. It really is."

He paused for a moment, as if waiting for her to deny the statement, and when no denial came he dropped his face into his hands and cried. Skye patted his back with consoling thumps. She half hoped one of the girls in the room next door would hear him and investigate. It seemed a shame that this spectacle, with all its illicit pathos, should be reserved for her alone.

"I love you," he said.

"Like you loved your wife?"

"I don't have a wife. This has nothing to do with her."

"I honestly don't think you're capable of love, Mr. November."

I imagine his face in the room's slant light, the irony of her accusation registering even through his grief. And then Skye told him. About seeing him kiss Ms. Latham and writing the letter to Mrs.

November. She told him about piling into the backseat of her car—
sliding her guitar on top of so many suitcases. How she'd known in
that instant that his wife was leaving, that Skye had driven her away.

"Except it was really you who drove her away," Skye said. "Being
unfaithful."

The melting perimeters of a crying man turned sharp. On alert.
Listening to Skye, Mr. November's unremarkable eyes turned a sudden and electric blue. For the first time Skye thought that he must
have loved Mrs. November: such was the palpable rage—hanging
in the air, thick and jagged between them. For a moment, she felt
so certain he would hit her that she closed her eyes, bracing herself
for the blow.

"I don't understand," Mr. November said instead, anger clipping
his voice as sorrow had elongated it. "You wrote her that letter because you wanted to be with me?"

Maybe if she'd said yes, he would have forgiven her. But Skye
shook her head. "I did it to protect her," she said.

He placed his hands on her shoulders, fingers straddling her
larynx.

"How righteous of you," Mr. November said. "I guess I could do
the same thing. I could tell Mrs. Chilton about you and me. I could
tell her about you and Catherine and the coke. Using your logic, that
would be the moral course of action."

"There isn't any coke," Skye said, frowning toward her sock
drawer, where I'd let her stash the last of it.

"I feel like I could kill you," Mr. November whispered.

Skye thought about carrying out her initial threat and screaming.
Instead, she pulled backward, out of his grasp, and lay down. Then
she yanked the covers tightly over her head.

"Please just go away," she said, her voice muffled under the thick down quilt.

He sat there for what seemed forever, his fingers pressing through the fabric and around her throat. From under the covers, Skye couldn't tell whether he meant the touch to be threatening, conciliatory, or erotic. Finally she heard him get up and fumble around her room, like he couldn't find his way out in the dark. After a while the door clicked shut. She pulled the covers off her head and breathed in the clear, unfettered air.

Pale starlight misted in from above, just enough so that she could register the disturbances in the room — the things on her desk disarranged, her drawers left ajar. She got out of bed and plunged her hand into the top drawer, beneath her socks.

The coke was gone.

WE COULDN'T EXACTLY report a theft. "Maybe I should tell them about Mr. November," Skye said.

"Tell them what, exactly? That he threatened to kill you? Or that you've been dating him."

"Some combination of the two."

We sat together on bales of hay in Pippin's stall, skipping Mr. November's third-period class. I imagined him scanning the room, all jittery nerves, jerking his head up whenever he heard a door rattle anywhere in the building. Pining despite himself for Skye's appearance.

"You never should have messed with him," I said.

"Easy to say now," she said, as if the relationship had once looked like a good idea. I tried to imagine what would happen if Mr. November turned us in. Pippin dropped his head and snorted, then nibbled at the pocket of Skye's jeans. I expected her to jump, startled, but instead she grabbed onto his halter and stroked his muzzle.

"I used to come up here that week after you got hurt," she said. "Before you came back to school. I'd bring him carrots and sugar cubes and hang out on the hay. I always waited for him to seem scared—to kick me or something—but he never did."

Any other time, this would have interested me. I would have asked Skye questions, about how Pippin seemed in my absence and the way he'd reacted to her. But just then, I needed to keep her on track. There was no room now for the bad judgment that led to Mr. November in the first place. Skye's hand needed to be held, like a child's. She needed to be told exactly what to do and how to do it. I wished I could will myself into her body — pulling all the necessary strings and suppressing every unpredictable or dangerous impulse.

"Listen," I said. "The most important thing is, if we get caught, we can't say where we got the coke."

"I don't even know." Her voice sounded vaguely petulant. She pushed Pippin's head away and said, in a softer tone, "You should let me ride him sometime."

The request was too ridiculous to merit an answer. I grabbed her hand, trying to snap her back to reality.

"We can't say anything about Waverly," I said, not mentioning John Paul or Susannah or Drew—as if possibly Skye could have forgotten their names.

"Of course," she said. "But we have to say it came from somewhere."

"Remember that guy Van?" I said. "You can say you got it from him. Just make up more details, and tell them about his name and his car. Say he picked you up hitchhiking and sold it to you."

"Shit," Skye said. And then louder: "Shit!"

In the next stall, Laura's horse whinnied and kicked the wall. But Pippin just stood, newly Zen. Ears barely twitching.

"This can't happen," Skye said.

A hot day, she wore my clothes again—a filmy Indian skirt and a tank top. The skirt was too long on me, and hardly covered her calves. Her hair was skinned back into a ponytail and her face looked pointed and pale, her bearing so tremulous that I thought she might shatter into the air around us.

She threw herself back on the hay bale, arms out by her sides like a snow angel. "My father will die," she said. "If this happens right before he resigns? Everyone will think that's the reason. I've put him through enough. First he will kill me, and then he will die."

Her father, I knew, would take her home and brush her off and send her to another tony school. Whereas my father: I couldn't even think what my father would do. Given the way he'd reacted to my relatively minor infractions, and the fact that cocaine—of all drugs—belonged to the world of Studio 54 and debutantes and movie executives, all the glamorous and nonworking rich he most despised.

"Look," I said. "Maybe it won't even happen. Maybe we're getting all wrought up over nothing, and Mr. November was just bluffing. He probably just took it home and snorted it."

"Maybe he took it over to Ms. Latham's," Skye said. "The two of them sat up and snorted it together, then made passionate love on one of her ratty hook rugs."

"No," I said. "Men can never get it up after snorting coke."

"I've heard that's a myth," she said, and we couldn't help laughing.

Not wanting to go to the dining hall, we walked to the orchard for lunch. We ate apples and smoked cheddar cheese and steaming slices of pie. Then we walked up the hill and went to our different classes—AP French for me, AP history for Skye.

We didn't hug before parting. I didn't turn to watch her walk away, curls tamed into that long, long ponytail. Narrow shoulders gleaming with perspiration from trotting uphill to get to class on time.

EXACTLY FIFTY MINUTES LATER, I bumped into Laura on my way to Human Behavior.

"Did you hear?" she said. "Mrs. Chilton took Skye out of history."

The dean of students had poked her elegant gray head into the classroom. Skye turned four shades of pale, pushed her chair back, and followed her out of class without even collecting her books.

There was no point in my going to class; I went to White Cottage and sat on my bed. Knowing that soon someone would come to get me and that when I returned it would be to pack my belongings. I thought about giving myself a head start but realized that would be a premature admission of guilt. So there was nothing to do but wait. It seemed the sky outside should grow dark, but the days had finally grown longer. Sunlight beamed stubbornly through my windows.

The bells tolled class. I sat on top of my cool French linen, sweaty legs crossed. The warped floorboards and simple white walls—spackled with thumbtack holes—had been home to a hundred girls before me. And I recognized the moment as a reprieve. I knew that whatever happened in the next few hours would define my life for a very long time. Somehow in that brief span of moments my belief system shifted in a way that hadn't occurred when I'd left Waverly, or started Esther Percy, or broken my arm. Not when I'd pledged a new life of purity, sitting on the stone wall with Skye. Only in my room, waiting to be summoned, did I arrive at a clear understanding. This time, these moments, were not my life but its threshold. Whereas I had believed myself to be entirely formed, I was actually very much an embryo — sections of my brain and being, years away from becoming whole. Years from now, I would not be able to fathom the things I had done, participated in. One day, danger and its irresistible wake would no longer be something I keened toward. For some reason this gave me comfort as I looked around at my scarves and my pictures, my tapestries and schoolbooks, my stack of record albums. I tapped my fingers on my knees, patiently waiting to bid good-bye to everything I had known before.

WHEN SKYE WALKED into her office, Mrs. Chilton sat behind her desk with Ms. Latham standing on one side and Mr. November on the other. Skye didn't wait for them to speak. She opened her mouth and told them everything. Of all her performances, this must have been the most virtuoso. She executed her betrayal in the most minute and compelling detail. No doubt if Mr. November had not been there she would have included him. Instead, she constructed her disclosure entirely around me. She told them about snorting coke off the toaster oven in my room in White Cottage. She told them about our trip to Cape Cod and her disappearance. She told them about the pot we had smoked in our dorm rooms and the mushrooms we had eaten over Easter vacation. She told them there was more coke on the way and that I had promised to deliver it to her.

While the small group of adults stared at her, entirely floored. They had called her into the office because of the unauthorized charges—totaling more than two thousand dollars—that had appeared on Ms. Latham's credit-card statement, and which had been traced back to Skye through the customer service staff at L.L. Bean. Ms. Latham was there as apologetic accuser, Mr. November as Skye's faculty adviser.

There must have been a long silence at the end of her arresting monologue. I imagine Mr. November staring at the floor—insides hollow from the stolen coke and his own impending doom. Ms. Latham wishing she'd gone directly to Skye instead of to Mrs. Chilton. And Mrs. Chilton herself, wending her hands together, anticipating the brewing storm. Saying in a stern but coaxing tone to Skye that the important thing was for her to tell them the original source of the coke: the name of the dealer, the person who had procured it.

And Skye told them what she had decided, from the very beginning, to be the truth.

Here's what I know about what happened next: Mrs. Chilton asked Mr. November to walk Skye back to her room. She sent Ms. Latham to collect me.

"Miss Morrow," Mrs. Chilton said, as I walked into her office. She sat in a wicker caned chair, her posture impossibly precise. Her skin was darkly tanned and deeply lined from years of vigorous walks and sailing trips. But through the crinkles and folds, her eyes shone a youthful cerulean blue.

I took the chair facing her desk. It was upholstered in chintz and much more comfortable than her own. The dean's office at Waverly had been shrouded in academic stillness—leather, velvet, and antique. This room didn't have that quality, exactly, nor the bustling air of industry of my father's office. Everything here looked used in a worn, unvaluable way. There was a collection of china cats on one shelf. Doilies covered worn patches on armchairs. It seemed cozy and civilized. A gray-haired place, perfect for tea and compliments.

"You know why you're here?" Mrs. Chilton said.

"Skye's in trouble?"

"I'm afraid she is," Mrs. Chilton said. "Very grave trouble. As are you."

I didn't say anything. A landscape portrait hung behind her in a darkly burnished frame. Horses and spaniels, perhaps on a fox hunt. I allowed myself a brief route of escape: Pippin and me, sailing down the cross-country course. I laid my hand on top of my cast, newly pristine after Cape Cod Bay and Maushop Lake had destroyed its predecessor.

"You've had quite a year," she said. "How's your arm?"

"It's fine," I said. "Getting better."

"I'm so glad to hear it." Palpable sarcasm. Maybe she thought I deserved permanent impairment.

"Thank you," I said.

I wonder if she was at all tempted, to see how long I would go without telling her anything. To sit there with me, casting her concentrated combination of kind and stern, until finally my guard broke down and I admitted to knowing the reason for this audience. It would have been a long wait. Forever or more. I never would have said a word.

"Skye tells us a story about cocaine," Mrs. Chilton said, after several minutes had ticked silently by.

I didn't answer.

"She tells us that you and she have been using cocaine throughout the school year. That you've obtained it more than twice, from your friends at Waverly."

I blinked back at her, my fingers resting on the arms of the chair. My shoulders at ease, as if what she said had nothing to do with me. As if English were not my native language.

"She tells us that a young man by the name of John Paul Saxton has been selling the cocaine to you and to your friends at Waverly. She tells us he has more. That you plan to bring more cocaine here, to this campus."

The strongest sort of sting behind my eyes. My teeth found my front lip, evincing the tiniest drop of blood. The back of my throat went dry.

"Do you have anything to say about this, Catherine?"

My fingers clenched, quietly clawing the armrest. I realized there were marks, where previous interrogants must have done the same.

And I thought of John Paul. I thought of the first day he'd sat next to me and offered his hand. I thought of his head bent over books. I thought of him rescuing Pretty Girl and saving goals on the soccer field. I thought of him on Cape Cod, ready to face any necessary consequence to help find Skye.

When John Paul and I had been caught in bed, the headmaster at Waverly called us into his office to lecture us on the importance of parietal rules and the many reasons for staying chaste. He had talked about birth control and sexually transmitted diseases. He reminded us repeatedly of our tender ages. And from the moment we sat down in our chairs, spaced two feet apart, John Paul had held my hand. While the headmaster stared, persisting with his intrusive and embarrassing lecture. John Paul's arm reaching across the air between us, clasping my clammy fingers with a warm and comforting grip.

Nodding as the headmaster spoke but refusing to be cowed. Making his quiet, obstinate, and gentlemanly stand: the right to his own feelings. For me.

I knew that John Paul would protect Susannah and Drew. He would sit in that same chair, alone this time, facing Waverly's headmaster. He would firmly and effusively deny selling coke but would not offer an alternative theory. Susannah and Drew would return to school, pockets full of coke, nothing left in John Paul's room but the scrapes of Scotch tape that had held up posters of Pelé and Bob Marley. They would huddle together and discuss coming forward. Confessing. But they never would. The damage had already been done. John Paul wasn't coming back no matter what they did. Why take themselves down with him?

Skye's story would stand as truth.

I thought of John Paul's meager house. His exhausted mother. His father, across the Atlantic, denying the existence of a son who might make him so infinitely proud. Would this fiasco convince Monsieur Filage that he'd done the right thing in denying him?

John Paul. His hard work and his kind soul and his ruined future.

My youthful love of justice violently rebelled against everything that would happen next. A surge of hatred welled up, toward Skye and her assumptions. If only I'd told her the truth.

I was seventeen years old. Love burgeoned huge, frightening, and all consuming. It lunged in every direction—like a multiheaded creature banging horns against itself. I loved John Paul and I loved Skye. I loved Susannah and I loved my parents. And it never occurred to me to love myself, because I had no means of disentangling my identity from the fierce and secret and divergent emotions I felt toward all of these people.

I wanted to answer Mrs. Chilton, but my body seemed surprised by that intention. It only provided the barest sort of grunt, a crackle from somewhere in the middle of my throat.

She asked if I wanted water. I shook my head, and managed to emit words. I asked her if she'd contacted Waverly.

"No," she said. "Not yet."

"Because it's not true," I said, "about John Paul."

She moved her head the slightest bit to the side, understanding I'd admitted that everything else was true. My mind reached to Van—that mercurial mystery ride—but I knew the time for alibis and scapegoats had come and gone.

I don't know what I thought would happen: if John Paul and his scholarships would be rescued, if Skye would be punished for falsely accusing him, if Susannah would be able to forgive this final infraction. Because without so much as taking a breath, I did the thing that came least naturally: I told Mrs. Chilton the source of the coke. And felt unexpectedly sorry for her as her elbow slipped, just slightly, off its slim wooden armrest.

She asked me more questions and I answered them without emotion. A truthful robot.

John Paul was already gone. Susannah close behind him. Now Skye, and soon my parents. I stood up as Ms. Latham entered the office. I let her put her arm around my shoulders. My entire body buzzed with my betrayal—but I believed I'd done the only possible thing.

Walking back to White Cottage with Ms. Latham, I imagined Mrs. Chilton had already picked up the phone to call the headmaster at Waverly. That Susannah and Drew would return from their trip to face the same kind of audience I had just endured. That like me and

Skye they would be expelled—perhaps facing another year of high school, their college acceptances withdrawn.

It never occurred to me that higher authorities than headmasters would be called on.

And in the time it took to bring me to Mrs. Chilton's, to exact my confession and betrayal. In the time Mr. November made his glowering escort of Skye back to her room. In the time it took to phone both sets of parents and deliver the news, and for Ms. Latham to help me pack my things. In the time it took for federal agents to be deployed, meeting Susannah and Drew when they deplaned at Logan—with two hundred thousand dollars' worth of coke, zipped into their pockets and stuffed into their shoes.

In that time, Skye made her way to the stables. Where she climbed onto Pippin's back and vanished.

20

THEY SEARCHED THE SAME PLACES, and dozens more. They searched Esther Percy and Devon. DC and Boston. They swept through our barn daily and scoured the old-growth forest. They interviewed all of us, repeatedly—officials hovering close while the battalions of reporters and news trucks and satellite dishes camped on campuses and at the ends of driveways. Except for John Paul, we all lived in houses with long, private drives. Facing the street—with all its intruding eyes—must have been unbearable. If they hadn't tapped our phone, I might have called him.

Meanwhile, I was finished with disclosure. I had many audiences with various police officers but never uttered a word about Senator Butterfield's impending resignation or his nameless paramour. The only thing I cared about was recovering Pippin. If Eleanor hadn't stayed true to bitter, goody-goody form and turned in Mr. November, his relationship with Skye would have gone undiscovered.

I did tell them every place Skye and I had been on Cape Cod. One of the Butterfields' sea kayaks was missing, and I tried—honestly but without success—to remember if we had left Drew's kayak where it lay or carried it back to the boathouse.

All I could really think about was Pippin. When I imagined officers combing the woods from Sesuit to Provincetown, and prowling
the jetty caves and dragging Maushop Lake, I didn't hope for the
girl's recovery but the horse's. I pictured Pippin—galloping through
a darkened forest, foam dripping from his bit. I imagined him shot
by a poacher's stray bullet. I saw his delicate flexor tendons crushed
in a steel-jawed leghold trap. I pictured his heart, giving out with fear
and confusion, and the running that Skye wouldn't understand was
too much for him. And even if the accompanying image were Skye,
a mile or so behind, head cracked on a small but jagged rock: I didn't
care, as long as Pippin was found unharmed.

But what drove me crazy, that first night and in the weeks that
followed, was not being able to decide if Skye's decision to disappear
with Pippin had been born of necessity or revenge. I didn't know if
she wanted to hurt me or if it was simply the only way she knew: to
bring me along with her.

"The problem with Catherine," my father said, as they
drove me home from school, "is that she's never had to work a day
in her life."

From the backseat, my eyes stuck to the road, hoping for a glimpse
of Pippin behind the passing trees. But I could see my mother swivel
her head toward him, a reflexive instinct to defend me. Then she
turned without speaking, facing the window. A sigh to say she'd
already done everything she could, and notwithstanding disappointing results, her job was finished.

And despite her defection, and the guilt-ridden panic over my
horse, I felt relieved. My father had only returned to the same conclusion—a personal cliché that no amount of sweat would ever

knock out of his head. Even this most grave incident would be a conflagrated version of ones that had come before. When we arrived home, he got out of the car and slammed the door, heading into the house without a word. My mother waited for me, then looped her elbow through mine as we followed him.

He waited for us at the bottom of the stairs. I remember a vague sense of alarm at the veins in his forehead — the only moment of my life I'd feared for his health instead of his retribution. I thought of his drowned son — my unmet brother — and for the first time in years wondered about Marc's funeral.

My father looked so old, and so angry.

"Catherine," he said, raising a finger at me. "This is not going to be a vacation for you. Until you are back in school, you will be working in this house. You will be ironing and doing laundry and dusting and vacuuming. You will be performing menial and meaningful tasks from the time you wake up until the time you fall into your bed asleep."

I didn't say anything. He dropped his hand and turned to go upstairs.

"Dad?"

He stopped for a moment, didn't turn around. His back looked comfortingly broad — his same self, unchanged by my actions.

"I'm sorry," I said.

He laughed. A short, harsh, and unhappy sound that cut me off at the knees. My mother put her arm around my shoulder. He went upstairs and slammed the door to their bedroom.

"*Chérie*," my mother said, pulling me into a hug. "We're just so glad you're safe." I wondered at this pathology, the use of the plural pronoun, as if no parent could stand as a single entity.

TWO MORNINGS LATER, I awoke to my father standing over my bed. He wore his usual gear: suit coat, tie, disapproving scowl.

"Pippin's all right," my mother called from the doorway. Clearly she'd been forbidden to cross the threshold but wanted to soften the blow of whatever news my father was about to deliver.

He told me, in the flattest of tones, that my horse had returned to the stables at Esther Percy in the early hours of dawn. My father did not have a flair for narrative and knew very little about horses — despite having lived in such close proximity all these years. So he didn't tell me what must have been true. The way Pippin's coat would have been soaked through with sweat. I imagined Skye had saddled him inexpertly, without a blanket. He would have shown up with his back chafed, the saddle askew, stumbling with exhaustion and hunger.

"Don't expect to see him again," my father said. "I sold him to Captain Zarghami."

I stared at him. The groggy remnants of my troubled dreams hadn't quite lifted. My relief was already mitigated by imagining what Pippin had suffered; now its tide rolled back like an unnatural disaster.

"I don't believe you," I said. "Captain Zarghami wouldn't do that. He wouldn't buy my horse."

"I made him an offer he couldn't refuse," my father said.

I felt my brow knit together in confusion. It seemed so odd that my father would reference any kind of popular culture. I couldn't remember ever seeing him at a movie.

He reached into his inside pocket, and because of that allusion, and my own wasted exhaustion, I thought for the longest, strangest, and most emotionless moment that he was reaching for some sort of revolver. That he was going to shoot me in my bed while my mother watched. So that when he actually floated two fifty-dollar bills, they seemed to fall in slow motion—landing on my chest in payment for a horse worth thousands upon thousands and, beyond that, more than I could ever say.

My father left on business that day, with no estimated date of return. And I felt the most swirling combination of reprieve and anguish at his departure. After all: girding myself to face the truth, I knew it was I who'd put Pippin in danger. The fact that the horse had survived, unharmed, seemed a boon I didn't nearly deserve. Contradictions warred: the relief that Pippin was all right, the grief that I'd never see him again. I felt rage and hatred toward my father, and at the same time a strange sort of gratitude, that someone had finally managed to mete out an appropriate punishment. When my father walked out the door, leaving his disappointment and anger in a swirling cloud around my head, I felt glad I wouldn't have to face him for a while, and sorry that I couldn't be finished with him for good.

And then in the illogical way of children, I would expect him to appear at the dinner table and be inexplicably sorry to see his place empty.

"SUSANNAH'S HOME," my mother told me at dinner, two days later. I glanced up from my untouched food. I must have looked too hopeful. The letter Susannah had written from Venezuela—forwarded to me from Esther Percy—had seemed almost like a message from someone who'd died.

"Bail," my mother explained. She patted my hand and smiled sadly. Since my father left, she had been treating me like an invalid—alluding to my situation but never saying anything directly. She had already deemed my father's long list of chores impossible to perform because of my broken arm. We read the newspaper together in the morning, trading articles about the scandal.

That night we watched the evening news—segments showing both the Waverly campus and Senator Butterfield, ducking past reporters into a Cape Cod police station.

At ten o'clock she came into my room to kiss me good night. I lay awake for a full hour before creeping downstairs. When I opened the burglar alarm's control panel, I saw that she had forgotten to turn it on, and I wondered if the omission were intentional.

I walked past the garage and back toward the barn. I'd spent the past four years at boarding school and every summer immersed in horses. Nobody had ever gotten around to teaching me how to drive.

Pippin's stall stood empty, a painful and gaping hollow. I couldn't manage saddling and bridling Bloom one-handed. So I just slipped a halter and lead over her ears and rode bareback. A dense and misty night, the air smelled of damp blossom and newly regenerated leaves. I rode out through the woods in back, across Potter's field and into a neighboring meadow to circumvent the squad car at the end of our driveway, watching out for Skye.

On the road Bloom snorted peacefully, plodding the familiar back streets to Susannah's. I held the lead with my good hand, my cast resting heavily on one knee. Susannah's driveway was lined by linden trees, their silver leaves shedding sprays of dampness as we passed.

The house was dark except for her window. I knew exactly what she'd be doing: sitting at her desk writing a letter, to me or Drew. I rode Bloom into the narrow shaft of light cast by her deskside lamp and waited for her to look out the window in search of her next thought. I had only sat there a moment when I noticed the red ember of a cigarette under the oak tree. I peered into the darkness, expecting Charlie's form to present itself once my eyes adjusted. But the man who dropped the cigarette and stubbed it out with his toe was too tall and fair to be Charlie. I would have been frightened as he walked toward me, if his gait hadn't looked so easy and so familiar.

"Hi, Catherine," he said through the darkness, and I recognized Susannah's father. His faced weathered and peeling as she'd described him but also strangely *young* in his T-shirt and jeans. Exposed and jittery.

"Hi, Mr. Twining." I tried to keep the surprise out of my voice. As if I didn't want him to know I had any reason to find his presence unusual. As if I didn't want him to realize I'd ever known he left. "I thought you were Charlie," I said.

"No, he's still at school," he said. "I'm staying here in the guest room, during this whole big mess."

I nodded, not sure what to say. In the old days, he would have sent me away by now with a stern warning or perhaps even a phone call to my parents.

"Do you want me to go get Susannah for you?" he said.

"Yes please." I watched him walk, stoop-shouldered, into the house. Not fatherly at all, but cowed and dejected.

Through Susannah's window I could see him startle her with a hand on her shoulder. I lifted my heavy left arm and waved. She waved back and pushed passed her father. In a moment she appeared alone at the back door, wearing a long sleeveless nightgown. Her father still stood in the window, mournfully looking down at us. I felt a strong surge of relief—as if his guilt, his sense of responsibility, somehow exonerated me.

"Catherine," Susannah whispered. "It's wet out here."

I rode to the doorstep, and she pulled the rosebud material around her waist and climbed up behind me.

"Don't go down the driveway," she said. "The police keep driving by. As if she'd come here."

I rode around to the playground of the Lutheran church that bordered her backyard. We climbed off Bloom and onto the swings. I felt dampness gather at the bottom of my jeans when I sat. Bloom, untied, lowered her head to munch on clover and dandelions.

"I was just writing to you," she said. "So I feel like I've already told you everything."

"Actually," I said, "I want to tell you something first."

She turned toward me, expectant. But I couldn't speak. I couldn't get it out. She stepped back her legs and began to swing. High and higher into the air, her nightgown winnowing through the air like a ship's sail. I watched her for a moment, then pushed myself up, too, taking care to match her rhythm so we swung side by side. Moving back, our heels touched the leaves of the oak tree. Moving forward, they sliced through the air and up through the damp stardust that swirled all around us. The corner post rose and fell from the ground in noisy and precarious complaint, until finally we slowed down and came to rest, swaying beside each other.

"You told them," she said, after a while. "Didn't you?"

I wanted to speak. But I couldn't admit what I'd done any more than I could deny it. Susannah watched me a minute, then turned her gaze away.

"At first I thought it was Skye," she said, looking straight ahead. "But that didn't make sense, because Skye didn't know anything. And I knew you wouldn't tell her."

The mist picked up to a light rain. Bloom snorted, then continued her grazing under an elm tree. I tried to apply a number, to how many times Susannah and I had sat on these very swings. A sum far too infinite to compute.

"They found Rico's address with the coke," Susannah said. Her tone was informative, but also accusatory, letting me know that she was not my only victim. "My lawyer said I had to turn him in. It was the only way to save Drew and me."

We sat for a moment, imagining Rico's small home. The grim options available to him: betraying Colombian drug lords or surviving Venezuelan jail. Perhaps both. A world of consequences we couldn't even begin to contemplate. While we sat in the cool New England night, the wind gently rustling the greening leaves. Even in the rain, the sky no longer looked ominous. With so much actual danger at hand, worrying about the end of the world had been relegated to luxury.

We heard a low, lorn cooing in the tree behind us. "Gray owl," Susannah said.

"Susannah," I said. "Are you? Saved, I mean."

"No," Susannah said. "But I will be."

If she hadn't been angry she might have admitted fear. Vulnerability. But instead she predicted what she couldn't possibly have known. That she and Drew would spend hours in front of judges, and years in anxiety-laden limbo, but never see the inside of a jail cell. They would each repeat their senior year at public school and continue on to the very colleges whose acceptance letters lay unopened in the mail slots at Waverly.

Something of the same—that grim confidence in continuing liberty—must have existed in me. Because I didn't know that Captain Zarghami had begun campaigning on my behalf and that Middlebury would agree to admit me as a freshman without completing my sixth-form year. Still, I had the strangest lack of worry about anything other than Skye. In terms of my own future, that time had such a vacant and intermediary feel—like nothing before whatever happened next could possibly matter. Police officers and TV crews lurked around corners, and the sky hung terribly close above our heads. But these portents didn't have nearly the strength of the blue hydrangea mingling with Bloom's good, horsey musk. The stillness and certainty of midnight, only the wild and unauthorized among us.

"It's not like you chose John Paul over me," Susannah said. "He would have ended up in jail for sure. His life would have been ruined."

A display of fireworks in my chest, crackling joy. I couldn't have been happier if Pippin had appeared from behind the juniper bushes—saddled and unharmed, ready to be mine again. These past months of distance and anger disappeared in a single instant. Of course I chose Susannah to betray. Her disownment of me was no more likely than her incarceration.

"It's Skye's fault," she pronounced, unwilling—as I must have known she'd be—to break her firm rules of loyalty, despite my own grave and repeated violations.

I reached out my good hand, cold metal chain nipping the inside of my bare arm. Susannah did likewise, and we clasped fingers and swung gently, kicking our feet into the wet ground.

"Do you know where Skye is?" she asked—certain, for once, that I would answer.

"No," I said. "But I'm sure she's all right."

"Of course she is," Susannah said. "Her kind always is."

We both laughed—at the campiness of that phrase and how ridiculous it was to think of Skye as any particular kind. As if there were any tribe that could possibly claim her.

"You know," Susannah said, "I think my father is more upset that I went to Venezuela without telling him than he is about the drugs. Weird, right?"

"Right," I said.

"The worst part of this whole thing is having him puppy dog around the house all day, looking guilty. I hate feeling sorry for him."

She got off the swing. Stood up and walked in her bare feet down the road. I collected Bloom's lead rope and fell into step beside her — her white nightgown unnaturally bright in the darkness. We walked through the woods, the back route to her house. The rain came down, still light but fuller in volume. It flattened my hair to my scalp but barely dented Susannah's heavy mane.

At her house, she hugged me quickly, then ran inside. I mounted Bloom as she stole inside her kitchen door. Through the light in her bedroom window, I saw her fold my letter and put it into an envelope. She never hand-delivered letters, always mailed them, and I knew this one would find its way to the corner mailbox by morning, traveling the scant mile by circuitous way of the Old Lenox Post Office. Like a thousand letters before it. And after it.

The rain fell, Bloom twitching her ears in protest. Without being commanded the horse shifted around and began heading toward home. A lump in my throat swelled with sorrow and relief at my own undeservedness.

I could never have predicted it could feel so painful. So grand and enormous. So unexpected and inevitable. To be forgiven.

AND SO THAT TIME CONTINUED, Skye gone, the rest of us in limbo. Susannah's father returned, for the time being, to Venezuela. Her mother went back to work, leaving her each morning with a list of chores that Susannah would perform in a perfunctory and half-done manner before climbing into her VW and driving over

to see me. We would ride out to the woods together, always at a
walk. Entirely forbidden to see one another but with nothing left to
lose. To stop taking risks would have marked the true end of things,
concessions to parental rules even more unthinkable in the face of
such disaster. And anyway, the absence of Susannah's mother and
the insistence of mine on remaining a polite bystander made any risk
seem minimal.

Never did our eyes keep to one direction. We let our gaze rove
slowly all around us, expecting at any moment to see Skye, hiding in
the snag trees. Her intoxicating beauty, and her dazzling energy, her
disregard for the havoc wreaked by her ineffable mission. I looked
for her everywhere. A week went by. Then the rain came full force.
On the local and national news, pretty reporters in hooded slickers
stood in front of Waverly and Esther Percy and the Butterfield Cape
house, talking solemnly into their soggy microphones.

When I woke up in the middle of the night, I saw Skye standing
over me. I saw her at the end of our driveway, and behind the saw-
horses in the tack room. I saw her on the sides of highways, thumb
poised. I imagined her sneaking aboard boats bound for Europe.
Susannah's forgiveness allowed me to envision Skye seeking refuge
in the most unlikely places: Eleanor's room at school or wherever
Mr. November had been exiled. I had been so certain, for so long,
of Skye's impending doom. Now, faced with it, nothing in the world
seemed more impossible. Somebody, somewhere, was harboring
Skye. I knew it in my bones deeply as I knew myself.

I dreamed reunions. Reunions with retribution—my hands
around her neck, throttling. Reunions with rejoicing—our arms
around each other, dancing wild relief.

Every day, even in the downpour, Susannah and I rode. We rode across streams and up hills and around trees. We forgot about my arm and let the horses gallop across the golf course, the groundskeeper running after us with clenched fists. We rode out to the lake and dared each other to stand shirtless in its rising steam, arms outstretched, letting the mosquitoes feast. And we never talked about ourselves or what would happen to us. But only about Skye, and where she was hiding, and what would become of her when they finally found her.

At the end of two weeks, we rode back to the barn and saw my mother walking out to meet us. Her youthfulness fled as she held a Burberry raincoat over her head. She revealed no surprise or dismay at seeing the two of us together, and we knew she hadn't come out to catch us or to pretend she hadn't known all along. Without looking at each other, we both understood exactly what she would say the moment we were within earshot.

Susannah pulled her horse to a stop. I slid off Bloom's saddle and faced my mother. The mist erased age from her face, but she looked distinctly sorrowful, and for a moment I could picture clearly: the young mother arriving to collect her child from a party and refusing—in her grief—to let him be taken away.

Water dripped down all of our faces. I took off my helmet and shook my hair loose. The rain gathered and drenched it almost instantly. My mother reached to touch my face, but drew her hand back and touched her own chin instead. Then she pulled her coat tighter around her neck, and looked beyond us—as if reading superscript from above the trees.

"*Elle a été trouvé,*" my mother said. *She's been found.*

And despite everything we had known about Skye's well-being, there was no need to hear another word.

21

TIME WILL MOVE FORWARD. When my husband and I first moved to the seaside town where Skye spent her childhood summers, I mapped out a careful route for myself, running every day down Locust Lane. A cocker spaniel named Jib spent his afternoons panting on his owners' front lawn, and he would hove himself to his feet and join me a while—turning back once I got to 6A, and trotting home.

Each year Jib got a little grayer around the muzzle and accompanied me a shorter distance. Lately, he only pulls himself to his feet to say hello, then settles back into the grass after I scratch his ears. The other day, he wasn't there at all; my heart constricted in a lonesome pang.

Impermanence: it always comes as a terrible shock. There's no getting accustomed to it.

The Butterfields' house no longer rides the bluff. After Skye's death, her parents tore down the additions and had the original house moved to an inland site. The land was donated to conservation. An early herald of spring is the river of wildflowers that rises up through beach grass where the mansion once stood. Buried in its midst—if you know where to look—rests a small brass plaque:

ELISABETH SKYE BUTTERFIELD

1967–1985

SKYE LOVED IT HERE

The rest of the beachfront has not fared so well. New homes the size of luxury hotels crowd together. Revetment walls cover the holes where bank swallows once nested.

Out on the beach, the caves beneath the jetty—once full of star-fish—hold nothing but barnacles and seaweed. Cigarette butts and bottle caps. Mussel shells and snails.

I SPOKE TO John Paul for the last time the day before Skye's funeral. The phone rang at the perfect moment, in the late after-noon—early enough for my father to be at work, and late enough for me to be indoors. Ever since the news, I had been waiting to hear from him, knowing that he would not let such a tragedy occur without contacting me.

Sitting at the kitchen table while my mother sliced fennel, I rec-ognized his ring the way a lover sometimes will—and lamented my mother's closer proximity to the telephone.

"Bonjour, Madame Morrow," I heard him say from across the room. *"Puis-je parler à Catherine, s'il vous plaît?"*

I saw her face fall, impressed and saddened by his composure. I saw her weariness as my accomplice, and perhaps the first traces of self-blame. She didn't say anything. Just held the phone out to me, showing her age around the mouth and chin. Deep dark eyes, unable to deny me this conversation but clearly unhappy about granting it.

I pulled the cord far into the butler's pantry and climbed up onto the counter. Sat with my feet in the sink, and my body pressed against the window. The receiver tight as possible to my ear.

"Hi," I said.

"Hi."

We sat there for too long a while, listening to each other breathe.

"I want to say I'm sorry about Skye," he finally said.

"I know," I told him. And then, after another long moment of quiet, I said, "Are you okay?"

"Yeah," he said, but he didn't sound convincing.

He told me that he'd have to repeat his fifth-form year at Saw River High. "Junior year, I mean," he corrected himself. Waverly had sent him home without allowing him to pack his things. The dorm resident had found two sheets of acid while clearing out John Paul's drawers, along with some pot.

"They think I was selling, so there may be some legal action." He sounded unconcerned, like he still believed his association with the wealthy granted him their exemptions. "But who knows?" he said. "I'll probably still go to college. I just have to write a good entrance essay about the whole thing. Show that I've turned over a new leaf, that I've grown as a person. Blah blah blah."

"Sure," I said. "That sounds great."

Quiet then. Neither of us wanting to admit how different his situation would be from Susannah's and Drew's—the results that would pertain not to the gravity of their infractions but the depth of their resources.

And of course we were right. What I heard about John Paul in the subsequent years came in bits and pieces, through Susannah and Drew. His legal-aid lawyer couldn't sway the judge with impressive academic and athletic records. His second attempt at junior year was supposed to be interrupted by juvenile detention. And then his mother panicked and sent him to France before his sentence began, using what remained of her modest savings. John Paul changed his last named to Filage and became the caretaker of an estate near Aix. He never finished high school. Never went on to college. Never convinced his father to acknowledge him.

"What about you?" John Paul finally asked me.

"We don't know yet," I said.

There had been so little mention of next year that I'd begun to think somebody had called it off. That I would stay home forever, wandering through the stables and the dwindling forests, my adulthood not merely postponed but canceled.

"Are you going to the funeral?" he asked.

I told him I was.

"I wish I could go," he said.

"Me too." I fought back a small sob as I realized how comforting it would be to have him there, and registered his tactful listening.

"It's hard to believe," he said.

"I still don't believe it." A firmness to this admission, succinct and immovable.

"Well," John Paul said. "I'm really sorry." And then he said what nobody else had, in the time she'd been missing or in the two days since she'd been found: "I know how much you loved her."

I should have burst forth with a good, soul-purging cry. John Paul would have listened silently, hearing all of my regret, and that I had indeed loved Skye, not to mention himself—loved both of them uselessly, in the present tense as well as the past. I felt the tears gather just under the top of my ribs. There they stayed in an unshed well, slowing my breath but never coming forth. If I could have wedged myself through the phone's tiny holes, I would have found my way across the wires, into John Paul's arms. Where I would have curled up and rested a good long while.

"Thank you for calling," I whispered.

And then, because I could leave much but not everything unsaid. Because I had only just learned—by the barest increment—to reveal myself, I said, "Not just Skye. You, too, John Paul."

I swear I could hear him nod. I could hear his fingers tighten, holding the phone closer to his ear. I could hear him close his eyes and remember the scent and texture of my skin. I could hear all this, and his obligation to another girl, and most of all his inability to break promises—allowing him to be sad but never torn.

I put down the phone and untangled myself from the wall. Climbed out of the sink. I knew he stayed on the other end, listening to me cross back into the kitchen. Hearing the gentle click of the receiver as I sent him off to his long and luckless life.

I DON'T REMEMBER asking to go to Skye's funeral. Like everything else, it was decided for me. The night they found her, my father came home late from his business trip. We sat up in the kitchen—my mother, father, and I—and he announced that he would drive me to Cape Cod for the services. I sent my mother a pleading glance, which she returned with sympathy but not action, retreating—my dereliction at last great enough to make my parents allies. The following day she loaned me her black Jean Muir, hanging it with my father's dark suit in the back of his Mercedes, and waved from the top of the driveway as the car pulled away.

Do all funerals take place in blinding sunlight? That Saturday in May, blossoms erupted. Birds chattered. And I couldn't stop catching glimpses of her. Like the day my mother told me, when news of

Skye's death did not quell Susannah's fury but flame it—as if killing herself had been a personal affront to us—until I had to beg away from her and rest a while in my room. I lay on my bed—the Breyer horses and the blue ribbons absurdly childish and cheerful—staring at the ceiling, ignoring my mother's troubled call to dinner until the sun hung low enough to cast shadows. I opened my eyes in the pitch black, surprised that I had fallen asleep, still more surprised to see a form in the far corner, sitting on my toile de Juoy armchair, wealth of curls spilling quietly in the moonlight.

But when I sat up to speak, she was gone.

Driving east, it happened repeatedly. A form in the woods, running madly behind the flowering apple trees, trying to keep up with the car. Hiding behind a birch tree at a rest area outside Springfield. Standing by the side of the highway—clearly her own lithe, long-haired self, inexplicably morphing into a slender, balding man as we passed. I did not point out any of these sightings to my father as his car alternately crept and sped from the westernmost part of the state to its eastern tip—clogged with traffic. And he, during those five long hours—even when we stopped for coffee or realized that the standstill traffic in Plymouth had been caused by a three-car pileup —spoke not a single word to me.

It would be years before I found out this was his second trip to Cape Cod. That in the past weeks he had not been away on business but scouring the woods and beaches, joining in the search for Skye. That he had been standing within earshot at the discovery, yards away from the spot where they finally found her.

Still more years, and sadly after he was no longer here to tell. Not until I held my own newborn in my arms, her eyes glassy and exhausted after long hours in the birth canal, saved and whole thanks to the miracle of modern intervention. I understood then that my father's refusal to speak or even look at me did not stem from stern-ness or cruelty but a furious and fearful understanding of that worst earthly disaster, just barely averted: his rage at me, for placing the most precious part of his interior in harm's way. Shouting to the skies, this strangest and most shameless survivor guilt: his was the child that lived.

SESUIT'S SMALL CONGREGATIONAL church teemed like an anthill — limousines and police cars swarming outside. Mourners jammed in the apse, trying to sign the guest book or find a seat in the back. I don't know how Senator Butterfield saw me, my mousy head peering down the aisle as he stood in front talking to the minister. But he waved his hand, commanding me forward.

I pointed to my chest and mouthed. *Me?*

He waved more furiously, nodding. I left my father crammed against the back wall, and wove my way through the Boston lumi-naries. Almost everyone seemed bleached or gray. I saw Mrs. Chilton and Ms. Latham. And to my surprise, Mr. and Mrs. November, sitting close together on a pew that would be all too visible to the Butterfields. Mr. November did not look up as I passed, both hands clasping his wife's as if her hand were all that prevented him dissolv-ing into a puddle at her feet.

I kept walking toward the senator, not seeing anybody close to my age except for Eleanor — uncharacteristically lovely in a black skirt and lavender blouse. Her hair loose. When she saw me walk by, she narrowed her eyes and glared through her glasses, as if Skye's death had been murder rather than suicide. I slowed my pace, terrified the Butterfields would feel the same way.

From somewhere up above, through a tinny speaker, I could hear the first bouncing chords of "Sugar Magnolia." And Senator Butterfield did not berate me or offer any manner of blame. He gathered me into a hug that crunched the bones in my back. In my mother's sleeveless dress, the incongruous white cast on my arm, I felt insubstantial as air.

"Catherine," he said, his voice hollow with grief. "You'll sit up here with us."

Turning to look at the crowd — the balcony full to capacity, the people spilling into the foyer and out onto the grassy lawn — I knew that from this moment forward the Butterfields would keep me as a phantom daughter. That for my whole life I would have a connection to these people, beneficial to me but imperative to them. That they would write me letters and insist on visits, and curry favor on my behalf.

To them I represented Skye in her last incarnation. With every passing year they would search my face for signs of what she might have become. And I don't know if she would have been able to forgive her father for not resigning after all, but continuing in the Senate and toward aspirations beyond, helped in no small part by the sympathetic publicity Skye's death generated. The senator never told me himself that he had changed his mind, not knowing — or not acknowledging — that I had been privy to the original plan. I simply waited for the announcement of his resignation and instead watched his career unfold and then escalate. There were times when I glimpsed him on the evening news or on the front page of a newspaper, and something of Skye would rise inside me, a purist's injury, an indignation that he should continue in the same vein that had led to his daughter's anger and eventual death. But then I would think of all the things I might have done differently. I would think of my complicit silence, riding a wave that seemed of another's making, my arms outstretched — keeping my balance despite every misgiving.

And if only I had jumped earlier, abandoned that equilibrium for an uncomfortable *choice,* perhaps Skye would have been alive to castigate the senator herself, for all his moral failings.

And so I forgave him, in what may have been the first adult decision of my life. It felt like the greatest gift, brimming as I was with all the pieces of herself that Skye had left behind. Because to this day I am still aware, when I catch myself quoting a line of poetry or moving in a way that doesn't feel native. Whenever I do something unwise or quixotic or exhilarating, I nod to the remnants of Skye I still contain and pick up the phone to call the Butterfields.

That day at the funeral, I sat in the front pew between Skye's parents, each of them holding my hand. The minister spoke, and some relatives. The governor—only just embarking on his bid for the presidency—managed to break from his usual deadpan style and deliver a gentle and heartbreaking eulogy. Ted Kennedy read the 121st Psalm. There were others too, an old patrician movie star whom my mother would have loved to see. A soprano from the Boston opera sang "I'll Fly Away." James Taylor himself performed "Fire and Rain."

AND STILL I LOOKED FOR HER. Driving back to the house in the Butterfield limousine (kidnapped by my new parents, my father following somewhere in the throng behind us), I stared through the trees at Maushop Lake, frankly believing I might see her—sunning on Fisherman's Landing.

In one week, the Butterfields would announce their plans to raze the house and donate its shorefront acres to the Nature Conservancy. But for now the place abounded in human life: the effort of summoning her back, at least for these few hours. Waiters passed hors d'oeuvres, and women fanned themselves with funeral programs.

People clustered together, wineglasses in hand. From where I stood at the top of the beach stairs, it might have been a wedding or an anniversary party. A christening. Any of life's events meant to conjure a particular emotion and make it communal. I left my mother's black pumps on the grass and climbed down to the rocks and sand. Picked my way across the pathless stretch of beach where Skye and I had walked together.

Merciless sun, shining and beckoning. Casting white shadows and masking the rocks' seaweed and high tide dampness. Barnacles breathed, and swallows swooped around me like bats as I combed the bank for Skye's coyote. I expected tide and shore to have accelerated its decomposing, that its brilliant white teeth would be matched by brilliant white bones. I picked my way across roots and skate eggs and broken seashells. But even when I was sure I'd gone too far and retraced my steps, the remains were nowhere in evidence.

So I walked back toward the ocean. Dipped my feet in the water and felt the jagged rocks bite into my feet.

What courage it must have taken, to walk into those waters with no plan to return. The thin straps of my tank top slipping over her shoulders, my filmy skirt clinging to her legs and then fanning out around her. Cormorants drying their wings, eiders floating, laughing gulls dropping clamshells with startling retorts. The bank swallows and the heartbroken bedroom and everything she loved best resting yards away, watching her go. Wet clothes clinging to her skin like a reminder of everything sensual and adventurous: all the pieces of *life* to be abandoned forever.

I imagined Skye's head gloriously and finally empty. I imagined her swimming—far out as she wanted. One destination in mind. Kicking off my skirt in deeper waters and concentrating on the crawl she'd learned at Maushop Lake—less than a mile from where she now embarked. I saw her swim for hours, until the sea around her grew dark and frigid. Too many creatures and leagues to name, exhaustion and regret and determination finally bringing her down, down, down. A symphony of bubbles rising, filled with final breaths.

While I myself stood unmoving, gentle waves lapping over my ankles, not able to take another step.

Catherine.

A light voice, lacking urgency, clear and malleable as a mourning dove's coo. I turned toward the bluff—the sound of spring peepers chirruping from behind the eelgrass.

All around me, before my very eyes, the world erupted. Scents to drown out the detritus and decay at my feet: honeysuckle and rugosa rose. Everything that winter had subsumed, that had been dead far longer than Skye. All coming back to life.

Catherine.

The thrall of the mystic touched my fingertips, and I made my way over rocks to the sandy beach. And I heard the sound again, and I turned around. There, out on the rocks. I saw something just beyond the bluff—a rustle in the faded grass, a flash of light from breaking waves. And I drew in my breath and walked toward it, expectant, perfectly willing for Skye to show herself to me.

So much easier, at seventeen, to believe in that possibility—Skye not having died at all or else returning from death—than in that other and unfathomable finality. So much better to stand there on the shore, waiting for her to rise from the sea and hand over the secrets of immortality: to someone who'd proven she could keep them.

I didn't know, I couldn't hear: the shale of my bones—grinding down like mortar beneath my glossy and unwithered skin.

Acknowledgments

My agent, Peter Steinberg, is not only a tireless advocate but a talented editor and loyal friend. I'm very lucky to be represented by him. And I am in awe of my editor at Algonquin, Kathy Pories, who worked on this book with so much grace, enthusiasm, and insight.

Danae Woodward, my first friend, was also my first reader. I owe her so many thanks for her boundless support and encouragement. I am also deeply indebted to my dear, dear friends Leslie Rechner and Kate Splaine for their loving generosity.

Shannon Virginia Woolfe gave me wonderful, juicy details about the Medal Maclay circuit in the eighties and pointed me toward the book *Hunter Seat Equitation* by George Morris.

Mel Boyajian edited and proofread. She took care of my child, and even folded my laundry. I don't know where I'd be without her. I'd be equally lost without Heidi Gessner.

Thanks to my parents, for love and support above and beyond.

Thanks to everyone at the University of North Carolina–Wilmington's Creative Writing Department, especially Karen Bender, Wendy Brenner, Clyde Edgerton, Phil Furia, Philip Gerard, Rebecca Lee, Sarah Messer, and Robert Siegel.

Thanks to Kate, Tim, Oliver, and Phoebe Rogers, for the beautiful red house where so much of this book was written. Thanks also to Barbara Gessner, for continuing generosity and love.

Early readers who offered encouragement include Daisy Barringer, Kristina Edgerton, Amber Morgan, and Jeremiah Splaine (who corrected my French with the greatest tact).

Thanks to everyone at Algonquin, especially Andra, Brunson, and Elisabeth. Thanks to Joe, Markus, Lauren, Bess, and Shannon at Regal Literary Agency.

And thank you to David and Hadley Gessner, for everything.

Gossip of the Starlings

An Interview with Nina de Gramont

Reading Group Questions

An Interview with Nina de Gramont

The epigraph to your novel is taken from John Knowles's _A Separate Peace_. Did this classic influence your story? Why do you think boarding schools are such fertile ground for fiction?

There's a lot of inherent drama in a boarding-school setting, most notably the mystery of the privileged and all the unavoidable issues of class and wealth. In addition to that, adolescence is such a fraught and dramatic time in our lives. Not only are we at our most romantic and idealistic, but there's a burning need for adventure that defies perspective or consequence. This need is something fiction has addressed in teenage boys far more than girls. That's one of the elements I wanted to explore in _Gossip of the Starlings:_ that girls have the same primal urge toward secret society, and danger. Also ambition: Catherine and Skye are each very ambitious, Catherine more realistically, with her horse shows, and Skye more altruistically—wanting to save the world in her own misguided way.

Writing my book I was conscious of a debt to Knowles's classic, and the careful reader will find more than one homage. I wanted to write a novel that—like _A Separate Peace_—readers could discover at sixteen and then revisit at different ages, finding new angles every time. Phineas and Gene are archetypal characters, and I borrowed elements from each of them for Catherine, Skye, and Susannah. I also tried to use the backdrop of the Cold War as a looming presence the same way Knowles used World War II. Though obviously the latter was a more literal threat to the students at Devon, the Cold War informed and defined the political atmosphere during the Reagan years.

Other influences on *Gossip of the Starlings* include *Old School* by Tobias Wolff and *Endless Love* by Scott Spencer. The latter isn't about prep school, but it deals so beautifully with the outsized emotions and corresponding insanity of adolescence. Strangely enough, another book I kept in mind was Jean Stein's oral biography of Edie Sedgwick. There are wonderful passages about Sedgwick's experience at an all-girls boarding school and her effect on the other students, which gave me great psychological insight into Catherine's fascination with Skye.

Gossip of the Starlings takes place in the mid-eighties and involves prep-school students and cocaine. How closely do events in your book mirror the Choate cocaine scandal of 1984, when students were arrested for smuggling cocaine from South America?

Certainly the novel's plot was inspired by those events, which were huge news the year I graduated from high school. I did go to boarding school, and I knew some people who were peripherally involved in that scandal. But what happened at Choate only provided the barest template for *Gossip of the Starlings*. I intentionally didn't go back and research any of those news stories, or conduct any interviews, because I wanted the action to belong purely to the characters in my novel. While some of the events may run parallel to what happened in 1984, the motivations and circumstances belong purely to Catherine, Skye, and their very fictional world.

The title of the novel comes from a poem. Why did you choose it for a title?

The line comes from Shel Silverstein's "Forgotten Language," which is in *Where the Sidewalk Ends*. I had that book when I was a child and read it over and over again. Silverstein's poem describes such a yearning nostalgia for childhood — the belief in magic and the closer communion with the natural world: "Once I heard and answered all the questions / of the crickets, / And joined the crying of each falling dying / flake of snow, / Once I spoke the language of the flowers. . . . / How did it go? / How did it go?" The characters in *Gossip of the Starlings* are just on the cusp of losing their innocence. In life, it's a cruelly fast progression from believing in the Wizard of Oz to having that curtain pulled back. One day it seems perfectly reasonable that the tooth fairy flies through your window, and the next you notice her handwriting is exactly like your mother's. In my novel, many of the escapades, however unwholesome, are a form of mourning this loss, and a misguided way of clinging to the childhood belief in magical happenings. And of course Catherine, the narrator, is looking back from a remove of years, nostalgic for the adventures and idealism of her youth. One review of my novel said I employed "an elegiac tone," and "Forgotten Language" is certainly an elegy of sorts.

A reviewer suggested sharing the book with one's teenage daughter. Is that what you intended?

Just before I started writing this book, I reread several novels that had been important to me when I was a teenager, particularly *Endless Love* and *I Capture the Castle*. I found that while I loved these books as much as ever, my reaction to them was completely different. I interpreted events differently, and I wanted different things for the characters. When I wrote *Gossip of the Starlings*, I wanted it to appeal to teenage and adult readers in different and even contradictory ways.

One of my earliest readers sent me a letter after she'd finished the book that said, "I would have obsessed over it when I was sixteen. And I just know I will love it at sixty." Reading that was an important moment for me, because it described exactly what I wanted to accomplish.

Skye is such an interesting character. She seems oblivious to the way she affects everyone around her. You created her. How do you feel about her?

Personally, I love Skye. She's really the heart of the book, and whether or not a reader likes her from a moral perspective, I think her appeal to Catherine is very clear. One of the reasons I wanted Catherine to narrate from a present-day perspective was to accomplish an adult sort of sympathy toward Skye. From a teenage point of view, Skye is glamorous and dangerous and very powerful. But from an adult point of view, she becomes quite tragic. She has so much beauty and brilliance, and in many ways such good intentions. In her heart of hearts, Skye is an altruist, but when she tries to translate that altruism into action, it just goes terribly wrong. What Skye really lacks is perspective on her youth: she doesn't understand that this too shall pass. Everything that happens to her is infused in her mind with inflated depth and drama. At one point Catherine observes that Skye's skin doesn't seem expansive enough to contain all that's at war inside her.

And I don't quite agree that Skye is oblivious. I think she really does love Catherine. But like Catherine, her identity isn't fully formed; both these girls have a hard time separating themselves from the people they love. As Catherine says toward the end of the novel, "I was seventeen years old. Love burgeoned huge, frightening, and all consuming. It lunged in every direction—like a multiheaded creature banging horns against itself. I loved John Paul and I loved Skye. I loved Susannah and I loved my parents. And it never occurred to me to love myself, because I had no means of disentangling my identity from the fierce and secret and divergent emotions I felt toward all of these people."

It's not so much that Skye doesn't care who goes down with her; it's that she doesn't have the power to stop herself, and can't bear to go down alone.

Are there aspects of you in Cathcrine or Skye?

Catherine has a classic narrator's (and therefore a classic writer's) personality: she's introspective, observant, and very confident in her memories. On a surface level I would say she is the character who shares the most in common with me. Certainly I've never been anywhere close to as glamorous (or reckless) as Skye, but sometimes I was surprised by the elements of myself she possesses. I remember one scene in particular, where Skye is having an emotional break-down. I wrote about what I described as "the uncontainable mess of her—thoughts and emotions and needs and neuroses, all spilling out over their corporeal lines." I can remember, as a teenager and even into my twenties, that very distinct feeling: my emotions being so enormous in relation to my outside self. Containing them was simply not a possibility.

One thing I really wanted to do with this book was illustrate the nature of friendship between teenage girls, and the impulse they have to tell each other everything. Certainly that was something I lifted from my own past and friendships. Catherine knows Skye and Susannah so well she can narrate their lives as well as her own, sometimes even more vividly and with sharper insight. That kind of friendship is something I look back on with exhaustion and a little regret, but also with a degree of nostalgia. As an adult I am able to put up healthy boundaries between myself and even my closest friends. Obviously this is a better and more mature place to be, but there's something deliciously idealistic and innocent—albeit danger-ous—in the impulse to blur lines between two people.

In one scene in the novel, Catherine and her friends have an extended party at Skye's parents' house on the bay side of Cape Cod. It's a scene that manages to convey both the excitement and ennui of adolescence. Did you draw from your own memories of that time period? What were you trying to reveal about the characters here?

When my husband read the final version of the novel, he said he felt great sympathy for my parents. He wished that they didn't have to read it and experience all the retroactive worry of imagining me in the same situations. I was not the best behaved of teenagers, so I am drawing on some of my own experiences for that scene in particular. I wanted to establish the sense of freedom that comes from escaping rules, and at the same time illustrate the dynamics that evolve from new, self-imposed rules. In other words, Skye and Catherine may have escaped the bonds of one culture, but they've entered a new one. As a neophyte in the rule-breaking world, Skye doesn't understand the importance of the new parameters. She's as willing to flout her peers' rules as she is her parents', and that more than anything is what makes her dangerous.

The novel has such a sense of foreboding and impending disaster hanging over it. Was providing an ending that lived up to those expectations a challenging task?

I don't think I would have been able to get away with such an intense narrative tone if I didn't tilt my hand and let the reader know we were heading toward tragedy. The surprise lies in how the tragedy will play out and what emotional development occurs along the way. Sometimes I think it can be even more dramatic to *know* disaster is looming. As a reader, it makes me pay more attention to clues and nuance. I guess that's doubly true as a writer!

When did you first decide you wanted to be a writer, and what drew you to the craft?

I'm very lucky to come from a book-obsessed family. We had a small TV hidden away in an upstairs room, while our living room was lined with bookshelves, as were our bedrooms and hallways. My mother's answer to every negative emotion—fear, disappointment, embarrassment—was to turn it into a story. She would sit at the kitchen table with her Smith Corona and I would walk around her in circles, dictating while she typed away. I don't know if it ever occurred to me to be anything *except* a writer, unless it was a bookseller. I worked in bookstores for years before my first book was published. I know I will always feel most at home surrounded by tall shelves stuffed with books.

Your first book, *Of Cats and Men,* was a collection of short stories. Can you talk a little about the transition from writing short stories to writing a novel? Do you prefer one format over the other?

I wrote the stories for *Of Cats and Men* over a period of about three years. Leafing through the book, I can remember the order in which the stories were written by their length. Toward the end I started naturally gravitating toward longer and longer work, so that the final story I wrote for *Cats*—"Lieutenant Island"—was nearly sixty manuscript pages. From there it was a very organic leap to writing a novel. That was simply how my internal perception of plot and scope evolved.

I do love short stories—both writing them and reading them—and I wish there were more of a market for them in today's publishing world. I think I'll always write short stories here and there, but I don't predict I'll ever write another collection. Having written a novel and achieved a degree of confidence in that form, it would be very difficult to go back. It's great fun to conceive characters and really live with them for a long while. I'm also a bit of a freak in that I love revising—ripping a piece apart and putting it back together—and novel writing can provide years worth of precisely that activity.

Reviewers have noted that *Gossip of the Starlings* is impossible to put down. Did you feel the same way when writing it?

I am thrilled that readers can't put the book down. What could be more gratifying for a writer to hear? Of course the experience of composing a book is somewhat different, though I will say that I was consistently haunted by the story—which to some degree had been germinating for almost twenty years. When I first started writing the novel, it was the middle of winter, and I had a lot going on in my life. My daughter was about eighteen months old and I was in graduate school, so I spent a lot more time ruminating on the story than actually writing it. I finally got a block of time that summer, which we spent in an eighteenth-century farmhouse on Cape Cod. I would sit with my laptop in a huge red velvet chair, and I felt like the words just spilled from the rafters into my head. A lot of revisions waited for me in the future, but that first draft was like taking dictation. Despite the dark nature of the book, for some reason the early stage of writing it was like the early stage of being in love. I would think of the story and hum to myself, smiling.

Reading Group Questions

1. *Gossip of the Starlings* takes place at a boarding school, and most of the characters come from very privileged backgrounds. Often when a novel has this sort of setting, the narrator is an outsider. Here, the narrator, Catherine Morrow, comes from a wealthy family. How does this change the way the story is told? How is Catherine an outsider despite her own privilege, and how is this important to the story?

2. The novel's epigraph quotes John Knowles: "Everyone has a moment in history which belongs particularly to him." Why is the time period important in this novel? In what ways does the era play a role? What is the era in your life that played a pivotal role?

3. Although Catherine narrates the story, in many ways Skye is the main character. Skye seems bent on self-destruction and not overly concerned about whom she takes down with her. Do you consider Skye a likable character? What do you think is the motivation behind her recklessness? If asked to justify her behavior, what do you think Skye would say?

4. At one point in the story, Catherine says, "None of us were addictive personalities" (page 156). Do you think this is true? On the whole, would you consider Catherine a reliable narrator? What makes you believe her? What makes you question her?

5. Catherine narrates from a remove of years. How does her distance from the events affect the way she tells the story? How has the passage of time altered your perception of your own adolescence?

6. The novel's title comes from a Shel Silverstein poem, "Forgotten Language," which mourns the loss of childhood magic. In what ways is this story—despite its dark overtones—nostalgic for youth? In what ways is it not?

7. The characters in this novel live extremely privileged lives. Are the issues they face unique to upper-class teens, or are they universal? In what ways do you sympathize with these characters, despite their advantages? Does their wealth explain their delinquency, or does it simply make it harder to excuse?

8. In some ways, Catherine and Skye have opposite personalities. What parts of the other does each girl contain? Are they drawn together because of the characteristics they share, or because of the ways they differ?

9. At first glance, Skye seems to have the power in her and Catherine's friendship, but when the two girls become estranged, Skye is the one who falls apart. How does each girl wield power within this story? Do they bear equal culpability for how the story plays out, or is one ultimately more responsible than the other? Why?

10. The friendships of our adolescent years are often fraught with high drama and intensity. Why do you think this is? Do you remember similar relationships in your own life? How did they affect you then, and in retrospect, how do they affect you now?

11. From Catherine's perspective, adults play a peripheral role in these events, but several of them—including Mr. November, Mr. Twining, and Senator Butterfield, in particular—are clearly complicit. Could the seemingly more innocuous adults also be blamed for what transpires? In what ways do Mrs. Morrow, Mrs. Butterfield, and Ms. Latham—among others—contribute to what goes wrong?

12. Catherine is a talented and committed equestrian, and most often her moments of clarity are in conjunction with her riding. What are the connections between the appeal of a championship and the appeal of her outlaw life? How do her relationships with the two horses—Pippin and Bloom—mirror the conflict between Skye and Susannah?

13. John Paul is as guilty as his more privileged friends in terms of drug use and rule breaking, but even the adult Catherine stands firm in her assessment of what she calls his "gallantry." Do you agree with Catherine's perspective of John Paul, or does he ultimately deserve his fate?

14. The young people in this novel indulge in behavior that can easily be seen as immoral. Yet each one is also, in his or her own way, idealistic. Is this idealism at odds with their behavior, or is there a connection between their flouting of rules and their personal belief systems? How does this vary from character to character?

15. None of the characters in this novel has qualities that are commonly associated with delinquents. They are good students, headed to top colleges, with not only impressive achievement but active consciences. What causes them to break the law to such a serious degree? Is there any one event that might have changed the conclusion that Catherine seems to consider inevitable?

16. In the letter Skye writes to Catherine, she describes a house that she fell in love with when she saw it at night; in daylight, the house turned out to be ill repaired and unappealing, a disappointment. Skye asks Catherine, "Did that make the house I'd seen the night before, the one I'd loved, any less real?" (page 196). What does this question say about Skye as a person? How might she see this reaction as a metaphor in her own life?

Nina de Gramont is the author of the collection *Of Cats and Men*, which was a Book Sense selection and won a Discovery Award from the New England Booksellers Association. She is also coeditor of the anthology *Choice*. Her work has appeared in *Redbook, Seventeen, Nerve*, the *Harvard Review, Post Road Magazine*, and *Exquisiste Corpse*. She lives in North Carolina with her husband and daughter.

Other Algonquin Readers Round Table Novels

Mudbound, a novel by Hillary Jordan

Mudbound is the saga of the McAllan family, who struggle to survive on a remote ramshackle farm, and the Jacksons, their black sharecroppers. When two men return from World War II to work the land, the unlikely friendship between these brothers-in-arms—one white, one black—arouses the passions of their neighbors. In this award-winning portrait of two families caught up in the blind hatred of a small Southern town, prejudice takes many forms, both subtle and ruthless.

Winner of the Bellwether Prize for Fiction

"This is storytelling at the height of its powers . . . Hillary Jordan writes with the force of a Delta storm." —Barbara Kingsolver

AN ALGONQUIN READERS ROUND TABLE EDITION WITH READING GROUP GUIDE AND OTHER SPECIAL FEATURES • FICTION • ISBN 13: 978-1-56512-677-0

Water for Elephants, a novel by Sara Gruen

As a young man, Jacob Jankowski is tossed by fate onto a rickety train, home to the Benzini Brothers Most Spectacular Show on Earth. Amid a world of freaks, grifters, and misfits, Jacob becomes involved with Marlena, the beautiful young equestrian star; her husband, a charismatic but twisted animal trainer; and Rosie, an untrainable elephant who is the great gray hope for this third-rate show. Now in his nineties, Jacob at long last reveals the story of their unlikely yet powerful bonds, ones that nearly shatter them all.

"[An] arresting new novel . . . With a showman's expert timing, [Gruen] saves a terrific revelation for the final pages, transforming a glimpse of Americana into an enchanting escapist fairy tale."
—*The New York Times Book Review*

"Gritty, sensual and charged with dark secrets involving love, murder and a majestic, mute heroine." —*Parade*

AN ALGONQUIN READERS ROUND TABLE EDITION WITH READING GROUP GUIDE AND OTHER SPECIAL FEATURES • FICTION • ISBN-13: 978-1-56512-560-5

Breakfast with Buddha, a novel by Roland Merullo

When his sister tricks him into taking her guru, a crimson-robed monk, on a trip to their childhood home, Otto Ringling, a confirmed skeptic, is not amused. Six days on the road with an enigmatic holy man who answers every question with a riddle is not what he'd planned. But along the way, Otto is given the remarkable opportunity to see his world—and more important, his life—through someone else's eyes.

"Enlightenment meets *On the Road* in this witty, insightful novel."
—*The Boston Sunday Globe*

"A laugh-out-loud novel that's both comical and wise . . . balancing irreverence with insight." —*The Louisville Courier-Journal*

AN ALGONQUIN READERS ROUND TABLE EDITION WITH READING GROUP GUIDE AND OTHER SPECIAL FEATURES • FICTION • ISBN 13: 978-1-56512-616-9

Saving the World, a novel by Julia Alvarez

While Alma Huebner is researching a new novel, she discovers the true story of Isabel Sendales y Gómez, who embarked on a courageous sea voyage to rescue the New World from smallpox. The author of *How the García Girls Lost Their Accents* and *In the Time of the Butterflies*, Alvarez captures the worlds of two women living two centuries apart but with surprisingly parallel fates.

"Fresh and unusual, and thought-provokingly sensitive."
—*The Boston Globe*

"Engrossing, expertly paced." —*People*

AN ALGONQUIN READERS ROUND TABLE EDITION WITH READING GROUP GUIDE AND OTHER SPECIAL FEATURES • FICTION • ISBN-13: 978-1-56512-558-2

The Ghost at the Table, a novel by Suzanne Berne

When Frances arranges to host Thanksgiving at her idyllic New England farmhouse, she envisions a happy family reunion, one that will include her sister, Cynthia. But tension mounts between them as each struggles with a different version of the mysterious circumstances surrounding their mother's death twenty-five years earlier.

"Wholly engaging, the perfect spark for launching a rich conversation around your own table." —*The Washington Post Book World*

"A crash course in sibling rivalry." —*O: The Oprah Magazine*

AN ALGONQUIN READERS ROUND TABLE EDITION WITH READING GROUP GUIDE AND OTHER SPECIAL FEATURES • FICTION • ISBN-13: 978-1-56512-579-7

Coal Black Horse, a novel by Robert Olmstead

When Robey Childs's mother has a premonition about her husband, who is away fighting in the Civil War, she sends her only son to find him and bring him home. At fourteen, Robey thinks he's off on a great adventure. But it takes the gift of a powerful and noble coal black horse to show him how to undertake the most important journey in his life.

"A remarkable creation." —*Chicago Tribune*

"Exciting . . . A grueling adventure." —*The New York Times Book Review*

"Gripping . . . Echoes the work of Cormac McCarthy."
—*The Cleveland Plain Dealer*

AN ALGONQUIN READERS ROUND TABLE EDITION WITH READING GROUP GUIDE AND OTHER SPECIAL FEATURES • FICTION • ISBN-13: 978-1-56512-601-5